CHEDDAR OFF DEAD

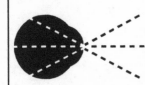

This Large Print Book carries the
Seal of Approval of N.A.V.H.

AN UNDERCOVER DISH MYSTERY

CHEDDAR OFF DEAD

JULIA BUCKLEY

WHEELER PUBLISHING
A part of Gale, a Cengage Company

Farmington Hills, Mich • San Francisco • New York • Waterville, Maine
Meriden, Conn • Mason, Ohio • Chicago

LIBRARY OF CONGRESS CATALOGING-IN-PUBLICATION DATA

Names: Buckley, Julia, 1964– author.
Title: Cheddar off dead / by Julia Buckley.
Description: Large print edition. | Waterville, Maine : Wheeler Publishing, 2017. | Series: An undercover dish mystery | Series: Wheeler Publishing large print cozy mystery
Identifiers: LCCN 2017017767| ISBN 9781432840525 (softcover) | ISBN 1432840525 (softcover)
Subjects: LCSH: Murder—Investigation—Fiction. | Large type books. | GSAFD: Mystery fiction.
Classification: LCC PS3602.U2648 C47 2017 | DDC 813/.6—dc23
LC record available at https://lccn.loc.gov/2017017767

Published in 2017 by arrangement with The Berkley Publishing Group, an imprint of Penguin Publishing Group, a division of Penguin Random House LLC

Printed in Mexico
1 2 3 4 5 6 7 21 20 19 18 17

To my nieces —
Anna, Cashie, Katie, and Pam —
who are the plucky heroines of
their own stories.

ACKNOWLEDGMENTS

I am grateful as always to the Mystery Writers of America — particularly the MWA Midwest and its stellar officers, Clare O'Donohue and Lori Rader-Day, who work hard to help mystery writers succeed, and to Margery Flax and MWA New York for being ever willing to address my questions and concerns.

Thank you to Berkley's Michelle Vega and Bethany Blair for their kindness and insight, and thanks to Danielle Dill for her work to promote the book. As ever I appreciate the guidance of my wise and wonderful agent, Kim Lionetti.

Thank you to my writers' group, small but mighty: Elizabeth Diskin, Cynthia Quam, and Martha Whitehead. Thanks to my dear friend Kathi Baron for being my writing counselor and constant cheerleader. Thank you to Lydia Brauer for her "friend smug-gery."

Thanks to the friends, family, colleagues, and readers who have spread the word about Lilah Drake.

Thanks again to Sheila Connolly and Sue Ann Jaffarian, who said such kind words about this series.

And thank you to my husband, Jeff, and sons, Ian and Graham — just because.

We are such stuff
As dreams are made on, and
our little life
Is rounded with a sleep.
— SHAKESPEARE, *The Tempest*

CHAPTER ONE

Bing Crosby was crooning "White Christmas" as I tried to fasten a Santa hat on the large skull of my chocolate Labrador, Mick. He wasn't cooperating. "Come on, Mick. I'm trying to get a Christmas card shot here," I wheedled, petting his nose. "Can you hold it on for just one minute?"

Mick nodded. This was Mick's special talent, but only one of the many things that made him lovable. He was able to convey, with one little humanlike gesture, the idea that he agreed with me, even approved of me. I had never encountered another dog who could nod like Mick.

I fastened the hat under his chin and took three quick snaps of him sitting in front of my shiny silver stove. I quickly reviewed the shots on my viewfinder. "Perfect! Very cozy and domestic. Thanks, Mick." I took off the hat and scratched his ears; then I gave him a rawhide chew, which he took into the corner of the kitchen for further investigation.

I washed my hands and went to my extra-large refrigerator (a new purchase for which I'd saved up funds for a year) and pulled out two huge trays of macaroni and cheese bake with crumbled potato chip topping. The casseroles smelled wonderful, and I realized I was hungry. Perhaps after I delivered them I could get myself some lunch. But before then I needed to get the food to John F. Kennedy Grade School, where Miss Jenny Braidwell taught third grade, and where her classroom full of students was convinced that their teacher was a terrific cook and baker. Miss Braidwell (who had once been my college roommate) made delicious, kid-friendly meals for all of her school events, and for many of them she was reimbursed by the school, since everyone at JFK liked Jenny Braidwell's cooking. No one knew, however, of Jenny's secret weapon: an old college pal who had made a clandestine agreement with Miss Braidwell to provide her with quality food — and an enhanced reputation as a super-teacher — in exchange for a generous sum of money.

At this point, all of my clientele were clandestine, but I was filling a niche. In the last two years I had learned a surprising fact: lots of people wanted credit for making food that they didn't have the time or the talent to make themselves. Some of those people had found me, or I had found them, and now I had a phone book full of clients. My father jokingly called this my "Undercover Dish" business.

I bundled the food carefully into the back of my aging Volvo, then went back into my hallway and called to Mick. "Want to come along for deliveries?" I asked. Normally Mick was my security guard, but today he only had eyes for his rawhide. I could hear him chewing it and making little satisfied growly sounds. Bing stopped singing, and my stereo, plugged into my iPod, selected another song from my shuffled playlist: "Blue Christmas" — the original Elvis recording. I definitely didn't want to hear a sad love song, Christmas themed or otherwise. It was time to leave.

"Fine, Mick. Party pooper. I'll see you in a while." I grabbed a little red bow off of my counter and clipped it onto my braid. Jenny had made it for me one Christmas. Her class had been making bows for moms and aunts and sisters, and she made one for me. Now I would wear it in tribute to Jenny and to the season. I locked the door of my little dwelling, which was actually an old gatehouse behind a much larger property, and climbed into the car; it smelled like cheesy heaven. Those little kids didn't know what joys awaited them.

I buckled in, flipped on the radio, and started backing out of the long driveway, headed for Dickens Street. A woman's voice on the Chicago "light" music station was speaking in soothing tones about the Christmas season. She informed me that it was 12:06. "It's December sixteenth," she warned. "Have you finished all of your holiday shopping? If not, remember that Dalby's has a full-service gift shop right next to the deli!"

Dalby's was a Chicago-area grocery chain. I shopped there often, and if I didn't get my act together, I realized, I would probably end up doing all of my holiday shopping at a grocery store. This made me briefly sad, so I lifted my chin and changed to the classical station; there was only one in Chicago, but it was fantastic. Right now it was playing something from *The Nutcracker,* and I pounded an imaginary baton on my steering wheel as I turned on Breville Road and headed north. There was a Dalby's on the left side of the street, highlighting the commercial message from the radio. I hadn't been to that particular store for almost a month because of an unpleasant experience that had made me avoid it.

At the end of November I had stopped at Dalby's in the evening to pick up some ingredients for a client's dish. While I marched down the spice aisle in quest of a four-pepper blend that almost always sold out, I caught a glimpse of a dark-haired man pushing his cart past the mouth of the aisle. I shrank against the wall of spices, but he hadn't seen me. It was Jay Parker, a police detective with whom I'd shared what turned out to be a one-evening event. I couldn't even call it a fling — it was just some rather passionate kissing that had suggested we might have a future together. Parker had later cast me off because I lied to him (for very complicated reasons), and the whole thing had been humiliating. The last thing I wanted, ever again, was to see him.

I found my pepper and decided to forgo the rest of the things on my list. I raced to the checkout lane, glancing furtively behind me to see if Parker was there.

The girl at the register was outrageously chatty, asking if I liked the cold weather and if I had any fun plans for Christmas, and though I gave her terse answers and forced a smile, she continued to chat, her hands moving at a leisurely pace. I was on the verge of strangling her when she finally handed me the pepper in a small bag and said, "Thanks for shopping at Dalby's. Have a nice day."

Normally I couldn't get one word — or even eye contact — out of a checkout person, but because I wanted to leave, Karma had made this one my best friend. I grabbed the bag from her and heard a voice say, "Lilah."

I froze. It was Parker's voice; I peeked behind me to see that he was in line, two carts back. His startling blue eyes met mine, and they had the high-voltage effect they always did.

"Oh, hi, Jay."

"How are you?" he asked.

The little white-haired lady between us, along with the checkout girl (whose name tag said *Hi, I'm Bonita*), watched without apology, openmouthed with wonder, probably at Parker's good looks.

"Oh, I'm fine. Just super busy. In fact, I have to run. It was good seeing you, though," I said. I was talking far too rapidly, which aggravated me and clearly amused the white-haired woman.

"Can you hold on for one second?" he asked. "Can we talk in the parking lot, maybe?"

I couldn't bear to look at him anymore. My eyes dropped to his cart, which was full of healthy foods like fresh vegetables and lean chicken breasts — and one giant tub of mint chocolate chip ice cream. "That would be so great, but I have to run and let Mick out; he's been cooped up for hours."

I dared a glance upward. His eyes expressed cool blue disbelief, so I added, "And I'm expecting a long-distance call. And some visitors."

"Lilah —" Parker said. A teenage boy came to pack up the white-haired woman's groceries, and he pushed me gently out of the way so that he could get to the bags.

"Oh, look at that — I'm in the way. It was great seeing you, Jay!" I said far too loudly, and then I ran out of Dalby's and into the parking lot — literally ran — so that I wouldn't have to encounter Jay Parker for even one second more. I thought I heard him call me once as I bolted toward the door, but I didn't turn back.

I sighed now as I drove past Dalby's. I hadn't seen Parker since that day, and I had shopped solely at Jewel since then in hopes that it would stay that way.

I was looking toward a happy Christmas holiday and a New Year in which I would establish a new me. I had a new job that I really liked, working for the best caterer in Pine Haven. I had a wonderful family and good friends, and I was about to visit one of those friends right now. I hadn't seen Jenny in person since November, either; she was always busy with school events, and I was always busy making or delivering secret food. But we managed to sneak in a lot of Facebook conversations and some deliciously snarky e-mails and texts. She knew nothing of my brief *thing* with Parker, and I didn't plan to tell her. It hadn't even been complicated by sex — just a lot of delicious kissing and some affectionate words. That tenuous relationship had proved to be an illusion. The fewer people who knew of my embarrassment, the better.

I pulled into the parking lot of JFK just as a light snow began to fall. It was lacy and delicate, like the kind inside a snow globe, and it lifted my spirits. I texted Jenny, informing her that the food was here. She wrote back, U R the best, and then, B rite out.

I sat in my car and waited, watching the snowflakes make their delicate journey from heaven to earth. Looking back, it's hard to remember what I was thinking as I stared through my windshield and contemplated the Christmas that was to come. It was one of those moments in life when I was so comfortably immersed in daily details that I felt no obligation to contemplate the bigger questions of life and death, the vastness of the universe, the mysteries beyond earthly comprehension. In retrospect it seems like that moment of quiet amid the snowflakes and empty cars was a last moment of innocence.

A second later Jenny appeared, along with a young man in a shirt and tie. He was cute in a studious and nerdy kind of way; he wore dark-rimmed glasses and his hair was messy, but probably not for fashionable reasons. I noted that Jenny seemed to enjoy speaking with him, and that her face was pink with pleasure after he leaned in and made some little joke to her. Then they were at my car. I had flipped my radio to the Christmas station, and this station, too, was playing "Blue Christmas," but the Michael Bublé cover instead of the Elvis version. Off it went, with a flick of my hand on the button.

I fell into professional mode, which was necessarily dishonest, in light of Jenny's companion. "Hey, Jenn. Your mom sent these over because they were taking up too much room in her house after you made them. I said I'd bring them since I live so

19

close to her and you were right on my errand route. She said you would be baking them today and serving them at your Christmas party. Is that right?" In reality, I had no idea where Jenny's mother lived.

Jenny nodded. "Thanks so much, Lilah. Ross and I can take it from here."

Ross was smiling at Jenny instead of me; his eyes were devouring her. Wow. I could see the wedding cake already: *Congratulations, Ross and Jennifer.*

"Are you a teacher, as well?" I asked as I slid out of the driver's seat.

Ross stuck out a hand, and I shook it. "Yes. Ross Peterson; I teach fifth grade. Jenny and I planned the lower grade Christmas party together. Between Jenny's delicious homemade food and the Christmas clown, the kids are going to be super excited. Plus we have our traditional visit from Santa. It's going to be a great party."

"What's a Christmas clown?" I asked, opening the back hatch.

"Oh, it's just an entertainer we found. She sings some holiday songs with them, and does a little magic and juggling and joke telling. It's a really cute and fun act. Then Santa comes in and gives out presents. They're with the clown right now, actually, in the school gym. She'll be with them for about an hour while Santa is still getting his makeup on. He's an actor, so he always makes a big deal about getting the look just right. So he goes second; now he's just waiting for her to be finished. The kids are at Level Ten excitement."

"That's fun. And where did you find Santa?" I asked.

Jenny slid out one of the trays and held it carefully in front of her. "Oh, that's Brad Whitefield. He's a friend of someone on the staff, so he got selected. He's an actor, like Ross said. He's done it the last few years. I guess actors have to take work where they can get it, right?"

Ross had the other tray now, and I closed the hatch. "Well, you guys enjoy the party," I said.

"We will," Jenny said, blowing me a kiss. "And Lilah, I wrote a note to my mom. Could you bring it to her when you see her today? I left it in a card on your front seat."

That meant my money, of course. People came up with all sorts of creative ways to slip me my pay. "Sure I can," I said. "Merry Christmas."

I watched them move carefully with the giant pans. I had warned Jenny that I would need those back within two days — lots of people wanted to "make" party food during

21

this season, and I had very little time to put it together now that I was catering full-time most days. My boss, who had been let in on my little secret, was generally kind about letting me make deliveries before I came into work; today she had given me the whole morning off.

I was about to get back in my car when I spied Santa himself, lifting my spirits as he emerged unexpectedly from a side door of the school, studying an iPhone in his ungloved hand.

He looked the part, although he obviously wore padding. Something about the whimsy of seeing Santa there in a school parking lot made me move forward, before I knew what I was doing, to greet him.

"Hello," I said. "Merry Christmas, Santa."

"Hey," he said. His voice was young; he couldn't have been out of his thirties, although it was hard to tell behind the beard. I wondered what sort of actor he was — someone who got regular work? Or someone who was perpetually unemployed? He looked up at me, and his phone tilted slightly — long enough for me to see some sort of elaborate graphic art on the screen, with what looked like the word *Kingdom* at the top. Then he moved again, and I couldn't see.

"I was just here delivering some food for the party, and I thought I'd come over. It's been a long time since I talked with Santa." I was being super friendly, which made me wonder if I was starved for companionship. The man was a stranger.

His eyes finally left his phone and looked up at me. "Hello. Are you — ?"

"I'm a friend of Jenny Braidwell's," I said. "She and I went to school together."

"Jenny — she's the one with the reddish hair, right?" he asked.

I nodded. Then he looked back down at his phone. "Santa has been playing his favorite game, but I guess it's time to face the text messages." He looked at me, squinting against the pale sun. Then he clicked into another screen and said, "Oh for God's sake. As if I don't have enough things to do!"

"I'll let you go, then," I said.

He sent me a rueful smile. "Sorry. I'm a rude Santa, aren't I? But it is just so irritating when people won't let up —" His phone beeped with an incoming text, and he read it. Then he looked concerned. "Looks like I'm running a quick errand," he said.

"Don't you have to be at the party?"

He looked at his watch. "Not for an hour. I guess I'll go deal with this and then come back. It's not far." He managed a friendly expression. "I'll walk you to your car, and you can tell me what you want for Christmas."

I laughed, and we moved back through the lot in the fairy-tale snow. We must have looked like the image on a strange Christmas card.

"So?" he asked me, looking suddenly like the real Santa, with round brown eyes behind his silver-framed glasses. His lips curved into a half smile. "What can I get you for Christmas, friend of Jenny's? We've got a little more than a week to make your dream come true."

"A second chance," I said, before I thought about it.

He raised his fake gray brows. "That's a tall order." He started to back away, his hands in front of him, jokingly, as if to push away my request. "I wouldn't mind one of those myself. I'm counting on it, in fact. The trick is not to rely on someone else, not even Santa. Make your own destiny — that's what I've learned."

"My own destiny, huh? That should be my plan for the New Year?" I had my key in my hand; I studied its shape in my palm.

"Of course. That should be the plan for every day. I'm a Zen Santa. Meditate about what you want, and it will lead you to personal enlightenment. Find your little island of escape. 'We are such stuff as dreams are made on, and our little life is rounded with a sleep.' "

"That's Shakespeare!"

"I've been pondering that line. Life is an illusion, and it is definitely short. And hey, what is Santa if he's not a gambler? He has to bet that he'll get to every house in time for Christmas — that's an impossibility, yet somehow he does it every year!" He winked at me and adjusted his beard. Now he looked younger. Maybe he was in his early thirties. "So we should be gamblers, too. We should gamble on ourselves — that's how you'll get your second chance."

"That's a really interesting point," I said.

He looked up at the sky for a moment, and some dusty snowflakes landed on his face. He laughed and wiped them away. "We have to pursue our dreams, right? I've been pursuing mine, and it's island life for me. I'm finished on Mainland." He adjusted a small ring that he wore on the little finger of his right hand. It was a plain circle made of some dark gray metal — perhaps hematite. "So that's my gift to you — realize the brevity of life, and let that reality guide your choices."

"That was far more profound than I expected."

"I know." He smiled at me, a benevolent Santa with sweet brown eyes.

I laughed. "Thank you. It was nice meeting you, Santa."

He shook my hand. Despite the cold, his ungloved hand was warm. "You, too. Have a Merry Christmas. I've got to run."

The grade school lot was long and wide, with cars on two sides, one row facing the wall of the school, and the other looking out at traffic on Breville. I waved as he headed down the school-facing lane of cars to a silver Toyota. Then I turned away and walked to my own vehicle; well down the lot to the only visitors' spots I could find. I had my key in the lock when another car pulled into the lot at the entrance near me; I saw a flash of blue as it went past. The clown has arrived, I thought. But no — Jenny and her friend had said that the clown was already performing in the gym, with all the children gathered around. A late teacher, perhaps.

There was the envelope from Jenny on my driver's seat; I reached in and picked it up, reading the note that Jenny had attached. Vaguely I heard the sound of a car window rolling down. Someone was going to chat with the man in the red suit. Then Santa's voice said, "Oh, here you are. I was just coming to you — seriously? Hey, give it back!" and then I heard a loud popping sound. Then an eerie silence.

I had already climbed into my seat, but I hadn't yet shut the door, and I immediately stepped back out and turned toward the lot; the blue car had made a U-turn and was driving right past my car, slowing slightly as it passed, then speeding up. I stared at it as it went by. There was a glare on the windshield; all I could tell was that there was one figure in the car. A moment later, with a squeal of brakes, the car exited the lot and drove out of sight. "Some people don't deserve driver's licenses," I murmured. I hadn't thought to look for a license plate, and now, from the corner of my eye, I saw that Santa wasn't where he belonged. He was prone, a red slash in the light dusting of snow.

Suddenly I was running, then kneeling in front of him. His eyes were open, but they weren't focused. "Are you okay?" I asked, even though I saw that a puddle of blood had started to form underneath him and an ugly rip marred the front of his suit. "Santa?"

I felt for a pulse in his neck; I did not find

one. I looked around, but the lot was deserted.

I scrambled back to my car and fumbled for my purse; I wasted precious seconds trying to find my phone and then attempting to dial three numbers with trembling fingers.

The emergency operator asked if she could help me.

"Yes — a man's been shot. John F. Kennedy School, on Breville Road."

I could feel her tension over the phone. "Is there an active shooter on the premises? Are the students in danger?"

"No — no. Whoever did it drove away. It's just him lying here, and — I think he's dead."

She promised to send an ambulance, and I went back to keep vigil over the man who had been Santa.

A slight wind lifted his beard and created the illusion of life and movement, but his skin had grown almost as pale as the snow that fell around us.

CHAPTER TWO

The school was in a "soft" lockdown; Jenny texted me so from inside. It did not seem there was immediate danger, but the police didn't take chances these days, not when children were involved. Meanwhile the parking lot was awash with blue and red lights, and Brad Whitefield was placed on a stretcher and put into an ambulance.

"Can you save him?" I asked.

The ambulance attendant looked surprised, then shook her head.

I had already known this, but it horrified me to confront the reality. "We'll need you to stay here," said a police officer, looming in front of me with an official air. "We'll be taking a statement in just a moment."

I sighed, feeling shaky, and sat in the driver's seat of my car with the door open and my legs sticking out into the parking lot, wishing I could go home. I texted Jenny again. Don't tell the kids what happened. Will they still get their party?

She texted back, assuring me that they were downplaying the flashing lights, at least to the tiniest children, and that the clown had already agreed to give out the special gifts that Whitefield, as Santa, had been set to deliver.

But they would all learn of it sooner or later, poor kids, and it would be woven into the tapestry of their grade school memories: the time that Santa Claus was shot to death in their parking lot.

More vehicles pulled up. Someone was cordoning off the lot and preventing street traffic on one block of Breville by setting out orange cones. A few parents showed up, then a few more, demanding to see their children. The police kept them on the periphery of the lot; a female officer had seemingly been assigned to them, and she continually assured them that all the children were safe and currently in lockdown for their own protection. The snowflakes continued to fall, but now they seemed a weird accompaniment to the evil that had just occurred.

A shadow blotted out the sun; I looked up to see Jay Parker in front of me. His blue eyes were wide with surprise. "Lilah? You're the witness?"

I shrugged. "I'm not a witness. As I told the other officer, I was facing away from him when it happened. I just glimpsed the car when it drove in and out. It was blue. Kind of a metallic blue."

Parker still couldn't get over it. "How is this happening again? How can you possibly have witnessed another murder?"

I stood up, hugging myself against the cold. "Are you suggesting that I somehow arrange to watch murders, Detective Parker?"

He huffed out some breath. "No. No. It's just — I think the odds of this happening are just astronomical —"

"Lucky me, then." My voice sounded quavery; Parker heard it, too, and his demeanor changed.

"Lilah, listen. I'm sorry you've had to go through this again. It must have been a terrible shock."

"I was alone with him, Jay, and I couldn't help him. He just lay there in the snow, in his Santa suit, like an evil Christmas card, and there was blood —"

He pulled me against him in a quick hug. "Okay. Come on — it's cold out here. I'll take you home and get the information there. All right? Give me one minute."

He disappeared into the throng of uniforms. I sat back down, suddenly weak-kneed. I wished that Mick were on the seat beside me.

Then a policeman who said he was Officer Wilson pulled me gently out of my car and asked for my keys. He would be driving my vehicle home, and I would be riding with Detective Parker.

I didn't question this; apparently they didn't trust me to drive a car after witnessing a man's death. I couldn't say that I disagreed with that assessment. Then Parker appeared and led me to his Ford. I climbed into the passenger seat and buckled in. Parker turned on the motor and fiddled with the heater, and soon enough I began to feel warm. He drove slowly out of the cluster of people and then out of the parking lot. He knew the way to my house; he'd been there on several occasions, so I didn't bother to give him directions.

Two blocks down Breville Road he cleared his throat. "Listen, Lilah —"

I interrupted him. "I'm sorry I didn't talk to you at the grocery store last month. I didn't want to be alone with you. I was afraid to be, I mean."

He sighed. "I know."

That brought another two minutes of silence. In my head Linda Ronstadt, angry yet melodic, asked when she would be loved. I finally said, "What did you want to talk to me about? Were you going to explain why you never called me again? Because I thought you made that fairly clear from the start: you considered me a dishonest person, and you weren't going to sully yourself with the likes of me."

Parker's eyes narrowed, but he kept them on the road. "You're purposely making me sound like a jerk."

"So what were you going to tell me? That you're not one?"

He turned onto Dickens Street, sighing again. "We're going to have to put this conversation on the back burner. I have an investigation to conduct. In fact, I would have asked Maria to do it, since I am obviously not unbiased in regard to you, but she happens to be on vacation."

"Huh." I stared moodily out my window. Maria was Parker's partner. She was dark haired and elegant and, as far as I knew, romantically unattached.

"But I will say this," Parker said, clearly irritated. "I wanted to talk to you to tell you that I missed you. And I saw you at the store, and you looked pretty, and I wanted it to be the way it was between us. That's why I called after you. But I see now that you're angry with me."

I had done a good job of putting October behind me, but now the memories came flooding back. I had made a pot of chili for a woman from my church named Pet Grandy. She liked to tell everyone that she made the famous chili that people wolfed down at bingo night, and that night in October had been no different — except that someone poisoned the chili and a woman died. Pet had asked me not to tell anyone that I was the chef. She wanted to preserve the illusion of her cooking skills. Against my better judgment, I had gone along with Pet's charade, and I hadn't told Parker that I'd made the chili, despite several opportunities to do so. When Parker found out, he walked out of my life.

I turned to him, surprised by the intensity of my feelings. "Yeah, I am angry. You know why? Because I thought about it, and no one is perfectly honest, not even you, the upright policeman. I did lie to you, and that was wrong, but I was trying to do right by Pet Grandy. She's a nice person who was put into a very bad situation. So at first I wallowed in guilt, but then I decided that if you really liked me, you'd be able to forgive me, because it's not like I was, in fact, a murderer."

All of this flowed out of me in almost one breath, and then, with the word *murderer,* I realized that someone had driven right up and shot that poor Santa Claus at point-blank range, and I started to cry.

Jay Parker's face turned red with some emotion — anger or shame. "Lilah, I'm sorry. Don't cry."

"I'm not crying," I sobbed, wiping my eyes on my jacket sleeve.

"Here we are. Home sweet home," he said with forced brightness, like someone comforting a cranky child. He pulled into my long driveway and up to my little caretaker's cottage, which pleased me every time I saw it. Back in October, Parker had visited me at this little house many times, and on the last night he visited he had kissed me and played with my long hair and told me that he wanted me in his life.

We got out of the car just as Officer Wilson drove my car up beside Parker's. He handed me my keys, gave Parker a brief wave, and then jogged back down the drive to a waiting cruiser. Parker focused on my car for a moment; then he walked around to the back hatch and stared at the rear bumper. I moved there, too, wondering what he was looking at. My bumper was undented and relatively clean. It bore a bright new sticker that said "Ask me about Haven of Pine Haven!"

"What?" I asked.

"Let's go inside," he said. Wordlessly we climbed the steps; my landlord, Terry, who lived in the big house on the same lot, had brought me a gift of a real pine wreath with a giant gold bow that now hung on the front wall of my home. On the door was a smaller pine swag with little dangling gold ornaments. I had lined the windows with gold lights, but they weren't shining now.

"Your house looks nice," Parker said. "Will you make me a cup of coffee so that we can talk?"

"About the murder, or about us?" I asked, still sniffling and fumbling for my key.

"Both."

"Fine." I let us into the house, where Mick confronted Parker in the tiny hall by planting two giant paws on his chest. No one was immune to Mick's charms — not even Parker. He smiled and practically embraced Mick, then settled for scratching his head and playing with his floppy ears.

"Hey, boy," he crooned. "Long time no see."

I marched to the kitchen, hung my coat on a back door hook, and started making some coffee. I opened my refrigerator and found half of a cake that I'd made for my parents' anniversary, which we'd celebrated two days earlier. It was an almond torte, resplendent with vanilla crème and a shaved nut and streusel topping. I took it out and placed it on a tray, slicing it into four pieces. I set this on the kitchen counter, which overlooked my little living room. Parker had sat there twice before, eating food that I'd made for him.

Now he wandered in, hung his coat next to mine, and washed his hands, clearly still uncomfortable with my sniffling. I let Mick out to wander the backyard and do his business; two minutes later he was at the door, ready to greet Parker and me.

While the coffee brewed, I turned to face Parker, and he sat on one of the stools in front of the counter. He had a laptop with him, and he set it on the counter to make his notes. "First things first, okay? Did you know this man, this Brad Whitefield, before today?"

"No. I don't even know what he looks like without the Santa suit."

Parker typed, then said, "And you were at the school because —"

"Jenny Braidwell was my roommate in college. Now she teaches at JFK, and she happens to be one of my clients."

"Ah." He typed some more. "And you were there because — ?"

"Because they were having a party, for which Jenny wanted to make some food. She's actually a terrible cook. I make it for her, and she pays me. I'm a secret caterer, as you know."

"I hear you're an aboveboard caterer now, too."

I sniffed. "Who told you that?"

"My mother, of course. She reminds me on an almost daily basis that you and she are good friends, and that I am a rude and ungrateful son."

I felt a burst of warmth and gratitude toward Ellie Parker. It was she who had tried to set me up with her son in the first place — and it had almost worked. Luckily Ellie and I had remained friends.

Parker was still looking at me. "By the way, that casserole that you made for Mom last Sunday — which my brothers still believe she made — was delicious."

"Thanks. It was a new recipe. Kind of a German theme, with the sauerkraut and the cabbage."

"People were raving about it all night. You're a very gifted chef."

"Okay. Go on with the questions."

He sighed. "So you made food for Jenny

Braidwell."

"Yes. Two giant pans of macaroni and cheese bake. Kids love it. Jenny came out with this other teacher named Ross, and they said that someone named Brad was going to be the Santa, and we talked about some other things. They said there was a Christmas clown. I didn't see her, just the Santa. He came out reading a message on his phone just as I was about to leave."

Parker sat up straighter. "What phone?"

"He got some texts while he was talking to me. They made him mad. He read one and said he was going to have to take a trip."

"Wait." He got out his own phone, punched in some numbers, and spoke tersely to someone who answered. "Finn? Miss Drake says that the victim had a phone. Right." He looked at me. "What kind?"

"An iPhone, I think. Black. But I think they took it from him."

"What?" Parker, about to relay the message, paused and stared. "Who took it from him?"

"Whoever was in the car. Because he said, 'Hey, give it back,' and then I heard the shot. They snatched something, then shot him."

Parker got up from his stool and went into

the hallway, where curious Lilahs couldn't hear what he was saying to Officer Finn. He talked for quite some time. The coffee was ready, so I poured two cups and set one next to the plate of sliced cake. When Parker returned, he sat down and stared at his plate without really seeing it. "Tell me everything he said," he told me, pushing the food aside to center his laptop.

"Um — okay. He came out and was looking at his phone. First he was playing some kind of game — like a video game. And it was about knights or something. Somebody's *Kingdom* — I didn't catch the name. But I was sort of trying to see it because the image looked pretty."

Parker's lip twitched.

"Anyway, he clicked out of that and started looking at text messages, and he was sort of complaining out loud and saying, 'Unbelievable,' and stuff like that."

"So he was upset by the text he had gotten."

"Yes. And whoever texted him must be the person who shot him."

"Why?"

"Because when the car pulled up he said, 'I was just coming to you,' as if the text had summoned him. And that would explain why they took his phone."

40

Parker thought about that. His eyes always seemed to glow when he was doing police work; I admired their blueness while pretending to look at my nails.

"And you're sure he didn't say a name, or anything that would indicate —"

"No, I don't think so. Anyway, when he came out of the school I went up to him —"

"Why was that? You said you didn't know him."

"I know, but — first of all, I like Santa Claus as a general rule. I see him as a positive symbol of love and unity."

Parker said nothing — just stared at me with those eyes.

"And secondly, I'd been feeling kind of sad, and I — I don't know, I just thought it would cheer me up to talk with Santa Claus, even if it was a guy in a suit at a grade school."

"Okay," said Parker. He typed a few words, which were probably "Lilah is weird."

"You said you wanted to hear this."

"Go on. What else did he say?"

"He was just — really put out. He said he didn't have time for whatever the person wanted, and now he was going to have to make a trip somewhere. He actually seemed

41

concerned about that part. So he started heading toward the parking lot, and we ended up walking together. He asked me what I wanted for Christmas, and — anyway, he made some comment about starting over. He quoted Shakespeare. He said he had gotten himself a second chance, and that you had to make your own destiny, not wait for some entity to grant it to you. Or something like that."

Parker was typing away. "What kind of second chance? What was he talking about?"

"He was a stranger in a Santa suit. It wasn't like I was interrogating him about each comment he made. We just exchanged a few words, and then I turned away and went toward my car."

"And it didn't make you turn around when you heard another car pull in? Weren't you curious to see who it was?"

"Well — no — because I was kind of deep in thought, and I don't know anyone at that school except Jenny, and she was inside. So I didn't really care. I just glanced at the car and saw that it was blue. I feel bad about it now, but when the car was leaving there was a glare on the windshield. If there hadn't been, I probably would have made eye contact with the person, but —"

Parker pushed aside his laptop and raked

a hand through his dark hair, then beamed his blue eyes at me with laser intensity. "Lilah, if you had made eye contact, you would be dead. To be honest, I'm surprised the person didn't try to — eliminate you as a witness."

"But I don't — I mean, they probably didn't see me, right? I was several cars away, and there was that glare on the windshield. If there was a glare for me, there was a glare for him, right? I didn't see anything inside, just a silhouette. One person."

He stood up and grabbed my hand. "You look pale. Come here. Sit down. That hadn't crossed your mind? That they might have seen you?"

"No. It's been a weird day." I sat on one of the stools; Parker took my coffee cup from the counter and handed it to me.

"Drink this. There you go. Look at me, Lilah."

I looked up at his earnest face. "I'm too abrupt sometimes. I shouldn't have frightened you like that. Obviously you're in no danger now, because the danger is past."

"And even if someone saw me, they wouldn't know how to find me."

"Right — I just have one small concern. When the car passed you — did it stay there long enough for the driver to see your

43

bumper sticker?"

I thought about it. Had the car hesitated for a moment before it tore out of the lot? Now it seemed to me that it had, but perhaps my brain was just making up that detail as a byproduct of fear.

"The Haven sticker? Why? Do you — oh, I see." Whoever saw the sticker would know where I worked. So if someone had been in too much of a hurry then, the Haven sticker might have given them a heads-up about where to find me in the future. "I don't know. I don't know if they saw it."

"I doubt it. You said everything happened very quickly. And whoever was driving would have been under a great deal of stress. They wouldn't have had time to notice small details."

He didn't totally believe that, and neither did I, now that I thought about it. Whoever had murdered the Santa might have second thoughts about trying to find me before I could summon up whatever clues I might have. He or she had left in a hurry, but it didn't mean they wouldn't come back — especially because when I saw the glare of the sun on the windshield, they might have seen *me* squinting into the car.

Parker sat down next to me and took a sip of his own coffee, then made a satisfied sound. "Still hot," he said. Then he forked up some of the almond cake and made a little moaning sound. "God, your food is good."

"Thanks."

He ate the whole thing, and drank some more coffee, before he said, "I should go. There's a lot of work to be done now."

"Okay."

"Lilah?"

"Yes."

"What did you tell Santa you wanted for Christmas?"

I considered lying, but then I decided, what the heck. Brad Whitefield had told me to gamble on myself, and he had also said that life was short. Moments later he had been proven right. "I said I wanted a second chance. That's why he was talking about it."

He didn't pretend not to know what that meant. He nodded at me several times, and his eyes darted around while he thought that over. Then he looked at me and held my gaze. "Maybe I want a second chance, too."

I shrugged. "It's probably too late." I said it to tick him off, but a tiny smile escaped me, and Parker saw it with his eagle eyes. He smiled, too.

"But maybe it's not, Lilah." He touched

the tip of my nose and said, "Your nose is cold."

I nodded. My nose stays cold all winter long.

"Can I come to talk to you, when this is over? About second chances?"

As always, his blue eyes had me half hypnotized. "I would like that."

Then Parker was all business. "I'm going to need you to call someone — your brother, maybe, or your parents. Have someone stay here with you for a few days. Hopefully we'll get to the bottom of this before long."

"Well, I mean — people have jobs. And I have a job. Oh no! I have to call work and tell them what happened."

"I'll talk with them if you want. Explain what happened. But are you sure you should —"

"It's a brand-new job, and they need me. The holiday, you know."

"Okay." Parker looked troubled. "But I'm going to drive you there and pick you up until I know you have someone who can come here. We don't want to take any chances until we —" He stopped and walked to my refrigerator, where a newspaper clipping was held on with a magnet. "What's this?"

"Oh — it's just an article about a friend

of mine. Angelo — you remember I said I knew him? He just got his own cable TV show. Just a local thing, but knowing Angelo, it will lead him on to superstardom. That was in the *Trib* about a week ago."

Parker scowled. He knew, from our previous association, that I had once dated Angelo. "I remember that he was a suspect in a murder investigation."

"Not really. We know who the real murderer was. Anyway, he sent me that, so I hung it up. He wants me to be proud of him, I guess."

He stared some more at the article with its prominent picture. It was a flattering shot: Angelo in a long black coat and a blue wool scarf, standing on the Clark Street Bridge; in the background boats could be seen chugging busily down the Chicago River. His black curls hung to his shoulders, and his dark eyes studied the camera with that special intensity of his. Women all over Chicago had probably fallen in love (and searched for him on Google). Parker looked as though he was about to say something else, but his phone rang, and he spoke tersely into it. Then he flipped it off and turned to me. "Let's go. I'll drop you at work, then I have to get back to the scene."

I nodded and went into the kitchen. Parker and I both bundled up again in our winter gear, and he studied some ornaments on my little Christmas tree, pretending not to be peeved about Angelo. Then he said, "Where is this place? Is it that little storefront right next to the Village Hall?"

"Yes. Haven of Pine Haven."

"Fine."

We were both gloomy in the car. In Parker's case, it was probably because he had to solve another murder. In mine, it was because (a) I couldn't forget the sight of a prone Santa Claus in the polluted snow and (b) Parker had not spoken again about second chances, nor did he seem particularly fond of me at the moment. What else was new?

Parker flipped on the radio, clearly uncomfortable with our silence. Gotye was singing "Somebody That I Used To Know." He was right at the part where the lover feels rejected and mistreated, and his pained voice echoed through the car. Parker flipped it off again with a flick of his wrist. "I thought there might be Christmas carols," he said, not looking at me. The song lingered in my head, though, because my brain holds on to music, absorbs it, and replays it, even when I'm sleeping.

I was scowling by the time we arrived, and

I didn't look at Parker when I said, "Thanks for the ride." I opened the door and stepped out onto the sidewalk. The snow had stopped falling, but the ground was covered with about three inches of white accumulation.

"Be careful," Parker said. "It's slippery."

I stole a glance over my shoulder and saw that Parker had gotten out of the car.

"What's going on?"

"I need to speak with your employer."

Not two months ago I had been in a similar situation with Parker; we had feared, due to a bizarre set of circumstances, that someone would poison me. Now it was happening again, I realized: outside forces were controlling my life, dictating my movements in the name of safety. Feeling like a prisoner in shackles, I followed Parker through the snow.

CHAPTER THREE

Parker got there first and opened the door; he held it for me, and I stalked past, stomping my boots on Esther's entry rug.

"Oh, Lilah — you're a bit late, aren't you?" asked Esther, her white hair disheveled and her face red from the ovens. She was toiling over a tray of bacon-wrapped scallops; we were doing a home wedding reception that evening.

Her husband, Jim, gray bearded and blue jeaned, worked beside her, his expression serene as he split figs with an expert hand, then began filling them with ricotta and drizzling honey on top. The more tense Esther got when under pressure, the more Jim seemed to grow calm. He was a good influence on us all when the schedule grew hectic.

Around the corner on the same big work space were Gabby and Nicole, two culinary students who worked for Esther part-time as interns. Their dark heads were bent over what Esther called mushroom fantasies — crisp little toast wedges covered in a mushroom-celery mix that the girls had sautéed in butter and sherry. The room smelled wonderful.

Before I could say anything to Esther, Parker raised a hand. "I'm Jay Parker of the Pine Haven Police Department. I wonder if I could speak to you, Mrs. Reynolds, and you, Mr. Reynolds? Perhaps in a different room?"

Everyone stopped dicing, chopping, and stuffing and looked up at us for a pregnant moment. Then Esther said, "What's wrong? Is it one of my children?"

I suppose that would be every mother's fear, always.

"Oh, Esther, *no!*" I cried. "It's just — I had a little — incident today, and —" To my utter embarrassment, I started to cry again.

Esther's eyes widened in horror. Parker said, "In another room?"

The four of us traipsed through a door and into Esther and Jim's private apartment, leaving poor Gabby and Nicole gaping after us. They probably went straight to their phones to run a Google search on the police blotter for Pine Haven. We sat on Esther's living room couches, and Parker filled them in succinctly on the day: my delivery, the ill-fated Santa, my unfortunate presence at a crime scene, the potential danger of my situation.

"I'm not saying that Lilah is definitely in danger. We'll know more after we gather some additional information, and I need to get back to that." Parker looked at his watch with something near desperation. "But I wondered if there was any way that you could keep Lilah to inside work today. I realize she probably helps you with deliveries or serving at parties, but perhaps she could take up more tasks here, and —"

"You can't be serious?" I said, gaping at him.

Jim spoke in his calm voice. "Lilah, he's being wise. We can get Gabby and Nicole to help us out at the reception, and you can man the phones here and start tomorrow's soufflés. It won't affect the timing of things in the least."

Esther didn't seem to have heard anything after the word *murder.* Now she came and sat beside me, taking my hands. "Oh, Lilah. You must have been so afraid."

I hugged her. Esther was always brisk and efficient, but she was quite maternal when the situation called for it.

"I have to go. I'll be back for Lilah tonight," Parker said.

"I can get my family to pick me up, Parker."

He stood; his keys were in his hand. "If you make other arrangements, call me. Otherwise I'll be here at the end of your shift, which will be — ?"

"Today? Around eight o'clock," Jim said.

"All right." Parker nodded at me. "Goodbye." And with one quick blue glance around the room, he took three long strides and was out the door.

"A man of few words," said Jim.

I said nothing.

"He's the one, isn't he?" Esther asked me. "The one who broke your heart?"

I tried to make light of it. "There's more than one person who answers that description, actually."

"It must have been so hard, having to be around him after such a tense situation."

"It was okay. He was decent." I still had my arms wrapped around Esther; I peeled them away and said, "I need to get to work."

Jim stood. "In a minute, Lilah. You've been invaluable around here for the last month and a half, and you've been overworking yourself between this job and your little sideline. Sit there and take some deep breaths. Then you come out and work when you're ready. And in the meantime, you can decide what you want to do for a ride. You're always welcome to stay here, if you wish."

"Thanks, Jim. Really, thanks." He strolled over and patted my head, then went out to complete his cheese-stuffed figs.

Esther took one of my hands and squeezed it. "Be honest with me. Do you feel up to working now?"

I nodded. "I desperately need to get my mind on something else. Give me some tasks, and I'll be much better."

"Sweetie. This is crazy! And not even two months after that whole incident at the church bingo hall!"

I winced, and Esther looked sorry. "I need to be quiet," she said.

"No, it's okay. It wasn't someone I knew — just a man who was playing Santa at the school where a friend of mine, Jenny, teaches. That's who I was bringing the food for; they had a big Christmas event today. She said the guy was a local actor named Brad Whitefield."

Esther stiffened. "Brad Whitefield. Why do I know that name?"

I shrugged.

"What age is he? Around thirty?"

"Probably. I mean, he had the Santa beard and hat, so I couldn't really tell, but he looked youngish."

"Oh dear. I'm going to call Mark. I think he might have known this man."

Mark was Esther and Jim's oldest child; he worked for a computer firm in the city. Sometimes he came by and mooched food and flirted with Gabby and Nicole and me; I liked him, although not romantically.

"Call him tomorrow, maybe. I don't want to get you off schedule."

Now Esther was looking at her watch. "I think we're okay. I think we're just fine. Now you do as Jim said, and rest here."

She got up, but then bent and kissed my forehead. "You and the two girls out there — you're like daughters to me, you know that?"

"Thanks, Esther. That's sweet."

She left, looking a bit shaken, and I leaned my head back on the couch and closed my eyes in their nice, quiet retreat of a living room. One of their cats, Penelope, leaped up and leaned against me as if in solidarity. She purred so loudly that it made me laugh; she squinted at me with her little white face, and it calmed me. I scratched her head for a while, then closed my eyes. I was on the verge of falling asleep when I shook myself and took out my cell phone. I didn't want to upset my mother and father — I had endured enough emotional scenes for one day. Their reaction could wait until tomorrow. Instead I called my brother, Cameron, whom I knew I could count on not to cry in my ear.

"Hello?" he said, sounding distracted. Cam was always distracted, and usually by his ridiculously beautiful girlfriend, Serafina.

"Cam. It's me."

"Hey, kid. We were just talking about you. We thought —"

"Cam, listen. There's been — an incident."

"What? With Mom or Dad?"

"No, no. I seem to have witnessed another murder."

"You have *got* to be kidding me!" Cam yelled.

"No. I wish I was."

I could hear Serafina questioning him in rapid-fire Italian; Cam turned away from the phone to yell some Italian back at her. Cam taught Italian as a foreign language at Loyola University. Serafina was an Italian in America, studying chemistry at the University of Chicago.

Finally he was back. "So what's going on?

Are you okay?"

"Yes, I'm fine. But — Detective Parker —"

I held the phone away from my ear as Cam let loose with a stream of invective. Then he said, "Why do you have to deal with that guy? Tell them you want to talk to someone else."

"That's not how it works, Cam." I felt a little glow at my older brother's protectiveness. He had been very angry at Parker back when the latter walked out on the fragile little something that we had.

"Fine. Then I'll deal with him. I don't want you talking to that guy."

"Anyway, will you let me finish?"

"What, then?"

"He wants me to stay with other people. Not to be alone. He wants to make sure I won't be . . . targeted."

"I have déjà vu. You just went through this in October, when you had to stay at Mom and Dad's."

"I know — it's crazy. It's going to ruin Christmas."

"No, it won't, *Sorellina*." Cam always broke into Italian when he said tender things. "We'll be fine."

"Well, anyway. Unless you want Parker coming to get me at the end of my shift —"

"I do *not*."

"Could you guys come and get me, and could I stay at your place for a couple of days?"

"Of course. Serafina would have insisted, anyway. And we have a new landlord, so you can bring your big, goofy dog, too."

"Oh, good. I was going to ask Mom and Dad to take him, but that would have involved explaining to them . . ."

"That can wait. What time should we be there?"

I told him, and he said that I should relax. Typical Cam. To him, everything could be remedied with a few deep breaths.

Still, I drew in a deep breath before I went into the kitchen, where four busy people stole secret glances at me as I readied my bowls and ingredients for the Gruyère and chive soufflés we were making for a family Christmas.

I began whisking eggs, and Esther pointed at me. "Once those are in the oven, Lilah, could you be an angel and chop the walnuts for the salad?"

"Of course. And I'll head to the location early tomorrow so I can help prep the salads in their kitchen."

Esther and Jim exchanged a glance. "We'll see," Jim said. "What might work better is if you also prep the dessert batter tonight; then we can just bake them tomorrow in their oven. You can stay where you are, and we'll call you if we need you. Will you be at your parents' house?"

"No — I'll be at my brother's in the city."

"See — that would be a big pain to get back here in time, especially with traffic on the Eisenhower. Just set up those desserts, and Gabby and Nicole can bake them on-site."

The desserts were also soufflés, which were to be baked in little individual ramekins and served at the table with a crème anglaise. This was one of Haven's specialties, and customers asked for it by name.

"If you're sure, Jim. . . ."

"I'm sure. This will be great. And the girls have already agreed to help tomorrow, right, kids?"

Gabby and Nicole, who were normally caught up in gossiping with one another, had summoned up sympathetic expressions and now both nodded eagerly, looking like twins with their dark ponytails. "We're excited to work on location," Gabby said, wiping a fleck of mushroom from her cheek with the back of her hand.

Esther looked at her watch. "Those look great, Gabby. You and Nicole go get your serving outfits on, and then we can all head over in our van. Jim and I will wrap these up." Before they could move, the door opened again, and Bart Andersen came strolling in, wearing his habitual smug expression. Bart was a high school freshman who washed dishes at Haven. I wasn't sure what Esther paid him, but he seemed pleased enough to be a wage earner while he was still fifteen. Bart was a nice kid, but he suffered from a severe case of overconfidence and teen narcissism, which we sometimes joked about in his presence. This never bothered him, due to the qualities previously mentioned.

"Hey, Bart. You've got your work cut out for you tonight, dude," Jim said.

"Whatever. I'm the greatest, so I'll probably be done in about five minutes," Bart said. When I had first started working at Haven, I had thought Bart was merely being ironic, and perhaps there was a slight dose of irony there, but in general Bart just liked to praise himself. The more he did it, the more I felt obligated to cut him down. Oddly he seemed to enjoy this.

"Are those three hairs on your chin your attempt at a beard?" I asked.

Bart stroked the red hairs I spoke of; they matched the red curls on his head. "The ladies aren't complaining," he said.

Everyone in the room started laughing, but as ever, Bart was impervious to mockery. "I'll be in my kingdom, serfs," he said, wandering into the sink room.

"That kid will go far," Jim murmured with grudging admiration.

"Far into denial," Esther said with a snort.

"Far away would be better," I said. "Am I stuck with him all day?"

Esther shook her head. "I'm only paying him for two hours."

"That should be fun."

Esther laughed, and then she and Jim got to work wrapping the hors d'oeuvres. Half an hour later she, Jim, and the girls were wearing their serving black and piling things into the Haven van.

"Thanks for keeping the home fires burning," Esther said, squeezing my hand. "Try not to kill Bart."

I smiled and waved, then went back to refrigerate my soufflé batter. I loaded some dirty dishes onto a cart and wheeled them back to the self-proclaimed king.

He stood at the scrub sink, his hands immersed in soapy water, his iPod making him immune to my approach. I pushed the cart until it made contact with his blue-jeaned rear. He turned, smirk in place, and pulled one earbud out of his ear.

"Bring them on, Lilah. I'm in the zone."

"Why are you in such a good mood? It's annoying."

He grinned at me. "I'm on vacation, dude! Not to mention, I just heard there was an incident at my old school! Don't get me wrong, it's terrible what happened to that man and everything, but it's also the most exciting thing that could have happened — and at my school!"

"You went to JFK?"

"Yeah. Graduated last year."

"So did you know — Mr. Whitefield?"

He sobered slightly. "Sort of. He played Santa a couple times for us, too. He was a nice enough dude, but also kind of a tool. I guess he was some kind of actor? But, like, super failing at it. I mean, if you have to take Santa jobs at grade schools, right?"

"Huh."

"Plus my mom kind of knew his family, and they think he's kind of a jerk."

"What do you mean?"

Bart rinsed off a dish, set it in the rack, and then turned to me fully. "When I was in fourth grade, he got married to this pretty hot lady. My family was invited to the church part of the wedding, and my mom actually went. She said it was really pretty and romantic and blah blah."

"So?"

"So when I was in seventh grade there was this rumor that he was in trouble with his wife and staying at someone else's house."

I felt my lips curling with my skepticism. "And how would your mom know that?"

"Because she's gossipy, and ladies are always scrambling at the chance to call her on the phone and tell her stuff. Her friend Betty was friends with Mr. Whitefield's wife, so that's how we knew."

"So he got divorced?"

"Nope. He got back with his wife. But my mom figures he was a cheater. My mom says once a cheater, always a cheater."

"That's not proof."

"No. I just heard some things. But I don't want to, like, speak badly about a dead man and stuff."

"You just did. You called him a tool."

"Yeah, well. He was a nice guy sometimes, too. When I was in eighth grade and he played the Santa, he gave me five bucks. The eighth graders didn't even get in the present line, because that was for the little kids. We were on the sidelines, singing carols for the little kids and crap like that. I went to the drinking fountain when Brad was leaving in his Santa suit, and he said that us older kids should get something, too, and he handed me five bucks."

"Huh."

"He said when you had a windfall at Christmastime, it was always good to pay it forward. I know, because I had to go home and look up the word *windfall.*"

"That's swell."

"You crack me up," Bart said, turning back to his dishes.

"Bart," I said, before he could plug his earbud back in.

"What?"

"The other stuff you heard — was it all about him having affairs? Cheating on his wife, I mean?"

"No, man. My dad says Whitefield was a major gambler and that he was in serious debt."

"And how would your dad know this? Is he a gambler, too?"

Bart smirked. "My dad is a lot of things."

That didn't sound good, but I didn't want to trod on that territory. "Thanks for the information," I said.

I went out into the kitchen and sent two text messages. To Jay Parker, I sent: A boy from JFK said Whitefield cheated on his wife and had serious gambling debts. Also I have arranged to stay with my brother tonight — no ride needed.

To Jenny, I wrote, Are you OK? Have things calmed down?

She texted back almost immediately. We need to meet. When are you free?

I typed, I'll be at Cam's for a couple days. MB after that.

OK. I'm fine — how about U?

Hanging in there. I hope all the kids are OK.

She decided to call me then, rather than text a long response.

"Hi," I said.

"Hey. The kids are all right. I think we handled it well, and they went home without being too traumatized. We made it clear that they were all safe. The little children were just told that we had a police incident, but that everything was fine. The older children were told there had been a shooting, and that it had not involved any students or teachers at the school."

"This is crazy, Jenny."

"I know. I have to run — call me soon," she said.

Nowadays people were always in a rush, including me and my family and friends.

This did not make me feel Christmassy —
nor did the day's tragic events. Perhaps a
couple of days away were just what I needed
to put me in touch with my holiday spirit.
Living at Cam's would give me a chance to
relax, breathe, enjoy the sights of Christmas
in the city, and get some perspective. Serafina would undoubtedly have decorated
their house with European flair, and I would
make a point of enjoying their hospitality. It
would be all right.

I just had to focus on the invigorating cold
air, the peace of Christmas, the joyful
contemplation of a New Year.

And forget that I had seen a man die.

CHAPTER FOUR

By eight o'clock I had prepped all the food for Thursday's gig. The salad fixings were chopped and stored; the soufflé batters, both cheese and chocolate, were refrigerated; and the ramekins were carefully wrapped for travel. Bart had finished and gone, and I had moved to Jim and Esther's impressive wine wall to find the bottles Jim had selected for the next day's event: a 2010 Côtes du Rhône and a 2011 Oregon Pinot Noir, both of which Jim had tasted recently and had found an appropriate match for this particular cheese blend.

My phone buzzed, and I saw that I had two text messages. One was from Parker. It said, Thanks for the info. In touch soon. Typical Parker. His Tarzan-like texts weren't that different from the way he communicated in person. He was definitely the tall, dark, and silent type, but he also seemed uncomfortable in any context beyond police work. I would have drawn the conclusion that Parker didn't have a romantic bone in his body, except that I knew that to be untrue. One just had to plumb the depths of Parker.

The other text was from Cam, and it said, We're on our way. I'll toot the horn when we get there.

I heard the horn about a minute after Esther and Jim got back, so I just had time to show them all of my prep work, and then Jim walked me out to the street where my brother waited. "I'm sure this is all just a ridiculous precaution," I said, but I was glad to have Jim's arm around my shoulder as I stepped onto the cold, dark street.

Then I was tucked into Cam's warm car and being softly serenaded by Andrea Bocelli while Serafina handed me a box of Frango mints, and my sweet dog, Mick, nuzzled my cheek.

"Thanks for picking him up, guys," I said.

"He was happy to see us," Serafina said. "I also put some of your clothes in a bag. Now eat a chocolate. I got them at the lab today from a friend of mine," she said.

"A guy who's in love with her, she means," said Cam, but without any apparent jealousy.

"He is too late," Serafina said, diving at Cam with one of her luxurious kisses, almost sending him veering off the road.

I tensed, holding Mick more tightly. "Geez! You guys are supposed to save me from death, not plunge me into it." It was only about eight thirty, but it felt like two in the morning, and I was exhausted.

Serafina looked at me over her left shoulder with wide brown eyes. "I'm sorry. But I love your brother so much that I couldn't resist him anymore. So I married him," Serafina said, flashing me a pretty white smile.

"Right," I said. Then I leaned forward. "Wait — what?"

Serafina stuck out her left hand, which contained a beautiful diamond ring and a thin silver band. "Cameron proposed to me last week, and I accepted. And then, because we are very spontaneous, and because we realized that I could apply for my permanent residency if we married now — we did it!! At city hall. Very romantic, and snowing."

"Oh my God — Cam! Serafina! I'm so happy for you! Mom is going to have a spaz!"

"She already did. We called her just before we came to get you," my brother said, meeting my eyes in his rearview mirror.

"Oh my gosh. So what — you've been on a kind of honeymoon? And I've ruined it by asking to stay at your love nest?"

"No! We love to have you, especially at Christmas!" Serafina cried, reaching back and taking one of the chocolates. She had a terrible sweet tooth, I'd learned. I held her hand and studied the ring — Cam had good taste. It was a large, center-cut diamond on a band that looked silver in the dark car.

"Is this platinum?"

"Yes. Isn't your brother a lovely man? He chose by himself."

I let her hand go. *My big brother.* I met his eyes again and saw his happiness. "Great job, Cam." I ate one of the chocolates myself and suddenly felt a little burst of my Christmas spirit coming back. The car was warm and merry; a light snow was falling; and my brother was a married man.

"We have to throw you a party!" I yelled. Mick nodded. Sometimes I was convinced my dog's special talent wasn't a random act he did in hope of treats, but an actual response to human dialogue.

Serafina giggled and Cam beamed, and their joy engulfed me; but I couldn't help but look over my shoulder every now and then to see if someone was creeping up behind us, ready to ram our car and send us off the road.

At their apartment Serafina took my coat,

poured Mick a bowl of water, and disappeared to make some tea and find some cookies. Cam said he had to make a phone call, and that I should make myself at home.

His apartment — now theirs — had always been one of my favorite places. It had high ceilings and a view of the lake. There were two bedrooms, but since Cam and Fina both needed an office for their respective careers, they had shoved a twin bed into a space meant to be a walk-in closet, so that their sleeping area looked sort of like a generous train car accommodation. Somehow, though, it was both cozy and romantic, and it added to the overall eccentricity of their home.

Their kitchen was generally untouched and the cleanest part of the place; neither of them had the time or the inclination to cook, so they ordered out often. I always felt a pang, looking at the beautiful stainless steel appliances and the red tile counter and center island, that there wasn't more food being prepared in that lovely space. It looked even lovelier right now, because Serafina, still dreamy eyed, was filling a kettle at the sink, her curly brown hair tumbling down her back in wild array.

After Mick found a spot on their kitchen rug, walked in circles a few times, and

71

curled into a little Labrador ball, I took a seat on a stool at the island and said, "Tell me about it. How did Cam propose?"

She turned to me, her face soft with love. "He was late home. It was the eleventh of December. It was that very cold night — do you remember?"

I nodded. I had made hot chocolate and sat with Mick against me for extra warmth, watching a rerun of *The Daily Show*.

"I was tired and had taken a bath. I was sitting in my flannel pajamas and big robe, looking not at all beautiful."

"Serafina, don't even start. There is no scenario in which you don't look amazing."

Serafina ran around the island and treated me to one of her trademark engulfing hugs; as usual, she smelled like flowers. "You are so sweet, my little Lilah."

Serafina acted as though I was decades younger than she was when we were perhaps two years apart. I doubted she was even thirty yet.

Now she sat down on the stool beside me and continued. "Anyway, Cam came home and said that he was freezing and was going to make a drink to warm him up. He asked if I would join him because he had good news that we had to celebrate. I said yes, lovely."

I smiled. Cam was my brother, and in a lot of ways I still considered him an idiot, as I had when we were teens, but I had a sense that he had done the engagement right.

"He turned out the lights, and we moved the couch near the windows so that we could look out at the night. We could not see the stars, but we could see the lake tossing, with its whitecaps. I asked what we were celebrating, and Cam said that he had fallen in love."

To my surprise, Serafina's eyes filled with tears. "I stared at him. I didn't think he was going to tell me that he had met another woman, but I didn't know why he was saying he was in love, since we had already said these words to each other, long ago."

I patted her hand.

"I asked what he meant, and he said that he had fallen in love with being in love, and he knew he wanted to love me forever. Then he told me there was no night so cold that he did not feel warmed by the love he felt for me, and there was no star in the sky so bright as my eyes. And then he handed me this box, with a diamond inside, and asked would I marry him."

Now my own eyes were moist. "That's wonderful." Cam wandered back into the room, and I said, "Nice proposal."

"Thanks." He shrugged. "I just couldn't wait anymore."

Serafina beamed at him, and my phone rang. I looked down at it and saw that Parker was calling. "Can I take this in one of the offices?" I asked.

"Sure." Cam glanced over my shoulder, read Parker's name, and scowled. "Do you want me to talk to him?"

"No, I do not."

I whisked away from them and heard Serafina hissing at Cam, "It is *her* love life, Cameron!"

I eased into Serafina's office and shut the door, then flicked on the phone. "Hello?"

"Lilah. I'm glad you answered. Where are you?"

"I'm at Cameron's apartment on Sheridan. Right near Loyola, where he teaches."

"Good security there?"

"Yes. We're on an upper floor, and people have to be buzzed in. What's going on?"

He sighed. "We followed your tip about the debt and found out that Whitefield owed money to Enrico Donato. Known as Big Rick Donato."

"So?"

"He's rumored to have mob connections. We actually don't have a lot on him. He keeps a very low profile; we didn't even know he was living in Pine Haven, among other places. He's said to own several residences in Chicagoland."

"What do you mean mob *connections*? He's a mobster? Like a horse head in the bed mobster?"

"I'm meeting with someone from the FBI tomorrow, so I'll get more information. Tell me this: the car you saw — was it big, like a limousine?"

I closed my eyes, thinking of the moment I had been trying to forget all day. "No — it was smallish — maybe a two door. And metallic blue, like I said."

"And you're sure you didn't see a face? Anything you could ID?"

"I don't think so, Jay. I mean, the moment was so confused, but I don't think I saw a thing. By the time I turned around and came out from between two cars, the other vehicle was leaving."

"Right. Okay. Are you working tomorrow?"

"No. Esther and Jim gave me the day off. But I can't stay here forever, obviously."

"And will you be alone there?"

"No. It's Wednesday, but my brother's school is off for the holidays, so I think Cam and Fina will be here."

"Give me the address." I did, sitting in the

75

chair and studying Fina's cluttered desk, which held everything from printed computer graphics to test tubes to a multitude of writing utensils. A giant gray gargoyle pencil holder sat to one side, holding a blue pen in its mouth. I started collecting pencils and pens and putting them back in the gray cup attached to the gargoyle. I found another little box of chocolates — hopefully Serafina had a good dentist — and slid it to one side. I was straightening her space without realizing it, feeling nervous and jumpy.

"Parker — how does an unemployed actor end up owing money to a reputed mobster?"

"How do you know he was unemployed?"

"Oh — well, just something Jenny said about him maybe needing the money. I don't actually know."

"In any case, we hope to know the answer soon so that we all have a merry Christmas."

"Yeah. Well, I have to go."

"Don't go out, Lilah."

"Okay."

"I'm not trying to scare you. I just — care about you. Okay?"

I studied the gargoyle, attempting nonchalance. It scowled back at me with a horrifying expression. "Okay."

"How are you holding up?"

"I'm fine, I guess. I've had better days."

"This will be over soon. Keep your chin up."

"Good night, Parker."

"Good night, Lilah."

I clicked off the phone. Serafina's desk had been neatened, but behind me were a table and chair covered with books, discarded outfits, mail, and more lab equipment. I left her office and peeked into Cam's, which was incredibly neat by comparison — his book-lined shelves were orderly, and his Renaissance knights collection stood guard on his windowsill in a surprisingly elegant display. The big brown leather desk chair was empty of any clutter, ready for Cam to come and sit in it and grade his papers or do his research on Alessandro Manzoni, Cam's favorite Italian writer, about whom he had already published several articles.

I wandered back to the main room and sat down. "Parker says that the dead man — Brad Whitefield — owed money to a mobster named Big Rick Donato."

Serafina snorted. "Americans! They think that every Italian is in the mob. They watch too much *Sopranos* and *Godfather.*"

Cam nodded at her, apparently agreeing,

and the teakettle whistled. Fina went to make the tea, and Cam turned to me. "So he thinks this was a mob hit?" he said, his voice low.

"I don't know. I just happened to tell him that this kid who does dishes at Haven said that he heard through the grapevine that Whitefield had debts. So I texted Parker, and this is what he found out."

"So he's — on it? I would hope that they can get to the bottom of this in a day or so, if they already have a suspect."

"Yeah, I guess. Assuming that these people really had anything to do with his death. Maybe it was an angry co-worker."

"Yeah, maybe." Cam looked disturbed, and rather tired.

Fina brought out the tea and some cinnamon toast. "This I can make," she said.

We toasted their marriage and the holidays and wished for many happy days to come. We drank our warm tea, and Serafina made me an equally warm bed on their couch. Cam ran downstairs with Mick, where they made a quick jaunt down the sidewalk. Then they ran back up, and Mick curled up at the foot of the couch, contented.

The last thing I saw was my brother switching off the lights and waving to me before he joined his wife in their little pleasure cave.

An Adele song floated in my head — the one where the girl is telling the guy who's moved on that it's not a problem, she'll find someone else just like him, but she's clearly still in love with him. It's melancholy and weirdly satisfying, especially the way Adele belts it out.

I closed my eyes, shook away the music, and attempted happy thoughts: In my imagination I had my own pleasure cave, to which I had lured Jay Parker, and he climbed in with me, his blue eyes glowing, while the radio played Sinatra singing "The Way You Look Tonight." Parker said, *I care about you,* and leaned in to kiss me, but the door was flung open, and a silhouette stood there, gun in hand.

You saw what I did, said the unknown person, and my eyes flew open.

CHAPTER FIVE

Thursday morning, the seventeenth of December, I woke with "Blue Christmas" back in my head. I opened my eyes to see Serafina bundling through her front door with a small pine tree, her dark hair speckled with white stars, her eyes shining with Christmas spirit.

"It's snowing?" I croaked.

"The most beautiful snow! So light, the flakes come down slowly, like little gifts from heaven. Come out and play in the snow, Lilah!" She leaned the tree on the wall and ran to me, assaulting my sleep-creased face with one of her affectionate Italian kisses.

"Ugh. How are you so awake? And so good smelling? I smell terrible, I'm sure."

Fina perched on the edge of the coffee table and studied my expression. "Lilah, you need to spend some time on yourself. Love yourself, as we love you, and you will thrive."

"Huh." I shoved my face back into the pillow, and Serafina laughed.

"I have my hair appointment today; you come with me."

"Why? Your hair is perfect. And also I can't go outside, right?"

"You don't have to. It is in the first floor of this building, where there are many businesses. I have gone to Rosalie's since I come to America. There are many Italians who go to her. We are like a family. Come, too. She will do amazing things to your hair."

My hair was one of my few vanities, and these days it hung to my elbows. I clutched the ends and looked at them. "I like my hair long. And so does — um, my mom. But maybe a trim. . . ."

"Rosalie is an artiste. She will make you in love with your reflection. So! I call her and ask her to put you in with me."

"Um — okay."

She hugged me, and then I made my way toward the bathroom and the shower. "Where's my brother?"

"He wanted to work on his book on campus. He says he will be home for a late lunch with us. We can decorate the tree together. It will be fun, so much." She was dialing the phone, and then she greeted

81

someone and walked toward the kitchen, speaking Italian.

I emerged from the bathroom twenty minutes later, feeling more presentable and more awake. Serafina handed me a cup of coffee, and she busied herself putting the tree base in a pot of water. Then she looked at a thin silver watch on her tanned wrist. "I have already walked your dog — he was a good boy. Now we should go. I like to get there early, in case she has extra time. You want all the time you can get."

She tugged on my arm, and I patted Mick, told him I'd be back soon, and followed her out of the apartment. We moved down the hall and into the elevator. We emerged on the main floor and crossed the carpeted lobby to one of many little glass-walled storefronts that dotted the first floor of the Parkman Building. This one said "Rosalie's Salon," in a pink, swirly font. Inside, a receptionist sat at a front desk, and behind her were eight chairs facing a wall-length mirror, which was adorned with rather garish silver garland, white lights, and giant dangling silver reindeer. Six of the chairs were filled. The other wall held a long church pew bench, where family members seemed to be waiting for the people in the chairs.

Serafina walked confidently to the desk and spoke to the teenage girl who sat there. "Hello, Balbina. Is she ready for me? Except I also bring my sister." She shoved me forward. "This is Lilah, Cameron's little sister. Isn't she sweet?"

Much to my dismay, several women appeared from nowhere and gathered around me, as though I were approximately two years old, and spoke loudly about my apparent cuteness. One of them pinched my cheek. I glared at Serafina.

"Rosalie," Fina said to a dark-haired woman in the group. "Isn't Lilah's hair pretty? She wants to keep it long. What can you do to make her irresistible to her boyfriend? I want him to not be able to keep his hands off of her."

"Don't let Cam hear you say that," I said.

Rosalie, who seemed fiftyish, had a dark mole above her upper lip that added to her air of elegance and mystery. She was studying my hair, weighing it in her hands. "Oh yes," she said. "We will make it beautiful."

She instructed Balbina to take me "into the back," where the girl rewashed the hair I had washed minutes earlier. To her credit, though, she had very soothing hands, and the shampoo she used had an alluring scent. I almost fell asleep in the chair, and then

Balbina was wrapping my head in a towel and sending me back to the front. I was settled into a new chair, and Rosalie began to towel dry my hair and peer at it in the mirror in front of us. Balbina stood next to me, pumping some lotion into her hands; moments later she was massaging my fingers.

"Oh, that's not necessary — but — wow. Oh boy, that feels good," I said.

Serafina, heading to the back to have her hair washed by some other young woman, said, "She needs the full treatment, Rosalie. Lilah has been under a great deal of stress. I can't say much about it, but she has been through a trauma."

All of the women sent me curious glances while I sent a warning look to Serafina. Rosalie combed out my hair and gave me a gentle head massage that left me feeling almost boneless. Balbina finished with my hands, which now felt smooth and smelled of eucalyptus. I let them drop into my lap. "Thank you," I murmured, and then I slid into a sort of trance as Rosalie began piling my hair up on my head in sections.

"A pretty color," she said. "Like a golden princess."

"Hmm," I said, my eyes closed.

"Giovanna," said Rosalie.

My eyes flew open, and I realized she wasn't addressing me, but the girl in the next chair, who had a cloud of red hair and wide green eyes.

"Yes," she said, turning a pretty and slightly petulant face toward us.

"How are the wedding plans going?" Rosalie asked.

Giovanna sighed. "They are fine. Nonno gives me a hard time constantly, and he has to be in charge of everything."

"Your grandfather loves you, and he is footing the bill," Rosalie said sternly.

Giovanna sighed again. "That doesn't mean he's in charge of my life. But I know you mean well, Nonnino."

She smiled into the mirror, and I realized she was looking at someone behind her. I shifted my gaze to see a gray-haired man waiting on the bench.

He sighed, almost as theatrically as his granddaughter had done. "It is sad to be only a checkbook to your family."

Giovanna's smile disappeared. "Stop playing the money card, Nonno. You know I love you, and you also know I would like to make my own decisions, and so would Nick."

"Decisions are dangerous. You must live with them all," her grandfather said. He wore a little gray flannel jacket with a white

85

shirt, black pants, and a pair of slippers.

"Yes, I know. I would love to make a really bad decision just to have the luxury of paying the price," Giovanna said, her voice rising.

"And it is Nonno's job to make sure you never have to pay for a bad decision!" Now he was sort of yelling.

Giovanna tossed her red head; her stylist had to pause in her snipping to avoid hurting her. "Nonno, you need to butt out! Nick is sick of this, and so am I! We're going to move away from Chicago and find someplace where we can live alone."

The old man sat very still for a moment, then wiped at his eyes. "Now I am a burden. A burden to my daughter's daughter, who never brought me anything but joy!"

"Don't start, Nonno!" Giovanna fumed, her green eyes flashing.

"If this were a reality TV show, I would watch it," I murmured to Rosalie.

Rosalie nodded solemnly. "I do watch it, every two weeks. Since she was about three."

The girl and her grandfather were oblivious to our discussion, because now they had descended into a full-blown argument in Italian. It went on for about five minutes, at which point Giovanna burst into stormy tears. Nonno appeared at my shoulder, shoving Giovanna's stylist out of the way and hugging his granddaughter around the neck. Then suddenly she was laughing, and so was he, and they pretended to strangle each other while they watched their reflections in the mirror.

I couldn't tear my eyes away. Serafina appeared on my other side and settled into her chair. "See, Lilah? We provide everything, including the theater!"

Then everyone in the place was laughing. Apparently Serafina was seen as quite the wag in their circle. I laughed, too, and then Rosalie's gentle hands were persuading my eyes to close gently, gradually, and I didn't open them until she had started her blow dryer. "I put in some layers," she said. "Nothing short — just something to give you bounce and fullness. This way, even if you wear it straight, it will be fluffy. You see?"

I did see. It was transforming under her hands into movie star hair.

"And then, if you want to curl it slightly, or put little kinks into it, it will fall perfectly into place." She moved deftly with a curling iron, her hand darting in and out of my hair.

"I could never do that," I said. "I just let my hair drip-dry."

"Hmm," Rosalie said, her face disapproving. She kept at it, clicking and clacking with the curling iron, moving with great speed and dexterity. "You should come to me always," she said. "I understand your hair."

"Okay." I looked at myself in the mirror and barely recognized the blonde woman who looked back at me, perfectly coiffed and elegant, but sexy, too. "Thank you, Rosalie. I will definitely be back. My current hairdresser makes me look like a dandelion."

"Hmm," said Rosalie. "Okay. You wait now while I do Serafina."

"Sure." I moved to the bench and sat next to old Nonno. He had returned, mollified by his Giovanna, who had sworn a few more times that she loved him.

"Your granddaughter is beautiful," I said.

He turned to smile at me; his face was slightly grizzled with gray hair, but he had surprisingly arresting eyes, which were also gray. "Yes, she is a beauty. Like a rose — full of thorns and pain, but so beautiful and irresistible."

"I heard that, Nonno." Giovanna stuck her tongue out at him in the long mirror.

Nonno shrugged. "You see?"

"Families can be complicated," I said.

"Yes. You have a big family?"

"Just my parents, my brother, and me.

And now Serafina, who married my brother."

Nonno nodded. "And no husband for you? Why is this?"

I did not like the direction of the conversation. "I don't need a husband."

He smiled. "A woman as beautiful as you? You should be on your fourth husband by now. Like Elizabeth Taylor."

In spite of myself, I giggled. "I do not aspire to be like Elizabeth Taylor. Although she was lovely. And so was Richard Burton."

"Yes. The man she could not do without, but she could not live with him, either."

"I get that."

"You have a Richard Burton?"

I sighed. "Long story, Nonno. Is it okay if I call you that? I've never heard that name before."

"It means 'Grandfather,' " he said. Then he stuck out his hand, which I shook automatically. "My name is Rick. I own the salon here" — he waved his hands vaguely at the room — "and I live on the top floor — at least at this time of year."

That explained the slippers. "That's a good setup. You can check on your business without really leaving your house."

"Yes. It is handy. But only one of my businesses."

"Wow. You are an entrepreneur. I guess that's how you'll pay for the wedding," I joked.

He threw his head back and opened his mouth, but no laugh came out. It was a pantomime of a laugh. Then he was serious again. "You live in Chicago? Here in the building?"

"No — I live in Pine Haven. I'm just visiting my brother."

"Ah, lovely Pine Haven. I also have a residence there."

"My parents would just love you. They're Realtors. They'd probably try to get you to upgrade."

He nodded, as though he had already discussed this with my parents. "That's not a bad idea. Always something to consider. Do you have a card for them?"

"Uh — yes." I retrieved the purse I had set at my feet and found a card in my wallet. "Here you go."

He studied it with impressive attention. "Daniel Drake. And you are?"

"My name is Lilah Drake."

"Lilah Drake of Pine Haven." He smiled at me with avuncular charm. I caught a whiff of scented tobacco. The phone rang at the front desk, and Balbina answered.

"I don't know — I would have to ask our owner, Mr. Donato. Please hold." Then she launched into a question in Italian, which began with, "Enrico, *per piacere* . . ."

He answered her in Italian. A feeling of unease began to spread through me. Enrico. Mr. Donato. Someone had just used that name. . . .

"Oh no," I said aloud.

He raised a thick pair of salty eyebrows. "Is something wrong?"

"You — I — nothing. Serafina, may I speak with you?"

She met my eyes in the long mirror and saw my distress. "Nonno, don't frighten Lilah with your war stories. She witnessed a terrible thing yesterday."

I opened my mouth, shocked at her comment, and for the second time I was surrounded by women, this time firing questions at me, some in Italian, some in English. The gist of it was that they wanted to know what I had witnessed.

Serafina seemed to realize for herself that she had said too much. She called the women to her and spoke in soft Italian, apparently trying to downplay her comment. Enrico Donato, the very man that Parker had told me to avoid, was looking at me with shrewd eyes. Moments earlier I had seen him as a cuddly grandfather. Now all I saw was the intelligence in his face, the largeness of his hands.

He spoke to me, so low that no one else could hear. "You are from Pine Haven, and Serafina says you saw something. I think I can guess what you witnessed. I have seen the local news. Something that happened yesterday, right in the open, right in that town. A shooting, was it not?"

I was trapped; my only defense was offense. "What would you know about it?"

He shrugged. "Nothing, I am afraid."

"I just realized who you are. So I may as well say this: from what I understand, the dead man owed you money. Perhaps a great deal."

He sat up straighter in his seat, his face weirdly interested — almost pleased. "I am sorry? Did you not just meet me? I am curious to hear how you would know this."

"I didn't know you until Balbina said your name. I was told that you were a gambler and that Brad Whitefield owed you money." I looked into his gray eyes and saw significant surprise, with a tinge of respect.

"And who might have told you that? And why would they have told you, a pretty young lady who was, what — in the wrong

92

place at the wrong time?"

"Never mind. How did you happen to think about the shooting just now? Is it because you were there?"

Now he looked extremely amused. "My dear, calm yourself. Your little hands are shaking."

I slid my hands under my legs. "Answer my question."

He feigned seriousness. "I'm not sure what you heard about me, but I assure you that I was not near young Brad yesterday. I was most sorry to hear of his death. Certainly it had nothing to do with me."

"Did he owe you money?"

"I suppose that is between him and me."

I nodded. "Well, just so you know, I didn't see anything yesterday. Only the aftermath."

Now he really was serious. "You are so convinced that I was in this place, doing this terrible thing. Why? Who has convinced you?"

Now it was my turn to shrug. "I suppose that is between him and me."

Enrico Donato laughed. "You are a spirited woman, like my granddaughter there. But perhaps you will pass on a message to your informant — I do not involve myself in these things, not anymore. I am an old man now, no? I live in quiet retirement. I leave gambling and quibbling over debts to the young." A brief shadow passed across his face.

"Do you have a son, Mr. Donato?"

He stood up and put out his hand. I shook it, mainly out of politeness. "This has been a most interesting conversation, Miss Drake."

"Yes, it has."

Giovanna appeared in front of us, her hair a glorious red halo around her curious face. "I'm finished, Nonno. What are you guys talking about? Are you boring her with your war stories?"

"I am not boring her, no."

His face was placid as he took out his wallet, apparently in preparation for paying at the front counter. "Miss Drake, I assure you that you have nothing to fear from me, nor do I know what happened to our friend. I hope that you have a lovely Christmas."

I nodded, and he moved away with Giovanna, who was whispering something in his ear. I kept my eye on him until he was gone, then whipped out my phone and texted Parker: I just met Enrico Donato.

About thirty seconds later I got one back that said, What? There in half an hour.

Then Serafina was standing and fluffing her even-more-gorgeous hair, and the two

94

of us moved to the front to pay, as Donato had done minutes earlier.

I promised Rosalie that I would, indeed, be returning, and then we left Rosalie's and traveled back toward the elevator, at which point I began hissing at Serafina, asking why she had mentioned my traumatic day, and had she known that Nonno was Enrico Donato?

"Oh! I suppose I have heard his first name before, but I didn't know he was the man Parker spoke of. I'm sorry, Lilah! But old Nonno is harmless as a fly. He's very sweet — and he dotes so much on Giovanna, his youngest grandchild."

"I don't even know what to say. Parker is going to kill both you and me, assuming that the mob doesn't kill me first," I huffed.

We had reached the door of her apartment; she turned to me now and said, "Did you get the impression that he would harm you?"

"No," I said.

Serafina nodded, turning the key and letting us in. "He is just a nice man. The police, they — what is it called? Jump to ideas."

"Jump to conclusions."

"Yes. Parker is too busy, anyway, to —"

"He said he'll be here in half an hour."

"Oh." She set down her purse and took off her coat, which she slung carelessly on the couch. If I knew my neat brother, he would hang it up when he got home. "Lilah, before he gets here, could you do me a favor?"

I was still feeling upset with her. Mick loped up to me with his usual friendly greeting, and I petted his ears. "I suppose," I said.

"I have a couple of dresses that I don't want anymore. I will give them to someone at work, or to Goodwill, unless you want them. Would you try them on for me?"

I sighed. I wanted to call work, find out what was happening, and get in touch with some of my secret clients. "Um — okay, really quickly."

She clapped her hands and disappeared down a hallway where, apparently, they had a clothing closet. Then she returned with the dresses. She handed me the first one — a winter-white pullover made of soft mohair. I eyed it dubiously. "I don't think this would look so great on me," I said. "And I'd have to pull it over my nice new hair."

She was already pushing me toward the bathroom. "I think it will look amazing on you. Just try it on."

With a loud sigh I went into their large

white-walled loo and stripped out of my jeans and sweater, then pulled on the dress and fluffed my hair back into place. The shade of white looked surprisingly good against my blonde locks. "I can't really see it," I said.

"Come out here; I have a full-length mirror in the hallway."

I emerged, and Serafina gasped. "Oh, I love it! It is so perfect on you, Lilah!"

I moved to the mirror she pointed out, and my mouth dropped open. Never had I realized how many curves I possessed until I slipped on the white dress. I turned this way and that, admiring my form and the lovely softness of the material. "Wow. Where do you shop? Sexy Women R Us?"

Serafina tinkled out another happy laugh. "I like feminine things. Wait, don't take it off. I have a necklace that is so perfect." She jogged away. She needn't have worried; I had no intention of removing the dress, perhaps ever. Between my new hairstyle and this amazing clothing, I was feeling like a new woman.

A knock sounded on the door; I knew it was probably Parker. "I'll get it," I called, and I jogged to the door, peeking first through the peephole to see Parker's somber face. I would have thought the man never smiled if it hadn't been for that one evening in the distant past. . . .

I opened the door, and Parker blinked at me. "Lolla," he gurgled.

"What?"

He cleared his throat. "Lilah. Are you going out?"

"What?"

"I said you need to stay in, Lilah. I wasn't joking —"

"I am staying in. Do you mean this?" I pointed at the dress. "Serafina just asked me to try it on. And I got a new hairdo."

He was glaring now. "I told you not to leave; where did you go?"

"We didn't leave the building. The salon is on the first floor. What do you think of my new look?"

Parker's eyes flicked away from me, but not before I'd seen some admiration. "Very nice. Tell Serafina you want to keep — that dress."

"Thank you, I will. Come in. It's just Fina and me for the time being." I led the way into the little living room.

Serafina emerged, smiling, and I said, "Do you two remember each other?"

Parker nodded, giving Serafina a brief wave, then taking off his coat and hanging it over a chair. He looked from her to his little laptop bag, from which he took his ubiquitous computer. He did not glance my way again.

His face had gone back to its scowling norm, and he said, as he opened up his computer file, "Now would you two like to explain to me how you ended up talking to the very man I suggested might be dangerous?"

Serafina and I both rushed to explain, taking turns, how we had merely wanted our hair done, and how Fina had not realized that old Nonno, whom she knew only as a customer's grandfather, was the man of whom Parker had spoken.

Parker typed and glared. "It seems like more than a coincidence."

Fina shook her head. "He owns the salon; it is one of his many businesses. He has a home here in this building. He sits down in his place of business every two weeks, watching his granddaughter get her hair done. And some other times he goes down there, as well. He likes being around all the ladies, I think."

I leaned toward him. "I thought you said you were going to talk to some FBI guy. What did he say?"

"It was a she, actually. And she said that in fact, despite their suspicions of Donato, he seems to have retired from active involvement, shall we say."

"He said that, too. He said he leaves these matters of gambling and money to the younger generation. I asked if he had a son, and he looked sort of disturbed. It made me think that if someone related to him did this, he was not aware of it. But it bothered him that I already knew his name. That really threw him."

"Did you tell him the police were investigating him?"

"No. I said I wasn't going to tell him my source because he wouldn't tell me his."

Parker's lip twitched momentarily. Then he typed something.

"He told me I had nothing to fear from him," I said. "I suppose I can believe that. He was just this little old grandfather. He was wearing slippers."

Parker's expression said he wasn't convinced that Donato was harmless.

I was about to protest some more, but my cell phone rang. "Oh geez," I said. "It's probably Esther calling. I was going to call this morning." I grabbed my purse, retrieved the phone, and clicked it on.

"Hello?"

"Lilah, *la mia bella*!"

"Angelo?" I cried. My ex-boyfriend had

not called me on the phone in more than a year. I wasn't sure how I felt about hearing his voice. We had spoken briefly a couple of months earlier, when he came to my house to discuss the murder, and the fact that he was seemingly under police suspicion. His visit had been almost pleasant, and we had managed to be civil to one another, almost like friends. Perhaps that was why he had felt emboldened to send me the article about his new television show. Perhaps we *had* become friends.

Parker, upon hearing Angelo's name, stiffened next to me, but continued to type.

Angelo's voice was relatively urgent. "I need to talk to you. You have some time now?"

"Uh — not really. I have the police here; it's a long story."

"Still about that lady who died at your church?"

"No, unfortunately. This is a new person who died. Anyway, I should probably call you back, unless you can give me the gist of why you're calling." I tried to sound brisk, not wanting to encourage Angelo or anger Parker.

"Quick, then. I have an opportunity for you to expand your business. I want you to appear on my show tomorrow. Make one of your sweet little recipes — something for the holiday."

"Tomorrow? I can't be ready tomorrow, Angelo!"

"But think what it would do for you. You can advertise for yourself, or for this new catering company. My show already has the high viewership, and good reviews. Don't pass it up!"

"This is crazy, Angelo. Let me think about it and call you back."

"Call within the hour. Otherwise I have to book someone else."

"Okay," I said. "Talk to you soon."

I hung up and felt Parker's blue gaze without turning. "Angelo wants me to appear on his cable cooking show tomorrow."

Serafina clapped her hands. "Oh, how exciting! I'll have everyone I know watching. What time and what channel?"

"I don't even know. He's giving me no time to think or plan — but it's a great opportunity." I finally turned to face Parker, who was now looking at his lap.

He cleared his throat. "Doesn't it seem like a bad idea to get involved with an old boyfriend? Especially one who treated you badly?"

I let his words float in the air for a while; arguably Parker himself had treated me rather badly. His face reddened as he seemed to hear the irony.

"I'm not 'getting involved' with him; I would be working on building my business. And I don't even know if I'm going to do it. I have to call Esther and Jim and ask what they think."

Parker shrugged and looked at his notes. "Let's get back to this," he said.

The phone rang again. Serafina giggled as I clicked it on. She had clearly enjoyed Parker's reaction to Angelo's call; she loved drama. Perhaps she thought it was Angelo calling back, but this time it was Jenny. "How are you doing, Lilah?"

"I'm okay. I'm here with a policeman, though. Can I call you back?"

Parker was scowling again, perhaps because I had referred to him as a policeman instead of something else. But what else was I supposed to call him? My love interest? My onetime fling?

"Just let me ask something really fast. Dave Brent, one of the teachers at my school, was planning this Christmas party. And even though this terrible thing just happened, Dave decided to have the party anyway. It's going to be most of the teachers and some of the staff and a bunch of other people. Anyway, I wondered if you'd like to go with me? It's on Monday, the twenty-first. Our first day of break."

"To your faculty Christmas party?"

"Just a party. The fact is, I'm going with that guy you saw me with — you know, my colleague, Ross Peterson? — and I'd really like you to get to know him. And Dave said we can invite friends and stuff."

"Jenny, I don't want to be a third wheel while you're there with Ross! And besides, it sounds like it would be the JFK faculty and me!"

"No, really — there's a whole crowd every year — people bring friends and dates and such. He has a huge place, and he loves to throw parties."

Parker tapped my arm. "Who is that?" he mouthed.

I stared, surprised at his rudeness. "Hang on," I told Jenny. I covered the phone and said, "It's my friend Jenny, the one who teaches at JFK. She invited me to the faculty Christmas party on Monday; she wants me to meet her date. But I think it would be beyond awkward to go there, to be around all those people I don't know, and they'll probably all talk about the shooting —"

"Tell her you're going," Parker said.

"What? Why?"

"And tell her you're bringing a date."

I stared at him for a minute, then told Jenny I'd changed my mind, and that I was bringing someone.

"Oh, great! Who are you bringing?" she asked.

"Uh — I guess Jay Parker," I said.

"Jay Parker. Okay, that's a new name. He sounds cute! I can't wait to meet him. Okay, how about if you guys stop by my house at about seven, and then we can go to the party together?"

"Sounds good. What do I wear?" I asked.

"Oh, just something festive. I'm going to wear a red dress, in hopes of driving Ross crazy."

"Okay. I guess I'll see you Monday night."

Jenny sent me some loud phone kisses and hung up.

I turned to Parker. "What the heck is going on?"

Parker held up a hand. "If I have the opportunity to talk to everyone who knew the dead man, at least peripherally, not as a police officer but as someone at a party, where their lips will be loosened by alcohol, then that is an opportunity that I will not pass up."

"So you're going to be, like, undercover?"

"Not exactly. But you won't be mentioning that I'm the police unless someone asks.

I'm your date, that's all." ·

Serafina watched us as though we were a Saturday afternoon movie. "Isn't she beautiful, Detective Parker? With her lovely golden hair and that perfect dress?"

"Yes, she is," Parker said, but he wasn't looking at me.

I felt a spurt of rebellion. "Are we finished here? Because I have to call Angelo." I tossed my newly silky hair. "And how long do I have to stay in this apartment? Mick and I need to go home."

"I don't know how long, Lilah. How long would you like to feel safe?"

We exchanged a glance that was not entirely friendly.

Parker turned to Serafina. "Is it all right for Lilah and Mick to stay here a little bit longer?"

The fact that he included my dog made some of my anger dissipate. I smiled down at my Labrador, who was smiling up at me from his place on the carpet.

"Of course they may stay as long as they wish! It is always fun to have family, especially at the holidays."

"Great." Parker packed up his computer and then stood up. "Then Lilah, I will expect you to stay here. Let me know what time to pick you up Monday, and I'll escort you to the party. Meanwhile, you can go call your boyfriend." '

So that was it. Parker was still fuming about Angelo.

"I'll do that. And maybe, since we'll be attending a party, you can take that rod out of your spine just for one evening."

We glared at each other. Parker said a polite good-bye to Serafina, then strode out of the apartment without another word to me.

He closed the door, and Serafina clapped. "Oh, Lilah! He is so much in love with you."

"What?"

"He couldn't take his eyes off you in that dress! And he is very jealous of the old flame, no? He cannot bear the thought of you with that man."

"Well — why can't he ever just be normal and affectionate? I'm so tired of his scowling face."

Serafina nodded, her face sympathetic. "But his job is so hard, isn't it? And it's Christmastime, when I'm sure he would rather be doing something else."

I nodded. "Yeah, okay."

"But he is going to a party with you soon."

"Yeah — for *work.*"

"But he is not going as a policeman, is he? He will be a different person. Perhaps he will be glad to escape into his role as your date. Hmm?" She leaned toward me with a mischievous expression.

Suddenly the room seemed brighter. "Serafina."

"Yes?"

"I need to wear something perfect on Monday. As perfect as this dress, but different, because he's already seen it."

"I have a whole closet full of perfect dresses," Serafina said.

CHAPTER SIX

I was at Angelo's studio at seven Friday morning, escorted by my brother (my guard) and clutching ingredients in Tupperware bowls. I made Cameron wait in the lobby with some Italian book he was reading; the only person he hated more than Parker was Angelo Cardelini, and I didn't need Cam glaring and making me nervous. He said he was fine with this plan, and he found a large chair near the stone fireplace across from the main door.

I rode up in the elevator, humming a song that had been in my head since I woke up that morning — a sad Beatles song called "For No One" that my father had always liked. Like many love songs, it was all about regret and missed opportunities. I sighed and tried to think up a happier tune. I forced a few bars of "Sleigh Ride" into my brain before the elevator doors opened.

In the studio Angelo pried my fingers off

of the containers and started setting out the food on his work space: a golden-tiled counter in front of a backsplash depicting a Tuscan orchard. A little Christmas tree sat on one side of the island, flickering with white lights and adding holiday charm to the set. The faux kitchen looked homey and authentic, and Angelo was a sexy chef, his hair tied back, his shirtsleeves pushed up, his overall appearance scrubbed and clean. He had a small studio audience already assembled in their folding chairs, and a quick glance told me that they were all middle-aged women. I had a feeling I knew why Angelo's ratings were climbing.

"You are in the second segment," Angelo said, consulting a clipboard that a woman wearing a headset handed him. "I will ask you about the dish: how you came up with the recipe, who you make it for, how long it takes, why it is good for an average family person to make at the holidays. Right? And you just answer naturally, as Lilah."

"Okay. And that's it?"

"Then you make it for us, before our eyes. I help now and then, with stirring or pouring. And we talk together, laugh, flirt, just like old times. The audience likes chemistry." He grinned at me.

I studied his face and realized that he was

quite good at this: the organizing of the show, the planning of the segments, the putting his guest at ease. I patted his arm. "I'm happy for you, Angelo. This is going to make you a big success. You're going to end up in New York."

He smiled. "You are sweet. Now Tabitha will take you to the dressing room because you look too tired to be on camera. She will work some magic with her brushes."

"Oh — okay. That's because I didn't have a lot of notice for this." I gave him a significant glance, which he shrugged away.

"You will be great. And the red dress is perfect — very Christmassy!"

"Thanks." The woman named Tabitha, she of the headset, appeared and led me to a tiny back room with a couple of chairs in front of a large mirror. She sat me down and turned me toward a bright light. "Okay — let me see that face," she said. "You have terrific skin, but I'm afraid I'm going to gunk it up with some stage makeup. Be sure you wash it off really thoroughly when you get home. This stuff is industrial strength."

I laughed, but Tabitha told me to hold my face still. I studied her, as well. She looked to be about thirty, with a round, childlike face and a long brown ponytail. Without being able to pin down exactly why, I decided that she looked like what my brother called "a theater person." She wore a nondescript outfit of gray corduroys and a green turtleneck, and she had an air of authority that made me think she wore many hats. When she finished working on my face, I ventured a glance into the mirror. "Oh, that's too much," I said.

"Nope. On TV it will look just right — trust me."

I studied my reflection dubiously, and my eyes wandered to a newspaper clipping on the table in front of the mirror. The headline read,

Local Man Gunned Down in School Parking Lot

I gasped at the first picture I'd ever seen of Brad Whitefield without Santa makeup. I had purposely avoided television, on Cam and Fina's advice. "Oh my," I said. Brad Whitefield had been a handsome man — brown haired and brown eyed, with a charming, dimpled smile. The caption identified him as

Pine Haven Resident Brad Whitefield, 32.

Tabitha followed my gaze. "Isn't that terrible? I actually knew that guy — Brad. He and I were in a production together in the city. He was in the cast, and I did the makeup. We got to be friends." She shook her head, and I looked at her in the mirror.

"You were in a show together — is it running now?"

She busied herself with her make-up case. "No — this was a production of *A Christmas Carol* that we did at the Goodman last year. But Brad was in something now, too. A Shakespearean play. He was actually quite a good actor."

"He was doing Shakespeare, and yet he was playing Santa at a grade school?"

"The grade school thing paid good money for two hours. He did it the last few years. It was actually a great way to get some Christmas cash. I asked him once if he needed an elf, and he laughed. I suppose he needed the money, because that was what he and Cleo always fought about."

"Cleo?"

"His wife. They had some hard times in the past, but I think they were pretty solid lately. Poor Cleo."

"Did she — ?" I didn't get to finish my question, because Tabitha looked at her watch and then signaled me to follow her. She led me to the wings of the little stage, where we watched Angelo doing his first segment. This was called "Kitchen Dilemmas," during which Angelo read a letter from a viewer and then solved her (or his) kitchen problem. This letter was from a woman named Darlene who had made one of Angelo's recipes but had been disappointed when half of the food stuck to the dish. I realized that Angelo was a natural for television. He looked right into the camera and said, "Darlene, the problem is not the way you are greasing your pan; the problem is in your ingredients. You cannot make that dish without olive oil, which adds moisture to the food and keeps the casserole from sticking to your glass bakeware. And you know which olive oil you should be using, don't you, Darlene?" He pointed to his audience full of fascinated women, and they all cried, "Angelo's Gourmet!"

This was the name of Angelo's own food line, and it was quite good; I used it in my own cooking.

Angelo smiled into the camera at the absent Darlene, who was probably going to faint when she watched the show and saw the sexy attention Angelo paid to her. Then he was saying, "For our next holiday segment, I have invited an old friend of mine, a Chicago chef and caterer named Lilah Drake. If you haven't heard of her yet, be ready to hear of her in the future. She is talented, young, and beautiful, and Chicago will not be able to keep her much longer!"

The crowd clapped and cheered. Angelo held up a hand. "Today Lilah is going to show us how to make a holiday brunch casserole that will feed eight and warm their hearts during this season of love and companionship. Lilah, come on out!"

I walked out on rubbery legs, not sure where to focus my attention. And then, to my vast relief, Angelo took over. He embraced me warmly and said, "Just look at me, not the camera," into my ear, then pulled away to tell his audience that we were lucky to benefit from the expertise of someone who was currently a caterer for Haven of Pine Haven. "But you also have private clients, do you not, Lilah?"

"I do, Angelo, and I must tell you — it's difficult to juggle catering with Haven during the day and then working on my own projects at night — but it's taught me to be very organized, and that pays off in the kitchen."

"It does, I agree. Now, this casserole is similar to a quiche, is it not?"

"It is. And, speaking of organization, it can all be prepared and refrigerated the night before, so that the next morning the chef can focus on whatever — setting a holiday table or putting on festive attire, or just relaxing with a cup of tea and a good book. We all deserve to relax once in a while, especially at the holidays, right?" I ventured a look at the studio audience, and they clapped. Heat rose in my face, and I basked in Angelo's approving glance.

"Show us how it's done, Lilah."

"All right. Before anything else I would advise you, when you're ready to bake, to preheat your oven for at least five minutes. You want this to go into a very hot oven, because it will affect the consistency of your casserole."

Angelo turned a dial on what seemed to be a fake stove. We already had a completed casserole that he would show as the "after" specimen. I had baked it at one o'clock that morning. "Done! And how do we start?"

"Well, you'll want to beat your eggs quite well. You can use an old-fashioned egg beater, or a fork. If it's the latter, remember that you should use your wrist for the most efficient mixing. I'm putting ten eggs in the bowl, along with my heavy cream, and I'll need you to add in the paprika and salt, Angelo."

Angelo grinned at his audience. "You see how she puts me to work? I once dated this

116

woman, and I can tell you, she is the boss in the kitchen."

The women in the audience practically screamed with laughter, along with what was probably a barely sublimated desire for Angelo. The room seemed electric since his mention of our former romance. I tried not to glare at him. "And as I recall, you rarely listened to me, which is why we are a *former* duo."

The women laughed again, and Angelo clapped his hands with theatrical glee. "She has spirit, friends. All right, let me get these spices in here before Lilah gets stern with me."

Somehow he was making everything sound sexual, and it was getting on my nerves. I tried to list the next ingredients in a very boring way, but Angelo managed to find double entendres in almost everything and to point those out to the crazed studio audience, who were stomping their feet by the time I said something about shredding the cheese, which they seemed to interpret as a euphemism for sex.

I finally just laughed and went with the flow — Angelo's smirking and the women shrieking — because it gave a certain manic energy to what might otherwise have been a placid and boring list of ingredients. Perhaps

Angelo had planned this from the start: to use our relationship and our fairly attractive demeanors to his advantage. I wondered if he was thinking of it as a sort of audition for one of those morning shows in which an attractive duo sits on a couch and relates the news and the trends of the day. Who knew how far Angelo could go? He had the looks and the instinct for the cameras.

I poured my whipped eggs into the glass pan. "Once you've put in the eggs, add your bacon mixture, and then your little bowl of shredded cheese and spices. Keep some of the cheese off to the side to sprinkle on top when the dish is baked. I can tell you, Angelo, that this is not only delicious, but an elegant meal for your holiday table. And you can see that there wasn't that much preparation — we've gotten it all ready in less than ten minutes."

"I've preheated my oven, Lilah *mia,* and so can we slide the dish in?"

"Yes. Just put that in, and then I think you have a finished version to show your audience?"

"I do." Angelo pulled out the casserole I'd baked to a golden-brown. "Look at that, ladies."

The audience actually said, "Ahhhhh." I wondered if Angelo had given them wine.

"And how would you serve this at your table, Lilah?"

"It's delicious with some fresh fruit or a nice green salad, perhaps with some nuts and crunchy peppers as a complement to the warm, chewy casserole. And as a beverage you can serve fruit juice or a nice holiday champagne."

"I have one here that I think will taste delicious — a Charles Heidsieck Brut. Will you toast with me, in honor of Christmas and the old days?"

Angelo sent me a sparkling smile, then winked at his audience, encouraging them, and soon they were all cheering us on, so of course I lifted a glass and clinked it against Angelo's. "Merry Christmas, and a happy New Year," I said.

"And to you, lovely Lilah. Good luck in all your endeavors." We sipped our champagne, and then Angelo leaned in to kiss me on the lips.

"Lilah Drake, everyone!" he said to his cheering audience.

I waved and made my way offstage.

Tabitha stood there, dumbstruck. "That is the best show he's done yet, hands down. I'll bet you a million dollars the producers are going to want you back!" She patted my shoulder. "Great job!"

"Thanks, Tabitha. Now I'm going to go home and take a nap."

"Yeah, we tape super early. But it's going to be great. Make sure you watch at nine o'clock."

"I will, thanks." We went back to the makeup room, where I retrieved my purse and coat. I saw the newspaper clipping again and paused. "Hey, Tabitha. Would you be able to find out for me what show Brad Whitefield was in? The thing is — I knew him slightly, and so did some friends of mine. I wanted to let them know that he was actually doing better than they thought. Some of them thought he was an out-of-work actor, but it sounds like he had pretty steady gigs in Chicago, didn't he?"

"Oh yeah. Brad never had trouble finding a new show. He really was talented. I heard him audition a number of times, and he would just take whatever script it was, whatever crazy lines, and make it sound totally natural, like he was just making it up himself as he went along. He was good. Cleo told me that he'd had a couple of calls from Hollywood in the last weeks, when scouts saw his Shakespearean performance. But anyway, I don't have to look it up. I have a playbill from his new show."

She jogged out of the room and returned

two minutes later with a program from *The Tempest.* "Brad was Prospero! What a great role. It was out in the suburbs, not the city, but it was getting lots of good press." She looked away for a minute, and I realized she had tears in her eyes.

"You guys were close friends, huh?"

"We kept in touch, ever since our first show together. And yeah, I knew him pretty well. Better than he even knew I did." She wiped at her eyes and gave me a rueful smile.

"Really? Listen, I happen to know the cop who's looking into Brad's death. He might want to talk to you about your last conversation."

She shook her head. "Nothing significant there. We were just shooting the bull. Besides, I'm not a huge fan of cops."

I hesitated; Tabitha could offer a lot of information about Brad Whitefield. "Well, listen — if you remember anything significant, you can call me. Let me give you my number." I found a piece of paper in my purse and jotted down my cell phone number and my e-mail.

"Okay. Thanks. If I remember anything."

"Even if you don't think it's important. I know that Detective Parker likes to have every little piece of the puzzle — and you can count on him to find your friend's killer." I thought about it and said, "And if you find out any funeral information — I think I'd like to go and pay my respects."

Her eyes looked moist again. "Sure. I'll let you know, and if I hear of anything or think of anything else for your police friend, I'll call. Thanks, Lilah. And thanks for being on the show."

"Sure."

I left the studio and went to the lobby, where Cameron had fallen asleep in his chair and now resembled a handsome homeless man. The guard at the check-in station seemed to suspect this very thing, so I approached him and explained that Cam was my brother, and had been waiting while I taped *Cooking with Angelo* on the fourth floor. He nodded grudgingly, and I woke my protector so that we could return to one of Chicago's many notoriously expensive parking lots that charge eighteen dollars for the privilege of parking for two hours.

"Unbelievable," Cam said, shaking his head at the parking sign. "Anyway, how did it go with Mr. Charming?"

"I really have no idea. I was so nervous I barely knew what I said, and the audience would have cheered no matter what happened because they clearly all wanted to sleep with Angelo."

"Guys like him really get my goat," Cam said, unlocking his Volkswagen.

"Why? Because they attract beautiful women? Seems to me you might have Angelo beat, if I start counting your girlfriends. Let's see — who was the first one? Amy Parkman, in seventh grade?" We climbed into the car; I was giggling.

"Don't start," said a scowling Cameron.

"And then there was Jennifer Pietrowski. She was really pretty. I remember envying her ability to use a hair straightener," I mused, buckling in.

"We never really dated," Cam said. "I just liked her." He backed out of his spot and started moving forward.

"Ah. Well, if we're going by who we *liked,* then I might have the longest list of —"

A loud noise, like glasses shattering, caused me to jump, then turn and see that the backseat was in fact covered with glass, and the right side passenger window was gone. Cam swerved the car in reaction. "Whoa! What was that?" Cam peered into the backseat and saw the glass. "Lilah, I think —"

"Drive, drive, drive!" I screamed.

Cam drove, faster than I thought possible, down the circular parking garage lanes and out into Chicago traffic. I saw my own fear reflected in his eyes. "Is anyone behind me? Look, Lilah!"

"I'm looking. I'm trying to keep my head away from the window, because I don't want it to get exploded like that —"

Cam's hand touched my leg while he steered with the other one. "Okay, okay. Let's both take a deep breath. Then get Parker on the phone."

I took out my cell with trembling fingers and pressed 2 on my speed dial.

His voice was beautiful music. "Parker."

"Jay?"

"Lilah. What's wrong?"

"Someone — I was with Cam — and someone —"

That was as far as I got before I started bawling in Parker's ear. He said, "Lilah, put Cameron on."

I handed Cameron the phone, and to his credit he managed to speak calmly to Parker while he negotiated Chicago traffic and kept his eye on the rearview mirror for potential sniper fire. Suddenly my brother seemed like a superhero, or an adroit spy. "Yes," he was saying. "We're all right. Whoever it was must be a pretty bad shot, because it didn't come close to Lilah. The bullet burst the back passenger window."

124

"Close enough," I said through my tears.

Cameron looked at me. "That's what Parker just said."

Parker told us to get back to Cameron's and he would meet us there.

Cameron agreed and hung up the phone. He handed it to me, I slid it back into my purse, and then I clutched my brother's hand. "I love you, Cam."

He squeezed back. "It will be okay, Lilah. And I love you, too."

We got back to Cam's apartment, and he parked illegally in front. "I'm not taking a chance on walking from another parking garage," he said.

Philip, Cam's doorman, appeared at my window, recognizing Cam's car. "Mr. Drake? You okay?"

"Philip, we just had a close call. Can I leave the car here until the police come?"

"You got it, Mr. Drake."

I had developed a residual case of the shakes, and Philip, with some special instinct I didn't think a man in his early twenties possessed, seemed to realize I needed to be handled gently. He opened my door and helped me out of the car, then walked me up to the entrance, speaking calmly to me all the while. My eyes darted everywhere, seeing an enemy in every passing pedestrian.

Cameron jogged behind us, and we all breathed more easily once we were in the building. I thanked Philip, and he returned to his station. We walked past Rosalie's Salon, and I saw Enrico Donato's face watching me through the window. I stared, openmouthed. Had he done this? He knew who I was. He knew what I saw (or didn't see). Could he have coldheartedly arranged for my execution? But if that were so, and he was really a mobster, would he have hired someone so clearly ineffectual?

While I mused, he came toward us on his slippered feet. "Miss Drake? Are you all right?"

"Were you hoping I was not?" I asked, my voice sharp.

"What happened?" he asked. His skin had turned white.

Cameron put his arm around me. "Listen — it's Mr. Donato, right?"

"Yes."

"My sister and I just had a shock. We were — attacked. So I just want to get her upstairs and hand her a stiff drink and get her calmed down."

He moved forward. "Who attacked you?"

"We don't know," I said, suddenly weary.

"A bullet came through our car's window. Rather near my head. Are you saying it wasn't you, or one of your men?"

"Lilah!" my brother said, his face a picture of warning.

Donato didn't even look at him. "I can assure you, Miss Drake — it was not. But I will make it my business to find out. Believe me. You are a friend of mine. Do you understand? I owe this to you and to young Brad. And we will be watching out for you. Keeping you safe."

Perhaps it was a sign of my odd state of mind that this former gangster's words brought me great relief in that moment. Someone else would watch out for us; someone else had our backs.

Cam did not want me talking to Donato. "We need to get Lilah home. The police will want to talk to her soon. Thank you for your concern," he said to the old man as he pulled me toward the elevator. I sent one last inquiring look to Donato, who still stood there with quiet authority, studying me. Then I turned and went with Cameron.

When we emerged from the elevator on the fourth floor, Cam stopped me in the hall outside his apartment. "Listen — we have to tell Serafina about this."

"Oh God. Cam, I can't deal with her right now."

"I know. So let me go in first and warn her that you'll want some recovery time and that she shouldn't kiss or hug you until you're ready."

"That will probably kill her," I said, with a weak grin.

Cam grinned, too. "She can hug me; I'm used to it."

"Go — break it to her gently."

Cam went in. I heard his voice greeting his wife, then a pause, then Serafina's voice, high-pitched and frightened. Then lots of heartfelt Italian.

The elevator pinged, and I stiffened, but it was Parker who turned the corner and ran toward me now. I threw myself into his arms without thinking; his coat was still cold from the outdoors, but it was open, and I burrowed inside it, to his warmth.

"Lilah," he said, his voice gentle. I felt something soft on the top of my head — Parker was kissing my hair. "I'm so sorry. I should have gone with you today. Or convinced you not to go."

"You couldn't have known someone would shoot at me!"

"I know now. And you won't be alone again."

I leaned away from him. "What?"

"I'll be assigning an officer to you indefinitely."

"How about assigning yourself?"

He smiled down at me. "That is a very appealing thought. But I can't look for this person and protect you at the same time. I'll be here as much as I can, of course."

This would have been thrilling if I weren't so afraid of being murdered.

"I'm so much trouble," I said.

"This is our job. To serve and protect, right?"

I smashed my face against his chest, which smelled nice, even through his shirt.

"It's okay, babe," Parker said in what could only be called an intimate tone.

Cameron came out then and ruined it. He stood stiffly in front of us and said, "Oh, hello."

"Mr. Drake." Parker shook his hand with me still clinging to him. "Can we go inside? If you'll give me the exact location, I'll send a unit there to look for the glass; they'll try to get a sense of where the shot came from. I've already sent them pictures of the vehicle — the one right in front of the building, right?"

"Yes — thanks for coming so quickly," Cameron said. I could sense the mixture of his disapproval and his grudging respect.

I pulled away from Parker with obvious reluctance and saw — because I was looking for it — the micro-expression on his face, which had included a tiny smile. I'm sure my brother never saw it. I was getting good at reading the subtext of Parker.

We went into Cam's apartment where Serafina, who had clearly been briefed by her husband, held back behind the pretty red-tile counter despite her obvious desire to come and swamp me with "thank goodness you're alive" kisses. "Would anyone like tea?" she asked.

"Yes, thanks," Parker said.

"Me, too. Thanks, Serafina." I sent her a grateful look, and she gave me a little wave. Cam followed Parker and me to the living room, where Parker and I sat on the couch and Cam claimed a chair across from us.

Cam described the area where we'd been parked, and our detective did some rapid texting. Then Parker put down his phone and said, "Now. Any ideas about who might have known you were there?"

I shrugged. "Anyone could have known if they made a point of following us from Cam's apartment."

"And who knew you were here?"

I started counting on my fingers. "My

friend Jenny; Enrico Donato and his whole clan; my family. That's all I can think of, aside from my coworkers. Oh, and the people in the studio could have followed Cam and me to the parking lot."

"Right," Parker said. He made some notes on his little computer. "Donato is just downstairs, right? I'll talk to him next."

"Um — I talked to him in the lobby. I asked if he tried to have me killed."

Parker sighed.

Cam said, "Yeah, that was a weird exchange. But the guy seemed genuinely shocked. He did say that he would put his men on protection duty."

"Great," Parker said drily.

"Are you telling me that this guy is seriously in the Outfit? Little Mr. Donato from the hair salon?" Cam looked sort of excited about it.

"He was reputedly active in the syndicate in the eighties and nineties. Then he was off the radar for a while. Lately the word is that he is retired."

"He seems worried, though," I said. "He got very pale when I told him someone shot at me."

Parker turned to me with an exasperated expression. "You don't need to tell strangers these things, Lilah."

"I was angry! I wanted to know if he was responsible. I don't think he was."

"But he could have hired someone who was."

"I guess."

Parker sighed again. Then he tried a new tactic, asking, "Why would anyone at the studio have followed you?"

I sat up straight. "Yeah, I forgot to tell you. The woman who did my makeup — Tabitha something — said she was good friends with Brad, and that he wasn't an out-of-work actor at all, but was getting regular work in the Chicago area. She said he was starring in *The Tempest* at some theater in the suburbs."

"Okay." He typed.

"And she was nice, she was fine, but I got the sense that she knew more than she was saying. She said she's known Whitefield for years. They met doing a show — she was makeup and he was talent. But she seems to do all sorts of stage tech stuff."

"Hmm. I'll need to talk to her; you're right."

Serafina had crept forward. "Lilah, I'm sorry to interrupt — but do you mind if I put on the show? I taped it because I was working out. It played an hour ago."

"It did?" I stared at her. I could barely

remember the whole TV show escapade — it seemed ages ago. I grabbed my purse and pulled out my phone; sure enough, there were about twelve text messages, mostly from my mother and from Jenny, all of them saying things like You look beautiful! and You and Angelo looked great together! (that was Jenny) and That was the best show ever!

"Oh geez," I said. "Yeah, I guess you can put it on. I'll have to face it sometime."

She flipped on her television and clicked on her recording of the show. There were Angelo's opening credits and some images of him striding down Michigan Avenue to the strains of some invigorating Italian music. Then the final screen image was a freeze of his face, looking very handsome, and the words Cooking with Angelo.

Parker cleared his throat and started skimming through his notes.

On the screen, Angelo waved at his studio audience as they clapped wildly; then he began reading the "Kitchen Dilemmas" letter from Darlene. I was amazed anew at what a natural Angelo was on camera; there was nothing stiff about him.

Parker, on the other hand, was growing stiffer by the moment.

Angelo introduced me, and I walked out. "Oh, Lilah, look how pretty you look on

133

television!" Serafina yelled, clapping her hands.

Cam nodded. "You do, Lilah — you look great."

Parker said nothing, but he glanced up at the screen when Serafina said that.

I said, "Tabitha was right. You can't tell how much makeup I had on — but look at my face now. I had tons of gunk on —"

I stole a look at Parker's shirt and saw the telltale makeup smears. "Oh, Jay, I'm so sorry. I got makeup on you."

He looked down and then shook his head. "No big deal. It will wash off." He wasn't making eye contact; this was never a good sign with Parker.

I needed to get him out of this room before Angelo kissed me on-screen.

"Don't you have to go call in? There's a phone right over there in Serafina's study."

Parker's blue eyes were on his computer. "This isn't the 1970s, Lilah. I called on my cell."

"I just thought — you probably need some quiet so you can fill people in on what's happening. Maybe get some feedback about Donato or something. I don't know — just away from the chaos."

"All I hear is a whistling teakettle," said Parker, giving me his cool blue stare. Fina ran to switch it off, then returned.

Angelo was already getting pretty flirtatious on the screen, and Cam and Fina were caught up in the drama. "Despite the host, this show is good," Cam said. "I'm going to start watching it for cooking tips. Fina and I don't cook enough."

"And you have such good chemistry," Serafina said. "The way he looks at you — oh, the audience is eating it up." She sent a little sidelong look to Parker, whose jaw had tightened significantly. I realized she was trying to help me by making him jealous, but that wasn't a good plan with the inscrutable Jay Parker.

"We really don't have chemistry," I assured them. "It shows that Angelo is a good actor."

Fina went to the kitchen to make the tea, and on-screen Angelo showed the audience my finished casserole.

Then we were wishing each other happy holidays and Angelo was leaning in to kiss me. Even on television I could see the way that I blushed when he stole that kiss. It had been a blush of anger, but it looked like attraction.

Parker set down his computer and stood up. "Can I help you make the tea?" he called after Serafina.

135

Shoot. I locked eyes with Cam, who had figured out what was happening. He sat down next to me and spoke in a low voice. "What does he think, you're going to pine for him until you die? Screw him. If he wants you, he should fight for you."

"You sound like your wife."

"You're right," said Cam, looking surprised. "But it's true. He has to stop getting angry at every little setback. Life is full of setbacks. He needs to take you as you are. So you're attractive to other men — duh."

Now I sighed. "It's more complicated than that. We had just sort of agreed that when the case was over we would — try again. And now he sees this."

"Oh," Cam said.

"I didn't know Angelo was going to kiss me."

"It's not a big deal. He still needs to get over it."

We continued speaking in low voices, but we stopped when Parker and Fina came in with the tea. Parker handed me a mug and said, "Here you go, Lilah." His voice wasn't unfriendly, but it had lost the intimacy that had thrilled me in the hallway. Then he said, "Serafina, if it's all right, I will use your office for a moment."

"Oh, of course," she said. "Let me move

some things off of the chair." She ran ahead of him to manage the clutter. I sipped my tea and narrowed my eyes, watching Parker. A moment later Fina came out, and Parker shut the door.

"Oh boy," I said.

Mick, who had been sleeping through our whole exchange, now yawned and ventured out of his basket to set his head in my lap. I rubbed his silky ears and said, "Mick, I think I'm in trouble."

He looked at me with his sweet, soulful eyes — and nodded.

CHAPTER SEVEN

Parker stayed at Cam's apartment that night; he said he would be around until the police appointed me an official guardian. Normally this would have been thrilling, but instead it was rather disappointing, since Parker spent a lot of time on his phone in another room, and he didn't really take part in our quietly festive movie watching and eggnog drinking.

I still felt a bit disappointed as I made some belated calls on Saturday morning, the nineteenth of December. The first was to my parents; I informed them of the event I'd witnessed, but I left out any mention of the second shooting. Cam and I had agreed to keep that from them for the time being. However, I had to admit to my mother that Parker was, once again, arranging for me to have a police guard.

"Oh my! Jay Parker. Are you — is that working out okay?"

"Yeah. It wasn't ideal, to be thrown together again, but it hasn't been that bad. We — we're talking again, sort of."

"Does he really think a bodyguard is necessary?" my mother asked.

"Long story," I hedged.

"Well, better safe than sorry. You've been through enough. Will this police officer he's assigning you be at our Christmas celebration?"

"Um — I don't know. You never know what can happen in a few days. Maybe they'll have someone under arrest by then."

"Hmm," said my mother. Then, brightening, she said, "You looked so wonderful on television. Daddy and I both said that you missed your calling. You seemed like a natural up there. Esther called me and said the same thing; and she said they've received a slew of phone calls at Haven since your appearance."

"Oh, Haven! I have to call her."

"You do that, sweetheart. But remember that you and I are making Christmas cookies on the twenty-third, right?"

"Right. See you then, Mom."

"Take care. Do whatever the police say to be safe."

"I will." I hung up and stared at the phone. I had told my mother all she needed to know, but I felt bad about omitting the truly serious parts. Still, neither Cam nor I wanted her worrying over it. What good had worrying ever done?

I dialed the number for Haven and spoke to Esther, apologizing for being out of commission.

"Lilah, you've had a lot going on. Jim and I both feel that you should just come back in the New Year. As you know, we're giving ourselves a little holiday anyway, so it's only a couple more days that we'll need to do without you — then it's vacation for all."

"Well — if you're sure —"

"I am. We can handle it. In the meantime, you've given us some amazing and free publicity — please thank Angelo Cardelini for me." Her voice was bright.

"You — got a lot of calls?"

"You have no idea! Jim and I have practically filled our bookings through June, with a few extra things squeezed in."

"That's wonderful!"

"Yes. And you did that for us, so stop worrying and sit back. Enjoy your family and the holidays, and let the police catch this culprit."

"You're the best, Esther."

"Merry Christmas, Lilah!"

I was smiling at the phone when Parker

140

walked in, fresh out of the shower. A manly scent trailed him — traces of sandalwood and cedar. I would have given a lot to get a peek inside his travel bag and find out what products he used. "Good morning," he said in his professional voice.

"Good morning." I sent him a smile, but he managed to not see it while he busied himself at Cam's counter, looking for coffee supplies. He seemed none the worse for wear, despite the fact that he had slept on the floor of Serafina's office.

"Will I be able to go out today? I have some deliveries to make to clients, and I need to get some ingredients. I think Serafina said there was a little grocery store down in the lobby. Is it okay to go there?"

"As long as I go with you," Parker said. "Officer Banks will be here later this morning; I'll introduce you to her, and she will accompany you wherever else you need to go."

"Thanks, Jay." I smiled again, and this time he saw it. He reciprocated with a smile of his own, wan and pale, but there.

The phone in my lap rang, and I answered it.

"Hello — is that Lilah?"

"Yes. Who is this?"

"This is Tabitha Roth, from Channel 40?

141

I did your makeup yesterday."

"Oh yes. Hello."

"Hi. Listen, you told me to call you. . . ."

I sat up. "Have you remembered something about Brad? Something the police could use?"

Parker's eyes darted to me, his posture alert.

"No, not really. But I ended up contacting an old friend of mine last night — someone from the cast of *The Tempest*. I know everyone on the cast, as a matter of fact. The fact is — the show has been canceled for the next couple of days. A bunch of us are going to meet today for lunch to have a drink in Brad's honor. You said you wanted to know funeral arrangements — and this might be all there is. The rest is going to be private. I don't know if you're interested, or if your cop friend wants to know."

"Yes, I'm glad you called. I'd like to go. I have — reasons I'd like to pay my respects to him, however that's going to be done. Where are you meeting?"

"Brad lived in Pine Haven, so we're going to a little bar there that he liked called Penny Lane."

"Sure — I know it. I'll meet you there at — what time?"

"Around one. Okay, see you later." She

hung up, and I turned to Parker.

"That was Tabitha, the girl I told you about who did my makeup?"

Parker nodded.

"She's getting together with some actors from the production Brad was currently in. They're having drinks in his honor at some bar — I guess almost as a little ceremony. There will be no public funeral. She thought you or I might want to sit in on their gathering."

His eyebrows rose. "That sounds good." He had his ubiquitous computer out again, and he scrolled through some things while the coffee percolated and filled the air with a rich aroma. "But I have a lot of things to follow up on, and I'm pretty backed up. . . ."

He didn't say it, but we both understood that he was behind in his investigation because of me. "But you said you wanted to go — is that because of your conversation with him? You don't have to feel guilty, Lilah."

"I don't, exactly. I just — I'd like to give some sort of formal acknowledgment of him."

"And I'll definitely want their names and their contact information. Officer Banks will be with you, and she'll get that information for me. I'm glad your connection gave you a call."

"Yeah — I'm kind of surprised she did. She said she didn't like cops. Anyway." I jumped up and grabbed my purse. "That means I need to get some stuff in the oven pronto. I'll have to deliver some casseroles before I meet with Tabitha, and I'll have a tight window to work in."

"Will you be making anything for the gang here?" Parker asked, his eyes gleaming with hope. One thing I knew Parker loved without condition was my cooking.

"Yes, as a matter of fact. I'm making a French toast casserole that I created for my friend Toby. He's been a client for a while. He has lots of kids and he has a dad specialty, which is this casserole, but since it's Christmas I'm flavoring it with gingerbread. It's delicious, and his kids will love it. I'll make two, and you'll have something to eat with your coffee."

"That sounds good," he said.

He accompanied me down the stairs to the lobby, where we found the little storefront that said *Mighty Mart.* It was barely a store at all, just one of those places that sells the staples for people who don't want to leave their building to get a couple of ingredients. I managed to find almost everything I needed and came up with substitutions for what I didn't have. Parker held a basket, and I dropped things in with feverish haste, worrying over timelines.

"Lilah," he murmured.

"Hmm?"

"That man in the doorway. Have you seen him before?"

I looked up, surprised. The man in question, youngish, dark haired, lounged just outside the Mighty Mart, leaning on the wall.

"No."

"He's been following us. He was on the stairway behind us."

"He's not a cop?"

"No." His brow furrowed, and his lips grew narrow. "Why am I thinking this might be the work of your new friend, Mr. Donato?"

I opened my mouth, but couldn't think of words. Parker took my basket to the counter and set it down. "You ring up. I'm going to have a chat."

He walked to the entrance and confronted the man outside, who looked not at all bothered by Parker's presence. I tried to keep my eyes on the cashier, but my gaze kept drifting to the doorway, where the two men held a quiet but intense conversation.

Finally the clerk handed me two bags and I moved toward the door. Parker, unsmiling, took my bags and steered me toward the stairs with his elbow. I waited until we were in the stairwell and said, "Well?"

"His name is Frank. He said he was asked by Mr. Donato to keep an eye on you and protect you. I explained that I am the police and he can scram."

I grinned at Parker. "Scram? Should he scram all the way back to the 1940s?"

That got a tiny smile. "If you see him around again when I'm not here, you call me, Lilah."

I shrugged. "If he's actually protecting me, why is that a bad thing?" We had reached our floor, and Parker held the door so that I could walk through.

Parker started to say something that was probably a lecture, but his phone rang, and he clicked it on and turned slightly away. "Parker." He listened for a while, and his shoulders stiffened. Then he said, "Okay. Yes — exactly. So maybe I can call you in about half an hour? I know." He took a few steps away and spoke in a soft voice. "Don't worry; I'll call you soon." And then, even more softly, "I love you."

I was outside Cam's door, so I was able to hide my distress by thumping the bags onto

146

the floor and fumbling for the key Cam had given me. Parker put away his phone and moved closer. I couldn't resist. "Was that your mother?" I tried to sound bright and unconcerned.

Parker looked at his shoes. "Uh — no."

That was all I was going to get. I blundered into the apartment and moved blindly to the kitchen, racking my brains to think of a person — any person — who might innocently elicit that intimate tone from Parker. He had no sisters, and I was sure he wouldn't speak to a brother that way. No — he had been talking to a woman, and that meant only something bad.

Parker moved toward me, his look wary. I got busy at the countertop, cracking eggs into a lovely red bowl from Serafina's cabinet. "You're quite proficient in the kitchen," he tried. "Such efficiency of movement."

"Thanks."

He seemed to realize that he was going to get nothing more from me, including eye contact, so he moved off to Serafina's office and shut the door. Even from this distance I thought I could hear him murmuring to someone.

I focused on my casseroles. The key to a delicious gingerbread is getting the right molasses (I used Angelo's Gourmet, which had earned a frown from Parker at the convenience store) and the perfect blend of spices. I did some careful measuring of cinnamon, cloves, and ginger, doubling up so that I could make two versions of this particular casserole. I preheated the oven and then dipped my bread into the ginger-bread concoction, laying it into glass bakeware, then drizzling it with a sprinkling of nuts and melted butter.

By the time I slid them into the oven, Serafina finally appeared, looking rumpled and sexy in a little red robe. It was official: there was no occasion in which Serafina did not look attractive. "Lilah? You're up so early!"

"Yes. I had to get started on some food deliveries, but I'll have breakfast for you and Cam. Is he at work?"

"No — he's in bed. We were up late, talking and talking."

Now it was Serafina who didn't make eye contact, but it was clear enough what she and my brother had been doing into the wee hours. "Oh. Well, hurry up and take your shower, and I'll make you both some coffee."

Forty minutes later they were all at the table and being regaled with Christmas songs from Serafina's iPod. I watched as

148

Parker, Cam, and Serafina dug in to the still-warm gingerbread casserole. Cam slathered his with additional syrup and butter, although I had already topped the dish with fresh whipped cream. They started to eat, and I held my breath until I heard the first "Ah," which came from Parker. He certainly was a loyalist about my food.

"Lilah, this is delicious!" Serafina said. "Such a wonderful way to start the day — warm food to warm the heart." Her words were highlighted by Perry Como, who was singing "Home for the Holidays" in his rich, reassuring voice.

"Thank you. Now I have to wrap up this other one and deliver it to Toby. I'll get your dish back tomorrow, Serafina."

She waved that off. "It is no problem. You know I barely ever cook. Cameron had those dishes when I moved in."

Cam grinned. "And I think I stole them from Mom."

The doorbell rang, and Parker left his food (reluctantly, I thought) to answer it. He came back in with a tall blonde woman who wore a professional-looking tan suit over a white turtleneck. She was also clearly packing a gun and a badge.

"Lilah, this is Wendy Banks. She'll be assigned to you until we find the person who shot at you and your brother."

I stepped forward and shook her hand. "Officer Banks," I said. Her grip was firm; she was clearly very strong. Suddenly I felt bad about the three anemic push-ups I had done that morning.

"Call me Wendy," she said. "It's nice to meet you."

"Have you eaten, Wendy?"

"I had some egg whites a few hours ago. What is that amazing aroma?"

Parker said, "Lilah is a very talented chef, and she made breakfast."

"Can I talk you into some of it?" I asked.

"You sure can," said Wendy, and after Parker made introductions, she was seated next to Serafina and digging in to a dish of my casserole. She seemed to be one of those people who mainly ate healthy, tofu-like substances but who enjoyed a good cheat now and then. "Oh wow," she said after taking a huge bite.

"No kidding," my brother agreed. They all ate in silence, and I finished wrapping Toby Atwater's food.

"Wendy, whenever you're finished, I have to deliver one of these casseroles to a client, and then I'm meeting some people at one. Parker can tell you about it while I get my coat."

She shoveled down the last of her food and said, "Thanks for this assignment, Jay. It beats the Dumpster search I had to do last week."

Everyone laughed, and I said, "We'll feed you as long as you're here. I really appreciate you doing this, at the holidays and everything." Nat King Cole was singing now about Yuletide carols sung by a choir.

Wendy glanced around Cam's cozy apartment, her gaze resting on Serafina's little pine tree, which looked distinctly European and charming. "This is the most Christmassy I've felt in a long time. I don't usually do much at the holidays." She shrugged, the picture of the lonely cop surprised by warmth and attention. Sort of like Parker.

A moment later everyone was getting ready to go out: Fina and Cam to do some shopping, Parker to get to his office, and Wendy and I to deliver a casserole. "Wendy," I said, "I normally take Mick with me as my protection. Do you care if he rides along?"

"Who's Mick?" she asked.

In response to his name, my sweet chocolate-brown dog came padding into the dining room and put his head on Wendy's lap. "Oh my gosh, what a beautiful Lab!" she said. "I had a dog like this when I was a kid, except he was coal-black. His name was

151

Claude." She started massaging Mick's head with great energy.

"Do you have a dog now?"

She shook her head. "Nah. My roommate and I have gone to the shelter a few times, but we never decided on anything."

She played with Mick's ears while I got his leash. "Here — can you hold him while I grab my food?"

Wendy walked my dog out the door, and I followed her, with one last glance at Parker. "Be careful," he said.

Toby was grateful for the casserole. We met outside of town by our usual spot — an overpass that created a shadow on the road and allowed for our mysterious exchange. He paid me, and I took my fifty dollars back to Wendy's black Ford 500. She grinned at me. "So you do this all the time — meet people in these clandestine locations and slip them food, like a drug deal?"

"Food is a kind of drug. Lots of people are addicted to it."

"No kidding," Wendy said. "I'm going to dream about that gingerbread tonight. You're really good." She turned toward me. "Hey, your sister-in-law told me you were just on television."

"Oh — yes. An old friend of mine has a

show called *Cooking with Angelo* —"

"Oh my gosh, we watch that show!"

"You do?"

"Yeah — my roommate and I like to watch it when I'm not on morning duty."

"What's the name of this mysterious roommate?"

She squinted out the back window as she pulled away. Her eyes had been darting consistently since we got in the car. I felt I was being protected by the CIA. "Betsy. Or Bets."

"That's nice that she watches. If you want, I can probably get her an Angelo T-shirt or something. He's all about merchandizing. I think he even has a trivet with his face on it."

"God, she would love that. That would be great." Her expression, which was as closed and cop-like as Parker's, briefly showed warmth and affection.

I got out my phone and scrolled until I found Angelo's number. "Let me text him now, before I forget. Tell me her name and address."

Wendy rattled off the information, and I texted it to Angelo, saying that Bets was a fan and a friend. "There. He's a pretty good businessman, and this falls under the heading of customer service, so I think we can assume he'll be on top of it."

"Thanks," Wendy said. "Now tell me about this lunch we're having."

"Oh, well — I guess you know that I was there when the guy was shot at the grade school? The guy dressed as Santa?"

"Detective Parker filled me in." Her face went into blank professional mode, and it made me wonder what else Parker had told her. Mick stuck his nose between our seats, and she petted it absently.

"Well, I happened to run into this woman Tabitha Roth, who travels in the same acting circles as the dead man — Whitefield. She and some of his former cast mates are having drinks in his honor, and she thought I might want to sit in, sort of as a fly on the wall. I had said I wanted to be notified of funeral arrangements, and — I guess this is it. The rest will be private. Parker thinks it will be good to be there in any case; he wants you to take notes, I guess, but he probably told you. And I can keep my eyes open, too. I have a tendency to note details — Parker will admit that's true."

"I guess we can compare notes afterward," she said. "This sounds like a good lead. God knows he can use the help at Christmastime; tons of people want time off this time of year, and we're kind of short staffed."

154

I looked out my window. We were passing a shopping mall, and the parking lot was packed. Beyond the sea of cars I could see Christmas lights twinkling at the mall entrance. "It's a bad time of year to get yourself killed."

"Now, don't get all depressed on me. We've got to keep alert and positive — it helps."

Mick sniffed at my shoulder, and I giggled. "Mick always cheers me up. He's my special boy."

"He is pretty great," Wendy said, and Mick nodded.

She was still laughing when we pulled up to the apartment. I called Serafina, who jogged down to claim Mick, and then we drove out of the city, back to Pine Haven and Penny Lane, the bar where the actors were gathering.

As we got out of our car, I noticed a dark-haired man a few spots down, leaning on his driver's door and reading the paper. Donato's Frank, following us to another location. Parker had warned Wendy about Frank, so I shook my head at her with a 'Do you believe this guy?' expression and we moved toward the door.

The moment we entered the bar I realized it might have been a mistake to come into such a large throng of people, but Wendy stood tall and alert at my side, and that provided far more comfort than I had expected. Annie Lennox's "Winter Wonderland" was blasting, mixed with the sound of many voices raised in jovial conversation. I scanned the room, generously festooned with pine swags and gold lights, and saw Tabitha waving. "There they are," I said. "Am I supposed to tell them you're a cop, or what?"

"Just say I'm your friend. They'll probably notice my gun sooner or later, but let them draw their own conclusions. The less they know, the better."

"Okay."

We reached the large table and grabbed two of the three empty seats. I did a quick scan of the chairs: even if I hadn't known these people were actors, I would have guessed. Tabitha introduced them one by one: Dylan Marsh, who had played the part of Antonio, wore a purple silk shirt, slightly open at the collar to reveal a tanned throat and some curling chest hair. He sported a well-trimmed brown beard that gave him the look of an evil prince in an old movie. He was jarringly handsome. Isabel Beauchamp, who had the role of Ariel, was tiny and delicate with a mass of blondish-red curls. She was brighter than the Christmas lights in a formfitting green dress with a gold belt that glistened in the bar's holiday glow. Claudia Birch, who had played Miranda, was tall and elegant, with dark hair and compelling dark eyes.

Next to them all, Tabitha looked rather plain in her jeans and T-shirt; it was clear why she was a behind-the-scenes person and all of these people were stage faces.

"Okay, now you know everyone," Tabitha said after her introductions. "Everyone, this is Lilah. She was an acquaintance of Brad's."

They nodded, not seeming to care much how I knew Whitefield. I waved vaguely at the table. "Thanks for inviting me. This is my friend Wendy."

"Are you a cop?" asked Dylan Marsh, looking at Wendy and smoothing his beard.

"Guilty," Wendy said lightly, lifting a finger for the waitress. "But it's my lunch hour, and I already had plans with Lilah when she got the call about your friend. So here we are."

I said, "I'm glad to have a chance to drink to Brad. He seemed like a really nice guy."

"He was a most talented man," said delicate Isabel. She had a British accent, I noted. "We will all miss him so much."

I nodded. "Will the show close down now? Prospero's the lead role, isn't it? I can't imagine how you would go on without him."

Everyone besides Wendy and me looked uncomfortable. Tabitha said, "Well, every production has understudies, Lilah. You can't take a risk on — someone getting hurt or sick or — dying."

"Oh, I see. So who is Brad's understudy?"

Dylan Marsh raised an elegant hand. "I am. I was Antonio, which is a much smaller part, but obviously I know the part of Prospero. It's the role I actually auditioned for. So my understudy will be the new Antonio, and I'll be the mighty sorcerer himself." He turned slightly red as he said it, but there was also some barely concealed triumph in his expression.

Wendy took a sip of her water. "Well, congratulations. The show must go on, sad as it is. Is it supposed to run for a while?"

Claudia Birch directed her dark, intense gaze at us. "We've gotten some wonderful reviews, and actually we've been extended indefinitely. It looks like we'll be taking the show on the road when it closes here. Our producer thinks we might end up on Broadway."

She said "Broadway" the way devout people say "heaven."

The waitress returned with our soft drinks; it seemed we latecomers were the only ones who hadn't ordered yet, so Wendy and I both asked for a pub sandwich.

"I guess cops can't drink on duty, huh?" Marsh inquired. He seemed weirdly fascinated with Wendy's profession.

"Nope," Wendy said. "But then people in your career can't really drink too heavily, either, can they? It would affect your performance."

They all snorted out some dramatic laughter. Little Isabel even held her ring-laden hands to her tiny abdomen, as though Wendy were causing her delicious pain. "Oh my. Actors are the most notorious drinkers, don't you know? Not so much we three here, but — some."

They all looked at the table again, and the conversation died.

"Brad, do you mean? Was he a drinker?" Wendy asked.

Marsh looked aggrieved. "Not anymore. In his early years, yeah, he had a reputation as a drinker and a brawler, too. But in the last couple years, he finally grew up. He got his act together. He made up with his wife; he stopped drinking and — other things."

"Gambling?" I asked.

Claudia Birch's dark eyes studied me. "I

159

thought you were just an acquaintance. It sounds like you knew him quite well."

"No — it was just — something I heard. That he had sort of an addiction. He seemed like a nice guy, though."

"Brad was more than a nice guy. He was a genius of an actor, and a good man. A passionate man. He had a zest for life." This was Isabel, who was suddenly near tears.

Claudia patted her shoulder and nodded in sympathy. "Brad was also doing his best to save his marriage. He and Cleo had some rocky times, but things were — finally getting back on course for them."

Dylan and Isabel remained quiet, thinking their own thoughts. I found myself staring at their clothing — his silk shirt and her jewel-toned dress — and imagining them as royalty in some fictional castle. Even in their off-hours they were transporting me to a pretend place. Tabitha lifted her glass. "He was like any genius: he had a dark side, but when he glowed, he glowed brightly."

This silenced everyone for a moment. I couldn't decide if the sentiment was mawkish or weirdly beautiful, but we all raised our glasses and clinked them together, and then drank to the man I had seen die.

Tabitha sighed. "Cleo might stop by, everyone, so be cool if she shows up."

The actors looked alarmed, and Tabitha held up a hand. "People who are grieving need support, even if we don't always know how to give it. Just be kind. That's what she needs."

Everyone nodded, and I realized what a strange grouping of people we were. For some reason I decided that Parker would hate all of the theater people, but I wasn't sure why I felt that way.

One oddity I noted was that all three thespians seemed to want to face the door. Marsh was at the head of the table and almost directly facing the entrance, but every time someone entered, he sat straighter and lifted his chin, as though he were confronting a glorious spotlight. Claudia and Isabel had both turned their chairs at odd angles so that they could keep their eyes on the incoming traffic. At one point Claudia leaned forward and blocked Dylan's view, and he actually hitched to his left and stayed that way, oddly off-center, until she sat back again.

I sent a covert look to Wendy, who smirked at me and took a bite of her sandwich.

A few minutes later, when it seemed we'd run out of polite conversation and passionate tributes to Brad, a woman walked in and moved toward the empty chair at our table.

She was a short redhead with a dusting of freckles and bright green eyes. She wasn't beautiful, but she was attractive, and seemed to have a vibrant and intense personality, which made her fit right in with the melodramatic crowd around us. She took off a voluminous green coat and hung it on her chair.

"Cleo," Tabitha said, standing up to embrace the woman.

Cleo sent her a moist-eyed look that spoke of gratitude, and they sat down. Tabitha introduced everyone at the table, and Cleo's eyes lingered on Wendy and me. "You two were friends of Brad's?"

"Not exactly friends. I got to know him in recent days," I said. "Tabitha and I happened to be discussing him yesterday, and — she invited me to share a drink in his honor."

Cleo nodded. "This was a nice idea, Tabby." She patted her hair, which did indeed look messy, and slapped at her cheeks as if to put some life into her very pale skin. "I needed to get out — I really did."

"How are all the arrangements coming along?" Claudia asked softly.

Cleo stole another surreptitious glance at Wendy and me. Something about us intrigued her — or bothered her? "It's going to be a private service and interment. Nothing for the public, I'm afraid. Brad didn't want anything like that."

Isabel raised her well-plucked eyebrows. "That doesn't sound like Brad. He loved the limelight, just as we all did."

"Brad was pretty complex, though," said Tabitha, her face earnest.

Cleo shrugged. "I guess when it comes right down to it, all actors are introverts at heart. He told me once that he didn't want a big deal made of his funeral. But of course he probably assumed that would happen when he was old." Her voice caught on the last word, and the table went silent. She dabbed at her green eyes with a tissue she had crumpled in her hand.

Dylan Marsh, who had been sipping his beer, froze with the glass halfway to the table, like a wax figure of himself, apparently uncertain how to process Cleo's grief.

Cleo snorted out a laugh through her tears. "Put it down, Dylan, before your arm starts shaking."

They all laughed nervously in response, and suddenly Cleo was facing me. "So how did you say you knew Brad?"

I felt the curious eyes of everyone at the table. "We met through mutual acquaintances, a short while before his death. He was nice to me," I said. "At a time when I was feeling down. He — gave me some good advice. I'll always be grateful for it."

She nodded, looking pleased. "Brad had a good heart. That's what I keep telling myself. He and I had our differences over the years, but all I can think of now is what a good guy he was when the chips were down."

"Were you excited about the prospect of traveling? I understand the play was going to go on tour," Wendy said, her voice appropriately solemn.

Cleo sighed. "No, not really. Brad loved the uncertainty of the actor's life, but I wanted to put down roots. It's one of the things we tended to fight about."

"You're not an actor?" I said.

Cleo's smile was sad. "No. I met Brad after one of his shows, but I work at a law firm. They've given me a leave of absence while I sort things out."

Claudia said, "But you *were* going to travel! Weren't you going to Hawaii in the spring?"

Cleo nodded with a little smile. "We were. I found the tickets in our desk drawer. Brad had been waiting to surprise me, but he admitted that he had made plans. His understudy was going to cover his role while he was gone, assuming the show lasted until March. It was — a very romantic gesture. I wish —"

I wanted to know what she wished, but Isabel spilled her water just then, and suddenly many hands were busy with mopping and dabbing, and the conversation ended.

I was watching Marsh. His face was necessarily theatrical, but it was compelling — I could see why he was successful in the dramatic arts. I found it difficult to look away, because his expression was constantly changing. First it had reflected sympathy for Cleo Whitefield, then a sort of bemused sadness as he gazed into his drink; now he looked up with an almost calculating expression. He caught my eye, smiled wryly, and looked down at the table, his lowered lids masking his demeanor.

I suddenly remembered that Antonio, the character Marsh had played in *The Tempest*, was the man who had usurped Prospero and stolen his throne. In fact, he had been willing to kill Prospero in order to get the power and acclaim of the dukedom. Now Marsh was replacing his own Prospero — Brad Whitefield. Was wanting a part a motive for murder?

Wendy was looking at her watch. "I guess

we should get going," she said to me. "It was nice meeting all of you. Mrs. White-field, I'm very sorry for your loss."

Cleo nodded. Wendy took a last swig of her drink and then stood up and began to shake hands with all the people at the table. I leaned down to reach for my purse just as Isabel held out a hand to clasp Wendy's. Her rings glimmered beneath the Christmas lights, and I noticed that she, like Brad Whitefield, wore a hematite band on her little finger. I wondered if it was a theater thing — some sort of symbolic gesture that the actors were making.

I was about to ask when Cleo Whitefield turned to me, her green eyes moist. "It was good of you to join in a toast to Brad. Since he didn't want a funeral, this is probably the only public acknowledgment of him that will be made. So it's nice — I feared it would be just me and Tabitha." She forced a smile, and I took her hand.

"I'm glad I could be here. Thank you for including me." I nodded to the group and made my way toward the door with Wendy. Tabitha ran after us.

"Lilah! Thanks for coming out. Did you get any helpful information?"

"I don't really know," I said. "I'll just report the basics and let the police process it as they wish. Thanks for inviting us."

Tabitha nodded.

Wendy said something to her, and she shifted her attention to my cop companion. I stole one last look at the table, where Cleo and the actors were leaning in toward one another and looking conspiratorial. Perhaps it was my imagination — but perhaps not. Dylan Marsh looked up at me, his evil genius beard glowing gold in the bar lights. He flashed a white-toothed smile that reminded me of a wolf's bared teeth.

"I think I'm feeling paranoid," I told Wendy as we headed to the car.

She was scanning the parking lot. "It was an odd group. The boss will want to hear about that lot. Here's our friend again."

She pointed her head toward Frank, who still leaned against a red Toyota.

"It's weird, right — that some gangster has one of his guys following me?" Frank saw us looking and waved. Then he continued to scan the parking lot, as Wendy had been doing.

"Weird and noteworthy," she said, her eyes narrowed. "I have all kinds of things to share with Parker."

"I'll let you pass on the information about about our lunch companions. You probably know better what to look for. To me it just seemed like an odd assortment of friends."

Wendy shot me a sideways look. "I wouldn't say that Whitefield had too many friends at that table."

"Really?" I thought about this as I reflected on the strange expressions that had passed over all of the actors' well-trained faces. Wendy's comment made me sad, and for some reason I thought of Brad Whitefield's Shakespearean quotation, "We are such stuff as dreams are made on."

As if to reinforce this sentiment, Wendy's Christmas station played Bing Crosby, who dreamed of a White Christmas as we drove through a light snow toward the city.

CHAPTER EIGHT

A heavier snow came on Sunday morning, and the four of us had bacon and eggs in Cam's little kitchen while we watched the flakes dance past the window.

"I'd like to go home today," I said.

Serafina pouted. "Why? Aren't you having a nice time?"

"Yes, of course. But I miss my bed, and now I have Wendy guarding me full-time, so I think it's okay, right?" I turned to Wendy, who was once again eating heartily.

She nodded. "I'll call to make sure. We don't do anything without Parker's approval." She wolfed down the last of her eggs, thanked Serafina and Cam, and took her cell phone into the living room, where she stood gazing out at the Lakeshore while she called the Pine Haven PD.

Cam looked uncertain. "She seems competent, but it makes me nervous to have you out of my sight. I mean, that was a real bullet, Lilo."

"I know. But I feel safe with Wendy. And I have clients to bake for today, and deliveries to make, and I need to talk to Esther and Jim, and a million other things. Even Mick probably misses his basket."

Mick, who was under the table waiting for wayward pieces of bacon, perked up his ears at the mention of his name.

Cam smiled. "We like having Mick here. Serafina is trying to talk me into getting a dog now."

"Mick has that effect on people."

I was watching Wendy, who had apparently been connected with Parker, and was now talking at great length. She had already shared her thoughts on the trio of actors, Tabitha, and Cleo — a bizarre grouping of people, now that I thought about it. And I was sure she'd mentioned Frank, who had managed to follow us to the bar the previous day, and who had been behind us when we left, as well. I wondered what she and Parker were talking about now.

What must Parker think of it all? I imagined that he was wearing his habitual scowl while Wendy spoke, and that he was doing something nervous with his hands — playing with a pencil or bouncing a Super Ball that I had seen in his car. I wondered what he was wearing, and if his scent was the same as it had been when he stayed the night at Cam's house. With a sudden jolt of fear, I wondered if I had done anything embarrassing while I slept that night — talked in my sleep or ground my teeth or snored — that Parker might have overheard.

"Lilah?"

I jumped. "Oh. You're off the phone."

"Parker says it's okay, but the rule is you go nowhere without me."

"I wouldn't want to."

"Fine. You can pack up your things whenever."

Serafina looked sad to hear this. I realized that she must miss her huge Italian family — she had something like ten brothers and sisters, and their house must have been packed at Christmastime.

I put my hand on hers. "You know I'll see you again in a few days. You and Cam should stay over at least one night at Mom and Dad's so we can have some fun — play board games and read Dickens aloud and all that Christmassy stuff."

Her face brightened. "That sounds beautiful. And I will make Italian cookies. The one thing I can bake."

"I'll want the recipe."

Cam stood up and stretched. "I need to

get out and run on the Lakeshore. The holidays make me fat."

Wendy shook her head. "I'm afraid I can't let you do that, Mr. Drake."

"What?" My brother looked as surprised as I felt.

"The bullet aimed at your car may have been intended for your sister. But it could also have been intended for you. Detective Parker would prefer that you keep to your home as much as possible until we've had a chance to investigate the incident."

Serafina nodded with a dark expression. "I've warned Cameron about this. He has some very angry ex-girlfriends."

Cam looked from Wendy to Serafina with wide eyes, then sighed. "I'll go stir-crazy in here. I have to get outside and run."

Wendy put her hands on her athletic hips. Today she wore a red shirt with a black suit. She looked professional and rather intimidating. "Understood. Perhaps just for the time being you can do your running on the staircases. Even better exercise, and you don't get wet from snow."

He scowled, but he nodded. "Fine."

Serafina swooped in and kissed him. "More time to spend with me," she said, and he grinned like the happy fool that he was.

■ ■ ■ ■

We drove up to my little cottage at about noon. Wendy checked the outside, then went inside with my key, her pistol drawn. This made me nervous, but it also comforted me. If someone was out there and prepared to use a gun against me, it was nice to know that an armed police officer was at my side, willing to wield her own weapon in my defense.

Wendy came back to the car, her eyes still darting. "All clear. Come on in. Cute house, by the way."

"Thanks! It's tiny, but we love it. Come on, Mick."

Mick sniffed some of the rocks and leaves that lined our driveway, then followed me up the front steps. I showed Wendy the layout of my place, then led her into my small but clean kitchen. I enjoyed a moment of quiet pride before I got out my calendar and started making notes.

"I hope you don't mind," I told Wendy, "but I have to get right to work. I have things to bake for clients who need their orders delivered today — just like yesterday, except this time it's a baked Reuben casserole and a pot of chili."

"Great! I'll be your taste tester, if you need one." Wendy was still in scanning mode, peeking into my backyard and examining the lock on my patio door.

"Of course. And I'd just like to say — thanks for being here. I know you guys are working hard, and it's Christmas and everything."

She shrugged. "This is the most interesting duty I've ever been given. And it has its culinary rewards."

I grinned as I gathered the ingredients for the big batch of chili I had to make for Perpetua Grandy. Pet was the woman at the heart of my dispute with Parker. It was Pet I had lied for; but it wasn't Pet's fault that I lied. She and I had remained on good terms, and I still cooked for her. She was one of my more eccentric friends, but she had an odd charisma that made all of our encounters entertaining.

I began slicing into two big white onions, then dicing them into smaller pieces.

"You're fast," Wendy noted, sliding onto one of my kitchen stools and watching me work.

"Practice," I said. I finished my chopping and scraped all of the onion pieces into a giant pot that I used for Perpetua's events. I flicked in some butter and began to sauté the vegetables. "There's something lovely about onions. I use them in every dish, both for flavor and for scent."

"What about garlic?"

"Not in this chili, but yes, I use it. Garlic can overwhelm, though, while onions accentuate. I don't like to overdo garlic. That's a rookie mistake."

"I should be taking notes," Wendy said.

I studied Wendy; she had a quiet air of authority and a no-nonsense look. I felt safe around her. "Now I have to draw on your expertise," I said.

"Okay, shoot."

"I've been trying to work this out. How would whoever shot at me know that I would be at that studio at that time of day? It seems to me like there are just a few possibilities. Choice A — the person who shot Whitefield hung around and followed Parker and me to my house, then followed me from that point on. But that doesn't make sense to me, because I was alone in the parking lot for more than five minutes. They could have just driven back in and shot me."

Wendy thought about this. "Unless they started driving away, then doubled back and found the police already there. And then they could have stayed on a side street and watched you."

"Ugh. That's horrible, but it also doesn't seem that likely to me. I feel like I would have sensed them. Plus, aside from the parking lot itself, there aren't a lot of places around Breville Road to just tuck in and wait to follow someone."

"Agreed. What's your B theory?"

"B is that it has something to do with Enrico Donato. He knew, as of Thursday when I got my hair done, that I was the one who witnessed the shooting. Based on the presence of Frank, it's clear that Donato has minions that will do his bidding. He could have assigned someone to follow me and take a shot when it was convenient."

Wendy stood up. "Is Frank still around, I wonder?" She left the kitchen and strolled to my front window. "I can't see the street that well from here, but I think I see his car. The guy is persistent; I'll give him that. I'll call the station and have someone send him on his way."

"If Frank is not protection, but someone who means me harm, why wouldn't he have acted by now? Unless of course he's the person who shot my window. But why would he let us see his face, in that case? And if Donato thinks I saw someone that I could identify, wouldn't it be too late? I've been around the police for four days. Clearly

I would have told them by now, so what's the point in eliminating me?"

"Don't forget another option — that the bullet was intended for your brother."

I opened a four-pound package of ground beef and set the meat into the pot, then started spooning it apart. "That doesn't make sense, either. Cam's a university professor and a nice guy. He has no enemies."

"You don't have enemies, either. You were just in the wrong place at the wrong time."

I thought about this while I mixed the meat with the onions. I pulled three tomatoes from a basket on my counter and began to chop them. "Well, if you're going to call Cam a C option, then there's at least a D option, too. That whoever shot at us on Friday had some other way of knowing we'd be there — maybe they found out from someone close to me."

"That's not likely, is it? Your parents and friends wouldn't tell strangers about you."

"First of all, my mother would brag about me to any passing pedestrian if she was proud of something I had done. I think she was pretty excited about the TV gig, although I only told her about it the night before, so there wouldn't be that many people she could tell. And also, what if it wasn't a stranger? What if the person is someone that we know?"

I dumped the chopped tomatoes into the meat and onions.

"Boy, that smells good," Wendy said. Then, "It's more likely that you've never met the person. The most plausible explanation is that the shooting was related to Whitefield's murder, and that whoever shot you is fearful that you might have information."

"But I would have told it to you by now!" I said, stirring the mixture on the stove.

"What if it's information you don't realize you have? Something that might only dawn on you later? In that case, it's still worth the risk to eliminate you."

"That's all very nebulous." I turned off the heat and began to remove the grease from the pot with a turkey baster, then deposited the extracted grease into an old glass salsa container. "And the question remains — if it's related to Whitefield's murder, how did the perpetrator know where I would be that early on a Saturday morning? Unless they followed me to Cam's from Haven, but I'm pretty sure no one did." I scowled into the food I was making. "None of this makes any sense to me. Do you think Parker is considering all these options?"

Wendy sniffed. "I know he is. I've never met a cop as sharp as he is. The guy lives his job. Last year at Christmas we had a big department Christmas party. Parker stayed for half an hour and then went to his office to work."

I started adding an array of spices to the meat, measuring them out by memory. "Is he — dating anyone?"

"Parker? I doubt it. I've never seen him with any companion other than his partner or his computer. Not that the ladies haven't tried. I've seen many a woman throw herself at the guy with minimal results. I get why they do it. I mean, I'm gay, but even I can see the appeal. He's tall and fit and he's got those eyes. . . ."

"Yeah. Anyway. It's just the other day he was on the phone, and it seemed like maybe he was talking to a woman."

She shrugged. "Stranger things have happened, but I don't know how he would maintain the relationship when he practically lives at the PD."

"Huh." I dumped in two large cans of Angelo's Gourmet tomato sauce, then stirred.

I could hear the smile in Wendy's voice.

"Sounds like you're pretty interested in him yourself."

I sighed. "Yeah, well. We have something of a history."

She was off the stool in a shot and towering over me. "Get *out!*"

"No. And this is between you and me."

"I am discreet. And curious."

"Two months ago I witnessed another murder."

"What?" She looked briefly mistrustful, as though I might have Munchausen syndrome.

"I don't know how this happened twice. I just happened to be there."

"The poisoning? In the church basement?"

"Yeah. I was there with my mom. We were witnesses, and that's how I met Parker. Anyway, we saw kind of a lot of each other because of the investigation, and it seemed like — things were getting a little more serious — and then it ended kind of abruptly."

She looked intrigued, but she was polite enough not to ask questions. "Now that you mention it, I thought I got kind of a vibe between you two at your brother's house. And he looks at you a lot — my gosh, it all makes sense now!"

"But I heard him talking to some woman

on the phone. And now I'm wondering if there's someone else."

"You said it was over with you two."

"But I . . . don't want it to be."

"Ah." Wendy nodded, then grinned at me. "You are just endlessly entertaining. As a case, as a food supplier, and now with this really interesting information about Parker."

"Don't spread it around."

She held up her hands. "I'm not the type. Although I will probably tell my roommate. But Bets will keep it to herself. She doesn't mix with people on the force."

"What does she do?"

"She's a math teacher. High school."

"And are you — a couple?"

"Yeah. For three years now." She looked pleased as she said it — contented. I felt a burst of envy for a relationship that seemed healthy instead of tormented.

"Do you have Christmas plans?"

She looked out the kitchen window with her hawk-like gaze, then returned to the stool. "Not really. Bets's family are in Kansas, and mine are in Canada. We only travel to see them every couple of years. Probably just a quiet meal at home."

"I'm having sort of a big meal with my family — you already met Cam and his wife, and my parents love meeting new people.

Why don't you two join us for Christmas? Especially because you might still be assigned to me."

I turned to catch her expression, which revealed genuine pleasure. "That would be wonderful! Thank you. I'll check with Bets tonight and get back —" She paused; Mick was growling in the next room. I tensed, and Wendy swept out without another word, her hand on her hip.

I peeked around the corner to see her pressed against the front door, looking out the small window. "A white car," she said. "Two occupants. They've pulled right up the long drive to your house, so they seem to be visiting you specifically."

"Oh God," I said.

"Before I go out there, take a look and see if you recognize anyone."

Shaking slightly, I joined her at the window and peered out. The first thing I noticed was the bumper sticker that said *JFK Honors Program.* The second was that one of the visitors was extremely small. I sighed with relief. "I know them. It's my friend Jenny and her nephew, Henry. She's probably returning my pans — I told her I needed them back. Could you let them in? I have one last thing to do in the kitchen."

I ran to the stove, added the final ingredients to my chili, then stirred it and left it to simmer. I grabbed a big glass pan for the casserole I needed to make for Gina Strauss, a client I'd met at a German food market in the city. Gina did a lot of cooking, but for a big German family meal, she needed to farm some of it out. However, she would never admit as much to her mother, so that was where I came in.

I got to work chopping some more vegetables, and Wendy appeared at the door. "Lilah, here are your visitors."

A little person ran past her and up to my legs, which he hugged rather dramatically.

"Henry!" I said. "You are the first nice thing to happen to me in quite some time."

"I know," said small Henry. "Do you have any cookies?"

Jenny was peeking through the doorway, holding the big pans in which I'd baked the macaroni and cheese. I grabbed my cookie jar and let Henry thrust his little hand inside. "Jenny, you can set those on the counter there. Wendy, this is my friend Jenny Braidwell. She teaches at the school where Whitefield played Santa. Jenny, this is Wendy Banks. She's a Pine Haven police officer."

Jenny set down the pans and shook Wendy's hand. "Nice to meet you." Then, to me, she said, "How are you holding up?"

"I'm getting back to work, which feels good. What's my little friend Henry doing here?"

"I'm babysitting him today. I told him I had to return your bakeware, and he was more than happy at the idea of visiting."

Henry already had chocolate on his face; he had moved to my refrigerator, where he was studying a variety of pictures that I had held there with magnets. "Who's dis guy?" he asked, pointing at the newspaper clipping of Angelo.

"He has a cooking show on TV. And he used to be my boyfriend," I said.

"Oh, he was gorgeous," Jenny said. This sounded disloyal, so she was quick to add, "But he was such a jerk. You're better off without him, Li."

Wendy's mouth hung open in surprise for a moment before she let out a laugh. "Bets thought you guys had chemistry. When I told her you were going to send her some of his merchandise, she texted me that she thought you two were going out. Wait until I tell her."

"We're not going out — make that clear — but once, yes."

Henry sneered. "He has long hair."

"Not everyone can have your natural

beauty, dear Henry," I said, grabbing him around the waist and kissing his head.

He squirmed away, but he clearly enjoyed the attention. Jenny's little nephew had sort of become my nephew as well, since I had seen him grow up and had sat in on many of Jenny's babysitting days.

I invited Jenny and the boy to sit down with Wendy and the last of my cookies and some milk, and then I finished up my casserole and put it in the oven. "There!" I said. "These should be finished and packed up in about two hours, and then I have deliveries to make."

Jenny shook her head. "I don't know how you do all that you do. I mean, I have a lot of lesson planning, but I don't have to shop and then cook and then deliver. That's time intensive and exhausting."

"Thank you! It is. But I also love it."

"You were so good on that TV show, Lilah. You looked really great on camera, and those studio lights made your hair look amazing. And speaking of your hair, do you have a new stylist? I love this cut."

"I do. I'll give you her card. You know Serafina, Cam's beautiful girlfriend?"

"You showed me her picture. She looks like an Italian goddess, basically."

"Yup. Well, they just eloped."

185

"Get *out!*" Jenny's lovely eyes widened.

"Yeah. And she took me to her stylist, and she's the one that did this."

"Oh, man, I want to see her. Too bad I can't get an appointment before the party tomorrow."

Henry gave us a sour look. "Ladies are always trying to look more pretty. They should just be pretty how they are."

Wendy held up her hand, and Henry gave her a high five. "I agree with Henry. You both look very attractive."

"Thanks," Jenny said. "I'm not normally the primping kind, but there is someone I'm trying to impress, and I'm going to a party with him tomorrow."

"It looked to me like you had already impressed him," I said. "Aside from the moment he was being introduced to me and talking about the clown, his eyes were on you."

Jenny blushed. "He's a nice guy. He's great with kids — it is his profession, after all — and he's got a good heart. He does a lot of charity work."

"And happens to be good-looking."

"That, too," she admitted.

I pointed at Jenny with a sudden revelation. "The clown," I said.

"What?" Jenny and Wendy said in unison.

"The Christmas clown. Ross told me that she was in the building, about to entertain the kids. But she probably got there early, right?"

"I guess," Jenny said.

"Will she be at this party tomorrow?" I asked.

"Uh — I don't know. Maybe. I think she actually is a friend of Dave's, so she probably will get an invite."

"Good. I want to talk to her," I said.

Jenny and Henry left half an hour later, and I got back to work. I carefully packed my chili pot into a sturdy cardboard box; then Wendy put it into the back of my car. I did the same with the casserole, and Wendy stowed that one, as well. Then, after she did a quick perimeter check, I left the house and climbed into my car with her and Mick, and we drove to St. Bartholomew Parish.

"I'll have to text Pet so she can run out to get it. She doesn't like people to see the handoff. She fears it will blow her cover."

"Got it," said Wendy, grinning.

Moments later Pet Grandy came bounding out into the snow, wearing a red velour sweatshirt and blue jeans. She waved discreetly at me but kept her eyes moving, making sure no one saw her take the chili.

She opened my back hatch, and I said, "It's the tall box, Pet."

"I saw you on TV," she said. "It was great. We'll talk soon — maybe next time you come to bingo night."

"Yeah — I'm sure my mom will drag me there in the New Year. Meanwhile, don't forget to return that Crock-Pot. You can leave it on my back porch under cover of night."

Pet giggled. "Merry Christmas, Lilah."

"Merry Christmas, Pet."

We drove to my next delivery, and I felt, somehow, that I had passed out of danger, and that things would be better now.

I flipped on the radio to hear Andy Williams belting out "It's the Most Wonderful Time of the Year." Wendy, to my vast surprise, started singing along in an unexpected soprano. I joined her, and Mick put his soft nose between us, seemingly to get closer to our music. We drove through snowy Pine Haven, admiring the Christmas lights, strung across the main streets, and the potted pines that brightened up the storefronts with their varied adornments.

I felt almost lighthearted, but I noted that Wendy's right hand rested at all times on her thigh so that it was never very far from her gun.

CHAPTER NINE

Bitter cold and blustery wind arrived on Monday morning; I felt bad sending Mick out into the yard at all, but he faced the gale with courage and did what was needed with more speed than usual. Then he trotted back in and went to his basket by the stove, which was nicely warm, since I was baking scones to go with Wendy's breakfast of cheesy eggs and bacon.

"You're going to fatten me up," Wendy said. She was already dressed in another pantsuit — this one a black knit set with a white blouse. "But it sure is good."

"It's the least I can do. And look how happy Mick is by the stove."

The phone rang, and I clicked it on while I peered at my scones through the oven glass. "Hello?"

"Hello, Lilah. It's Ellie."

"Ellie! I've been meaning to call you. Did you want to do some last-minute shopping with me?"

"Oh — do you know, I did most of mine online this year."

"That was smart."

"And so convenient! But listen. I'm calling with a confession, sweetie."

Ellie was my friend, and had been for the last three years, ever since we'd met at, of all things, a Tupperware party. She also happened to be Jay Parker's mother. Only Ellie and my parents were allowed to call me "sweetie."

"What sort of confession?"

"There's something I wanted to tell you, as my friend. But I knew you would worry. So I made Jay promise he wouldn't tell."

"What is it?" My internal alarm had my skin prickling. "Are you okay?"

She sighed in my ear. "I am, but I didn't know until this morning. My doctor was good enough to call before Christmas, because she knew I would worry. Tests came back negative. I had a cancer scare."

"Ellie! You should have told me. I would have been there in a flash, with food and consolation."

"I know, Lilah. You are such a good kid. But I just — I didn't want to worry you, in case it was nothing. Which, thank God, it was."

Then it hit me: Parker had been talking to her on the phone. It was her to whom he had said, "I love you." But I had asked if it was his mother, and Parker had said no.

"So — did you speak to Jay yesterday morning about this? On his cell phone?"

"Yes. He said he couldn't talk, but then he called me back a while later."

"Let me get this straight. Your son spoke to you, but when I asked if it was you, he said no."

"I guess he didn't want you to ask about it."

"So he *lied.* He lied to me."

"Well, he was protecting me, I guess."

"Right. The way I was protecting Pet Grandy when I lied. For which I got two months of silence from your son."

Ellie whistled. "I sense a little battle coming on. But just so you know, Jay had my feelings at heart."

"I appreciate that. But you were there, Ellie. You saw how he turned on me and decided I was a dishonest person."

"Which I know you are not."

"Thank you."

"Go have it out with him, and then you'll be back together by Christmas, and that's the only present I need."

"I *will* have it out with him. I can't guaran-

191

tee the getting back together part. We were barely together the first time."

"Do you want him back?" she asked.

I paused. "Yes."

She clapped into the phone. "Oh good. Oh, I'm so glad. Jay can seem like such a boring stick, but there's really so much more to him."

Wendy was wandering around the house again, looking alert. "Ellie, I have to go. But I will definitely see you before Christmas. And I'm so glad you're okay."

"Thanks, sweetie. Bye." I hung up and narrowed my eyes at a tree in my backyard. It was currently being lambasted by the polar wind, and it bent low under the barrage.

"Everything okay?" Wendy asked me.

"Hmm? Oh — yeah. That was Parker's mom. She and I were friends before I ever met him."

"Really? I can't imagine Parker having a mom. He seems like one of those people who just emerges at birth from an administrative office, fully grown."

I laughed. "Or springs from the arm of Zeus?"

"Something like that, yeah."

"Yeah, Parker clearly didn't have a babyhood."

We laughed, and my phone rang again. I clicked on, grinning at Wendy. "Hello?"

"Lilah?" It was Cam, and he sounded upset.

"What's wrong?"

"I just wanted to make sure you're okay. Serafina — was attacked."

Something wrenched in my stomach. "What? Is she all right? Is she there? What happened?"

Cam took a deep breath. "It seems like it was a mugging. She was walking down Sheridan with that expensive Italian purse —" In the background, Serafina made a wailing sound.

"Oh no! Did they take her red purse? It was gorgeous!"

Cam sighed. "You women are beyond me. Yes, the guy took the purse."

"Is she okay? Did he hurt her?"

"She's bruised up a little. He knocked her down, and she — fought with him. She didn't want to give up her bag." Cam's voice was shaken.

"Did you call the police?"

"Yes — we just finished with them. They're on the lookout, and Serafina gave them a good description. But I just had a thought — could this have anything to do with everything else that's been happening?

193

Could it be related to the shooting, and your Santa Claus?"

"But why Serafina?"

"I don't know. Unless there was something they thought she had. . . ."

"Did she keep anything of value in there? Besides money, I mean?"

"Credit cards. Some family pictures valuable only to her." Serafina wailed again in the background and spoke some broken Italian. "And I guess some items in her wallet — business cards, stuff like that. And her address book."

None of that sounded like a motive for targeting Serafina personally; and yet I wondered. Who else knew of Serafina's link to me? Who knew that if he wanted to send a message, he might consider attacking my family?

"Let me talk to her," I said.

Cam put Serafina on the phone. "Fina. Are you okay? Do you want me to come over and make you some chocolate cake?"

She gave a watery laugh. "Sweet Lilah, my little sister. You are good to me."

"Would you and Cam like to come over here for a while? Get out of the city?"

"No. Cam is watching over me. I'll be fine. But my purse, Lilah! My beautiful bag. It cost so much — my sisters saved up to give it to me when I left for America."

"They'll find it. Usually people take the money and toss the purse. They'll find it and return it to you."

"Oh, I hope. The worst is that he was Italian, my attacker."

Again my skin prickled. "Why do you say that?"

"Because I fought with him, and he spoke Italian. He said, *'Pazzo, pazzo.'* Means 'crazy.' "

"Fina, I have to go, but you can call me later if you want. I know how it feels to be attacked. It's scary. You tuck under some covers and have some hot chocolate and watch one of those Italian movies that makes no sense."

She giggled.

"And if you need me and Mick and Wendy to come there and protect you, we will."

"Thank you, Lilah."

We said good-bye, and I hung up the phone. Then I grabbed my laptop where it sat charging on the kitchen counter. I opened it up and typed "Enrico Donato in Chicago" in a web browser. His name was there, but the number was unlisted. Then, on a whim, I searched for the number of Rosalie's Salon. I doubted she would be open on a Monday, but I dialed anyway.

Someone picked up on the second ring; there was a hubbub of voices in the background. "Merry Christmas from Rosalie's! How can I help you?"

"Enrico Donato, please."

"Rick? Hang on — Rosalie, is Rick here?" she called. Some background murmuring, and then a man's voice.

"This is Rick Donato." It was his voice, soft and chilling. It brought his features back to me clearly, especially the intelligence in his gray eyes.

"Mr. Donato. This is Lilah Drake. I met you the other day in —"

"I know who you are, Miss Drake. How can I help you?" His voice, silky and polite, was sinister to me.

"You can explain why, if I have nothing to fear from you, my sister-in-law Serafina was attacked today outside her building." Wendy appeared next to me, looking alarmed. She held up her hands, as if to stop me from talking.

"What?"

"Yes, act surprised, but I don't believe you. Who else knew I was related to Serafina? Who else knew where Serafina lived? Who is conveniently located in the very same building as Serafina?"

His voice was colder now. "Did her at-

196

tacker suggest that he was using her as some kind of warning?"

"No. He took her purse. But he was an Italian man; she said so."

"There are many Italian men in Chicago, Miss Drake."

"Forgive me if I happen to see a pattern. Two attacks on my family within a few short days — shortly after I meet you and tell you that I was at the scene of the murder of a man who owed you money."

There was a pause, then Donato's smooth voice. "I understand how upsetting it all must be. But may I suggest that at this moment you are not being logical, and that you are likely to see many other possibilities for what actually happened. I gave you my word that I had nothing to do with Mr. Whitefield's death. People who know me are aware that my word is good."

"I don't know you."

"Which is why I am forced to tell you again — I have nothing against your family, nor am I responsible for any attacks against them. I will see that Serafina, who happens to be my friend, is protected. And I will do my best to find this man."

"Spare me any more of your promises. And stay away from my family," I said. And then I hung up on him.

I sat for a moment, until the red web of anger cleared, and then I turned to Wendy, feeling panicked. "Did I just hang up on a mobster? Did I just yell in his ear?"

"You did." Wendy took the phone from me. "Is Serafina okay?"

"Yeah. Just shaken up. And I guess I am as well."

"It sounds like it could have been a random mugging."

"Yeah. But the timing doesn't strike you as odd?"

"It does." She thought about it, staring at my phone. "I'll think on it. And I'll mention it to Parker. I think he's interviewing people all morning, but I'll try to get through to him at lunchtime."

"Interviewing people? Who?"

"Family, friends, neighbors of Whitefield. Possible witnesses who might have been on Breville Road at the time Whitefield was shot. Anyone who might have seen the blue car."

"It's a lot of work, isn't it? Painstaking work."

"It is. But Parker's good at it. He's methodical — that's how his brain works."

I nodded. "If you're finished with that plate, I'll do the dishes."

"No way. You cooked — I'll do cleanup.

You can go back to your calendar and work out your deliveries. Do we have any today?"

"No. I left today free because I'm going to a party tonight. With Parker, actually."

She had been clearing the countertop where we'd eaten, but she turned back, her eyes wide. "With Parker?"

"It's a fake date. He wants to be able to interview all the people from JFK without them putting up their guard. He's using me as a way to get in."

Wendy shook her head. "He could get to them any number of ways. Don't kid yourself. It's a real date. Parker, you clever devil." She grinned down at the counter while she wiped it with my sponge.

"Yeah, he's great," I said. Wendy laughed.

I opened the door to my half basement and went to my utility closet, where I retrieved a couple of rolls of wrapping paper. I brought them back up, found some Scotch tape, and moved to the living room, where I had a large coffee table. I grabbed the pile of presents I'd already purchased from where I'd stacked them next to my couch. "Do you have anything you need wrapped?" I asked Wendy. "I can do it while I'm handling these."

Wendy peeked around the corner, holding a dish towel. "I do have something, actually.

It's in my trunk. That would be amazing."

"Go get it. I'm a pretty good wrapper."

Wendy did her careful looking around, then opened the door, letting in an unfortunate blast of cold air. She returned a minute later with a small bag. I peeked inside to see a jewelry box and a bottle of perfume. "Nice," I said.

"Pretty safe gifts," she agreed. "I'm not the best at buying that stuff, but I'm learning."

For the next half hour, I achieved a sort of serenity in the act of wrapping. Folding paper, curling ribbon, tucking in pretty accents.

Wendy finished in the kitchen and came in to watch. "That looks great," she said.

"Do you have a pine tree at your house? Any sort of fir or pine?"

"Uh — yeah. In our front yard."

"On Christmas, or whichever day you give this gift, cut a little fragrant pine branch. Just a tiny one to tuck under this ribbon. It will smell amazing and look pretty."

"Wow," said Wendy.

My eyes flicked to the front door, and I screamed. Wendy's gun was in her hand before she had even finished turning. A man's face had briefly appeared in the glass of the door; he was a stranger with dark hair.

"Don't open the door," I hissed. "I don't know him. He shouldn't be here."

Wendy nodded. She went to the door and spoke loudly. "Step away from the door. I'm a police officer and I am armed. Step away from the door, and I will come out to you."

She looked out the window. "Okay, he's backed up into the driveway. He's showing me that he's unarmed."

"But is he alone? What if he has some henchman right next to the door?"

Wendy shook her head. "I checked. Wait here, and I'll figure out what this guy wants." She opened the door, gun still drawn. I heard her say, "I need to see some identification."

Then a silence. I was too afraid to go to the doorway, but I was amazed that Wendy could stand in the polar air and not sound like she was freezing to death. Perhaps her adrenaline was warming her.

I heard the man's voice — low, calm, slightly condescending.

Then Wendy's: "And what brings you here today?"

Some more talking from the man.

Two knocks on the door, and then Wendy's voice. "Lilah, it's me. I'm coming back in."

She entered; she had put her gun away.

"The man in the driveway says his name is Tony Donato. He claims to be the son of Enrico Donato. He says his father commanded him to come here and explain to you that he has nothing to do with Whitefield's death. He said he would like five minutes of your time."

I shook my head. "I don't want to talk to him. I don't want to talk to any of them!"

Wendy looked uncomfortable. "He says if you're unavailable he'll keep returning until it's convenient for you."

That was not an attractive image: Donato's face in my window, again and again, until I agreed to let him in. Besides, Wendy was here, with her gun, and she would be a witness to anything threatening that was said.

"Okay," I said. "Fine."

Wendy opened the door and ushered in a man of about forty. He wasn't tall, but he had an air of confidence and authority that made him seem larger than he really was. He had black curly hair and a tan that looked fake, but somehow it projected health and prosperity. He wore expensive-looking black pants, a black shirt, and a brown leather jacket with a flannel scarf, which he was busy unwinding. As he moved toward me and settled in a chair across from the couch where I sat, I caught his scent: Clive Christian No. 1. Cam had gotten it as a gift once from a student's family. Later we checked online and found that one bottle cost nearly a thousand dollars and was billed as "the world's most expensive perfume."

He smiled at me now, and I realized he'd inherited some of his father's charisma. "Thanks for letting me in, Miss Drake. Hey, I recognize you! I saw you on *Cooking with Angelo*! That's my wife's and my favorite cooking show."

"Yes, I was on the show Friday." I watched his face for any sign of discomfort, but he still smiled easily. "Right afterward, someone shot at my brother and me, shattering the window of his car."

His smile disappeared. "That's terrible; I'm sorry to hear that. Listen, I know you've directed your suspicions at my father. He's very upset about this. No matter what you've heard about him, he's a good man — a family man, a man invested in his community. And he's very sensitive about his reputation. He does not want you thinking he would take part in any violence."

"I'm sorry he's offended," I said crisply.

Tony Donato nodded. "So let me start out by telling you my relationship with Brad

Whitefield. Brad wasn't just a friend; he was family to us. And yes, occasionally he gambled at my house. We do sometimes play high-stakes poker, and I would classify Brad as someone who bordered on addiction. He did owe some money at the time he died — about five thousand dollars. Not a huge sum. And again, no matter what you heard, or what you think from watching movies, I do not extract money by roughing people up. I do have people sign contracts of debt if they are too long without paying. But there's another thing you should know about Brad and my family."

I was all ears. I leaned forward, convinced that Tony Donato was either rather simple or one of the most genuinely good-natured people I had ever met.

"My family has always patronized the arts. This goes back hundreds of years in the Donato clan, and we're very proud of it. My father and I lend our financial support to the Art Institute, as well as individual artists. We donate to the Chicago Symphony and to public television. And we both absolutely love theater. We have season tickets to the Goodman and to Steppenwolf, and we rarely miss a show. We believe in the arts, and Brad — well, he was going to go a long way. My father and I singled him out early on as someone we wanted to support in his career. His latest show — did you see it?" I shook my head.

"It was *The Tempest.* I don't claim to be a Shakespeare expert, but I know a good performance when I see it. And so did the critics. Brad was going to go all the way, and we intended to help him get there." Donato looked genuinely grieved. "So a little thing like a poker debt? When Brad had all this talent to give the world?" He shook his head. "The Donatos believe in the arts. We believed in Brad. And basically we had decided to forgive him the debt as long as he agreed to get addiction counseling."

Tony Donato was right: he did not fit my stereotype of a mobster, if in fact he had ever been one at all. I thought about Brad Whitefield; what had he said about gambling when he talked to me there in the parking lot? *What is Santa if he's not a gambler?* He had smiled, so charmingly, and said, *We should be gamblers, too. We should gamble on ourselves.*

Donato ran a hand through his curly hair and sent a rueful glance to Wendy, who sat on the arm of the couch. "I feel bad that you're here, right before Christmas, with all these fears and with police protection. But I give you my word as a Donato — I had nothing to do with Brad getting himself shot. That was something else. I know there was a fair amount of backstabbing that went on in the theater. Maybe something like that. Or some angry girlfriend. In the past, Brad wasn't necessarily all about loyalty. My father had a talk with him about that. But it was hard to hold anything against Brad. He had flaws, but he was just a lovable guy. He was family."

"So how do you think a grade school boy happened to know about Brad's gambling debt?"

He raised his eyebrows. "I have no idea. But let's face it, there were plenty of people in that room when we played the game. Any one of them could have gossiped. That stuff trickles down. Although from now on we might have to develop some sort of policy about that."

Wendy stiffened. "There are laws about gambling at home, sir."

Donato smiled at her. "Oh, we know them, believe me. And we are totally legal, according to the written law. We play within our own home, as part of an established party, and we only invite our friends — not the general public. In addition, we do not charge a fee to play — just the stake itself."

"It sounds like you've covered all your

bases," she said.

"Indeed we have. And so have our lawyers. If you two would ever like to be invited, as my friends and guests —"

"No, thanks," Wendy said.

He chuckled. "You look very disapproving of me, like my wife when I drink too much. But if we met in different circumstances, we would get along quite well. You are dealing with a preconceived notion."

Strangely enough, I felt this was true. While the elder Donato had a certain dignity and intelligence that made him compelling, this one had an easygoing demeanor that was hard to resist, even now. I waited until he made eye contact, and asked, "What was your response when you heard Brad was shot? Who did you think was responsible? Do you own a gun?"

Donato grinned at me. "Which question should I answer first? I own several guns, all legally licensed. The police have already examined them. My first response to hearing about Brad was to cry, because of the talent that was lost to the world."

To my vast surprise, Donato's eyes welled up as he spoke. I shifted my gaze to Wendy, who looked equally taken aback.

He removed a white handkerchief from his pocket and dabbed at his eyes. It was a curiously feminine gesture. Then he said, "As to who might have done it, I truly had no idea. Still have no idea. Even when I say that it might be an angry girlfriend — I don't really believe that. Because Brad had a way of staying on good terms with his exes. Cleo knew about his early affairs, but she was willing to work it out with him. She loved him. This is very hard for her."

I narrowed my eyes at him. The way Donato told it, not only were the Donatos just a friendly family who liked to throw happy poker parties and patronize the arts, but Brad was an ideal man who, though flawed, was endlessly forgiven for those flaws by his debtors, his past lovers, and mankind in general. "You're very good at selling things," I said. "After wrapping them in an appealing package."

Wendy nodded in agreement. "Where were you on December sixteenth, Mr. Donato, at about one in the afternoon?"

He shrugged. "I'd have to check my calendar. I don't know offhand. But that was, what — last Wednesday? So I was probably in Riverdale, meeting with a Realtor. I own some property there, and I am looking to sell it."

He wiped an imaginary speck off of his jacket, and I noted his wedding ring; it was a simple gold band, but it looked expensive. "How did your wife get along with Brad?" I asked.

Donato's hand froze in midair, and he scowled. "What sort of question is that? Are you suggesting that my wife cheated on me?"

Wendy and I exchanged a surprised glance. "No — I was actually asking whether she, too, was a friend of Brad's, or an admirer of his ability."

"Don't give me that look. Yes, I'm a jealous husband, and my wife likes that. It makes her feel wanted."

"Okay."

He smiled again. "Yes, of course. Talia thought Brad was very talented. She was a fan of his on whatever that social site is. The site of that Harvard kid."

"Facebook?"

"Yeah. Brad has a Facebook page — like a fan page. I guess all actors do. So she liked it, to show her support."

I didn't dare look at Wendy, but I sensed that she, too, found this interesting.

"Anyway. Is there any chance I've convinced you that the Donatos mean no harm against you or your family? And even if we had killed Brad — hypothetically, now — why would that involve you? You were no one to him, were you?"

"No. We really didn't know each other."

"So why am I even here? Why is this even an issue?"

His seemingly authentic confusion made me think he had probably not been driving the car in the school parking lot. But for all I knew, the young Donato, like Brad, might be a very good actor.

"It is an issue, but I'm not really at liberty to discuss it. Thank you for dropping by," I said, standing up and offering my hand.

"What am I supposed to tell my father?"

"Tell him we had a nice talk."

"That's not enough. The man will hound me. He'll send me right back here, so we should resolve this now. I've got stuff to do before my Christmas company arrives. Do we understand each other? In the spirit of the season, the Donatos wish you love and peace."

"Fine," I said. I went to my side table and picked up some business cards for Haven. "Then I'm sure you'd like to support my business, as well. Feel free to share with all of your Christmas guests."

Donato nodded. Apparently this was a language he could understand. He gave us his charming grin and moved to the exit. "Merry Christmas, ladies," he said. He opened the door and said, "Damn, it's cold out there." He jogged briskly to his car, climbed in, and pulled out of the long driveway.

"Do you trust him?" Wendy asked me.

"Nope. You?"

"No way. The guy's a player, and I don't mean sexually."

"But I don't necessarily think he committed murder."

Wendy nodded. "I'm going to call in. I have some questions for Parker; I'll see if he's already talked to Donato Junior."

"Maybe he should look into a connection between Whitefield and Talia Donato."

"You think?" She grinned at me. "Good call."

She took out her cell and moved to the kitchen; I could hear her speaking in low tones, sounding official.

I finished my packages and set them on the fireplace mantel; I put Wendy's on a side table near the entrance. My laptop was sitting there, as well.

On a whim, I grabbed it and sat down on the couch. I logged in to Facebook and typed in the name "Brad Whitefield." This brought up his actor page, which bore a handsome profile picture of him — a black-and-white publicity shot with the standard finger-to-chin thoughtful pose. His cover shot was clearly a still from the production of *The Tempest;* the cast was lined up, ready to bow, grinning at the audience. I recognized all of my friends from the restaurant — Dylan Marsh, looking especially evil in his Antonio costume, his pointed beard glistening with perspiration; Isabel Beauchamp, small and golden in the footlights, her face shimmering with some sort of glitter; and Claudia Birch, standing tall and looking proud to be a thespian. Brad stood in the center. His stage presence was clear even in a photograph; he dominated the scene, for one because he was the tallest person in the cast, but for another, because he was dressed as a sorcerer.

Whitefield, according to the page stats, had 3,458 "likes." That was pretty good for an amateur actor, I thought. The last person to leave a comment on the page had written, "Rest in peace, Brad. We'll miss you." I scrolled down to see that many other fans had left little eulogies on the page. I wanted to see who had last written to him when he was still alive.

It took a significant amount of scrolling, but I finally got to the sixteenth — the day Brad was killed. The last three people to post were his wife, Cleo; Talia Donato; and

Isabel Beauchamp. His wife had written, "For all of Brad's fans — check out this TV commercial Brad did back when he was eighteen!" She had posted a link, a rather blurry copy of a Chicago-area car commercial starring a young and gawky-looking Whitefield. Still, his talent had been apparent even then, and he hadn't been afraid to look right into the camera.

Talia Donato had written, "Break a leg tonight, Brad and the whole talented cast of *The Tempest*! We love you!" Hmm.

Isabel Beauchamp's post, the final one before the obituaries began, said, "I am loving this play and this wonderful cast, but oh, I think we could all use a break!" She followed this with an emoticon of a clearly exhausted person, whose eyes drooped with near sleep. My eyes flicked back to the cover photograph; this time I saw something I hadn't seen before: part of the backstage area was visible in the picture. And there, standing in the wings with a headset on, was Tabitha. "Wendy!" I called, but she was still on the phone.

Tabitha had told me that Brad was in "some show" in the suburbs. She had distanced herself from it, implied that she had the playbill because someone gave it to her. And when I'd mentioned Parker, she said she didn't really want to talk to any police.

What struck me now, looking at the picture, was that even in the background, in the shadowy backstage, it was easy to see the look of love on Tabitha's face. She was gazing at the line of actors with an almost worshipful expression. The question was — with which actor was Tabitha Roth in love, and why hadn't this come up in conversation?

CHAPTER TEN

I showed the Facebook page to Wendy, who also thought there was much to study in both the verbal and visual rhetoric.

Meanwhile I realized that the time of The Christmas Party — the one thrown by Jenny's boss Dave — was approaching, and I had to get ready. Serafina had given me a slinky dress in a daring emerald-green to wear, but it was far too cold a night; I longed to wear something warm. I rooted through my closet until I found a holiday favorite: a thin silver turtleneck flecked with shiny, diamond-like threads. I had often worn it on Christmas or New Year's Eve, and it looked nice on me. I donned it, along with a slim-fitting pair of black pants, which I tucked into some knee-high black boots. I added rhinestone earrings and a long, thin silver chain, on which hung a rhinestone star. The necklace was what my mother called "junk jewelry," but I had always loved it, and it complemented the outfit nicely. I fluffed out my hair, put on some eyeliner and soft pink lipstick, and went back down the stairs, where Wendy sat texting on my couch.

"Sorry," she said. "I was just saying hi to Bets."

"That's fine."

"You look great! Parker's going to be distracted."

I sighed. "I wish."

"Do you? You always seem kind of mad at him."

"And he always seems kind of mad at me."

"That's what they call sexual tension," Wendy said, her expression sage.

I laughed. "Anyway, I guess he'll be my guard while we're at the party, so does that mean you can go home, or . . . ?"

"No — he'll want me here, watching for any unwelcome visitors."

"Then let me show you what I have in the fridge, in case you get hungry." We went into the kitchen, and I pointed out the various cold cuts and fresh rolls, as well as some Tupperware containers with leftovers that might appeal to her.

"Looks great. Am I allowed to share with Mick?"

"In small doses. I don't want him getting

too spoiled. And whatever he eats, he should eat in his bowl." This was hypocritical, since I had been known to feed Mick under the dinner table on many occasions, but I was trying to convey the idea that I was a strict and attentive dog owner.

"Cool," Wendy said. "Do you want to watch some TV?"

"Sure. What do you like?"

"I was looking at your DVDs, and I noticed you have *Arrested Development*. Do you mind if I play an episode or two? Bets and I love that show."

I agreed, and we watched two shows from season one, marveling at the hilarious antics of a talented cast. I confided my crush on Jason Bateman and my admiration for all of them, particularly Jessica Walter. "They're such a great ensemble," I said. "They work so well together —" I paused, thinking suddenly of the cast picture on Brad Whitefield's Facebook page. Everyone had gone on and on about what a great cast it was. How would the chemistry change now that Whitefield was gone? Would Dylan Marsh be able to fill his shoes? If not, how would that affect their chances at going on the road, and eventually to Broadway?

Parker arrived at six thirty, looking distracted. He wore a bulky black coat, a red scarf, and earmuffs. "It's five below," he said when he came in. "Make sure you bundle up, Lilah."

I did, with a Gore-Tex vest and a parka, along with double-stitched mittens and a huge gray scarf, which I wound around my head several times. I waved to Wendy and followed Parker out to his car, which he had left running. I climbed in, unwrapped my scarf slightly, and said, "Ah — heat."

"It's a cold night." Parker turned toward me on the seat. "I know your friend wanted to meet us first, but wouldn't it be better to catch up with her at the party? Otherwise you have to thaw out and refreeze twice."

This was practical — at last, something that Parker and I had in common. "I'll call her," I said. I took off my mittens so that I could dial Jenny's number. There were bits of ice in the wind, and they clacked against the window of Parker's car.

Jenny answered with her bright voice, and since she was Jenny, she was forgiving of the change in plans. She provided clear directions to our destination, and I thanked her before hanging up. "Wow," I said.

"What?"

"This guy lives in Woodcrest."

"Fancy."

"How does he afford that subdivision when he works at a *grade school*?"

Parker shrugged. "The origin of people's money is always a mystery." He pulled smoothly out of the long driveway and into traffic.

I found myself tongue-tied. For one thing, I had no idea if this was a real date, or if it was just another evening with Parker being obsessed by his work. If it was the former, I had absolutely no idea what to do or say. I noted that Parker's car was nice inside, with comfortable seats that still bore a trace of the smoke smell from the habit in which Parker tried to pretend he had never indulged. Now that I thought about it, he patted at his pockets less often than when I had first met him and his hands had always sought phantom cigarettes.

Parker cleared his throat. "You look nice."

"Thanks. I went for warmth over style."

"You look very stylish."

"You look very Eskimo-like."

Parker sniffed out a laugh and flicked on his turn signal with a casual gloved hand. "Wendy says you met quite an odd assortment of people since I saw you last."

"God, yes. Did she already fill you in, or do you want my take?"

"Every detail helps." His eyes were on

traffic, but I had the sense that Parker, too, was at a loss for words, and he was relying on the safety of work talk.

"Okay. Gosh, where to begin — the eccentric actors or the seemingly sociopathic mobster who says he's not a mobster?"

"It all sounds entertaining," Parker said, shooting me a little grin.

So I told him: about Isabel and her fragile beauty; about Allison and her noble profile; about Dylan and his villainous beard. About Serafina and her mugging. And — very quietly — about my call to Enrico Donato.

"What?" Parker yelled.

"Why not? He said he's a harmless family man. So I told him I was about family, too. He should appreciate that. He must, because he sent his son to my house."

"God. I had no idea that's why Donato Junior came for a visit. Lilah, what if these men *are* dangerous? What if they don't like you getting into their business?"

I sat up straighter. "What if I don't like them getting into *mine*? Shooting at me and my brother? Mugging my sister? By marriage, but still!"

"Okay, calm down. I'm just saying — I worry about the chances you take. I don't know how to make you realize — I've seen terrible things, Lilah."

"So have I."

He braked at a red light and turned to me. "And I don't want you to have to see any more, nor do I want any more henchmen showing up at your door. I want you — to have a nice Christmas."

This was surprising, and I went silent for a minute. "That was sweet, Parker."

He opened his mouth, then shut it. The light turned green, and he drove through the intersection and turned right into the gates of the beautiful Woodcrest subdivision — the ritziest place in Pine Haven. "We're here," he said. "Party time."

And the moment that might have been something was lost.

CHAPTER ELEVEN

Jenny and Ross pulled up just after we did, and we walked in together. Jenny had apparently been here before, and she knocked briefly, then opened the door.

"They'll be way at the back," she said. "That's why Dave left the door open." She took off her coat in the large, impressive foyer, set it on a side table, and arranged her clothes in front of a marble-framed mirror that hung on the wall near the entrance. Her brown hair hung loose and glossy down the back of her red dress; her eyes were shining. "Come on in and I'll make some introductions. I'm sure everyone's in the party room, like last year, so we have a minute to get acquainted. This is Ross. You two met once before." Ross shook my hand, then Parker's.

"Let me take all your winter gear," Jenny said. "Ross and I know the drill. Isn't it horrible out there? Like a frozen nightmare."

She touched her cheeks, reddened with the cold, and then waited expectantly. We tucked our gloves and scarves into our coat pockets and handed Jenny our gear. She darted to a closet I had not seen before, opened it, and hung up our coats, with the help of the attentive Ross. Then she returned to us and met my gaze. "And who is your companion, Lilah?"

"Oh, I'm sorry. Jenny Braidwell, this is Jay Parker. Ross, Jay." The men nodded at each other.

Devoid of winter gear, Parker looked like a different man — a man I had never seen before. He wore an elegant dark blue button-down shirt tucked into a pair of charcoal gray pants, under which he wore dark boots. His hair, slightly flattened by his earmuffs, had been lightly slicked back in a stylish way. The blue of his shirt seemed to enhance the blue of his eyes, and the overall effect was dramatic.

Jenny waved some fingers in front of my face. "Come on this way — I'll introduce you to the gang." She grabbed my hand, and the men were forced to follow; I heard them making conversation behind us that sounded friendly enough. Meanwhile Jenny was hissing in my ear: "Where do you *find* them? I thought Angelo was sexy, but this guy — wow. He's got a Paul Newman thing going on."

He didn't. But he did look good. I peeked once more over my shoulder at the two dark-haired men.

"How about this place?" Jenny asked quietly. "Isn't it amazing?"

I took in the grandeur of the hallway we were traversing, from its shining hardwood floors to its oak-trimmed doorways. We were passing a table with two fat potted pines, glowing with holiday lights and lustrous red ribbon. They were the work of an expensive florist, and they smelled wonderful. "Yeah. Tell me again what teachers make per year?"

She giggled, then paused, holding me back for a quick burst of gossip before we joined the throng that I could hear at the back of the house. We waited for Parker and Ross to join us. "I know! But it's not Dave who makes the money — it's his wife. She's the president of Cartman Bank — that big one downtown, by Water Tower Place?"

"Wow. Well, that explains a lot."

"It's a great house," Ross said. "I came here to watch football with Dave a few weeks ago. His TV room is like a theater. Surround sound, all that jazz."

"Wow," I said.

Parker was looking past us, probably longing to interrogate people. "How many of your coworkers are here tonight?"

Jenny consulted Ross for confirmation. "I think — just about all of them. We're a little school; only eight full-time classroom teachers, and then some staff members. I think everyone made it tonight except for Jan Berthold, and she's super pregnant."

Parker chuckled. It sounded fake to me, but Jenny and Ross didn't seem to notice. "There are a lot more than eight people here."

Jenny nodded; we had all noticed the noise level growing as we approached the back of the house. "Yeah — like I said, this isn't just a work thing. He invites all kinds of friends and acquaintances, and people bring family, other friends, whatever."

We moved on, into a high-ceilinged, warmly lit room dominated by the largest Christmas tree I had ever seen. This stood in one corner, next to a fireplace that crackled with authentic flames. "Is that real?" I said, pointing to the tree.

The hostess, a woman with an elegant gray bob and a red velvet dress, homed in on me and floated over. She seemed a bit tipsy. "It is real! Can you smell it? David and I have a little place in Michigan, and there's a Christmas tree farm down the road. We order one from them every year, and they deliver it in a truck. It's our little tradition."

"Amazing," I said. "It's beautiful."

She stuck out her hand. "I'm Emma Brent. And this is my husband, David," she said, grabbing a bookish-looking man with silver-rimmed glasses and slightly stooped posture. "David, these are Jennifer's friends."

David was almost as jolly as his wife. "Nice to meet you! We're glad to have you here. Em and I love Christmas, and we always try to do it up like Fezziwig."

We laughed, and Jenny introduced Parker and me. "Lilah was just on television. On *Cooking with Angelo!*" Jenny said.

Emma and Dave beamed. "That's terrific. You must be so proud of her!" Emma said, turning to Parker, whose eyes had been drifting around the room.

Parker clicked back to attention. "Oh, I am," he said, slipping an arm around my shoulder. "Lilah is a woman of endless talents."

Emma proceeded to point out some of the people milling around the room, introducing them by name far too quickly for me to remember them all. There was a red-haired music teacher named Peter, who was plunking out Christmas tunes on the Brents' grand piano; there were two young women named Kathy and what sounded like Carol; there was an older man with a pipe — it sounded as though Emma had called him Biff. Then a married couple whose names I didn't catch, and two middle-aged women holding glasses of red wine and looking pleased with the world, along with a variety of random people who didn't work at the school at all but were, like Parker and me, just there as escorts or friends.

Parker still had his arm around me — a fact I would have resented if I weren't enjoying it so much. Now he pulled me into a corner and put his mouth close to my ear. "Talk to any of the women you can. You're charismatic, and they'll open up to you."

This was not the sort of dialogue I'd been hoping for. I pushed his arm away and said, "Make up your mind, Parker — is this business or pleasure?"

His eyes widened. "I told you why I wanted to attend. But it's always a pleasure to be with you."

I sighed. I was tired of Parker and his two-sided utterances. "Fine. I'll talk to the women."

Emma Brent came wafting past on a cloud of expensive perfume. "Did everyone have a chance to sign the card for Cleo? She's stopping by later, if she feels up to it. And if anyone else wanted to add to the cash donation, we'll be giving that to her when she comes."

"Who's Cleo?" asked one of the middle-aged women.

"She's Brad Whitefield's wife. You know Brad — our Santa every year?"

"Oh God, yes. Oh wow."

Several people formed a large, casual semicircle, apparently wanting to hear what was said about Brad. "Poor lady," someone said. "I still can't believe it about Brad. He was just a kid, really. And right outside the school!"

"Lilah was there," Parker said. I stared at him, stupefied into silence, but soon realized why he'd done it. The semi-circle readjusted itself around me, and people started asking questions. Parker slid away, the traitor, to watch from an objective distance.

"Oh my goodness," Emma Brent said, bending her tall frame and touching my shoulder. "You were there? When Brad was shot?"

"Um — yes. I had dropped something off for Jenny, and I just happened to be there when Brad was there. We talked for a while, and then I was leaving, and he was going

228

off to run some errand, and —"

One of the women edged forward, her face curious and sad. "Did you see it happen?"

"No — just the aftermath. I was the one who called the ambulance. I — there was nothing I could do for him."

Then all sorts of people were taking turns patting my shoulder and giving me sympathetic glances.

"You didn't see who did it — not at all?" asked David Brent.

"No, I'm afraid not. I was distracted. I heard the car drive in, but I didn't look up, and when I heard the gunshot, it didn't immediately register. I wasn't any help to the police."

"What a shame," said David. "But I suppose it's better for you in the long run. You wouldn't want to be a witness."

I saw Parker's face through the crowd of people, and I realized that he had done me a favor. Now a room full of partygoers was aware that I had nothing to tell the police. Perhaps that included the perpetrator, or someone who knew the perpetrator. Perhaps word would spread.

Apparently people still weren't finished asking me about Whitefield. Two young women sidled up to me and introduced themselves as Tara and Andrea — the kindergarten teachers.

"Nice to meet you," I said.

Emma whisked past again and stuck a glass of eggnog in my hand, then moved on to her buffet table and began arranging things.

The woman named Tara, a small blonde person with red glasses, said that she knew Brad. "We used to go out sometimes, a big group of us from Pine Haven. Brad and Cleo would go, too. Just to a pub somewhere, and we'd all watch a football game and have beer and chat."

"Ah."

"Did he — did Brad say anything to you? Before he — ?" Tara blushed.

"No. No, he — wasn't conscious. I shouldn't really talk about this at a party."

"No, of course not." The women exchanged a glance. Then the one named Andrea, who was also blonde, and plump, said, "I just can't imagine seeing someone die. I've never even been to a wake. I've never seen a dead person."

I sipped the glass of eggnog; it was spiked with something, but it was delicious. I drank it in about three gulps.

"Isn't that great?" Tara said. "Dave makes it every year. Talk about holiday spirit. He's bottled it."

I was feeling a little more Christmassy; when Emma came past five minutes later with a tray of cups, I grabbed one and deposited my empty. Then, with liquid courage, I began making the rounds. I asked Tara and Andrea how well they knew Brad, aside from the occasional drinks at pubs. They both shook their heads. "I never saw him outside of a group," Tara said.

Andrea consumed a little meatball off of a toothpick — standard party fare. I needed to get a look at Emma's buffet table and see who had catered this shindig. "I didn't know him at all. Just as Santa. But the kids loved him. He really did talk to each child. He was good at finding out the Christmas wishes of each one, and then we would take their picture, and I'd jot down the wishes on the back, for their parents. It was a cute tradition that we had. I'll miss him."

I thanked them and moved farther into the room. It was a lovely space, and the Brents had decorated with elegant flair. The long food table, covered in a red cloth and festooned with gold bows and glitter, held the basics of a high-class catered event: a large shrimp tray with a fancy-looking cocktail sauce; little baked wontons filled with walnut chicken; grapes rolled in cheese and coated with pistachios; fried ravioli with a marinara dipping sauce; a baked Brie with a cranberry topping and a scattering of bread and crackers. It was admirable, but nothing that Haven hadn't produced, and I felt confident that Esther and Jim could have made this table shine more brightly. I would be giving Haven's card to Emma before the evening was over.

I looked for Jenny, but she was with Ross, and they were precariously near the mistletoe that hung in the grand doorway. It seemed that he was trying to maneuver her over there. I was confident that Jenny was aware of his game and enjoying it. Considering what was probably about to happen, now was not the time for me to make small talk with her boyfriend. One of the middle-aged women moved past me, and I followed her. "It's a lovely party," I said.

"Oh yes," she said. "I'm just aiming for that window seat over there. Isn't it pretty? I love the way this room is lined with books and places to read them. But with Emma's stressful job, I wonder if she finds the time."

"That's a Catch-22," I said. "I'm sorry, I forgot your name."

"It's Hannah Ford. I teach fourth grade at Kennedy."

"Nice to meet you. I'm Lilah."

"I heard the introduction when you came

in. You and your husband make a lovely couple."

"What? Oh, Jay? No, he's not my husband. We — he — Jenny invited me, and —"

"Oh, just dating, hmm? Well, you have time." She looked at me with a placid expression that was somehow comforting. There was a certain stillness about her that made me expect her to produce a ball of yarn and start knitting. "I'm sorry to hear that you witnessed Brad's death."

"Did you know him?"

"As Santa. I also know his wife; she and I both took tickets at a community theater, years ago. I think that's how she met Brad in the first place."

"Ah."

"Poor Cleo. She was just smitten with Brad. I'm afraid that's the effect he had on all the ladies. Still, it was Cleo he chose. She comes from a rather prominent Chicago family, I heard."

The red-haired man, no longer at the piano, approached us. "Hannah, do you need to sign this card, or can Emma seal it up?"

"I already did, thanks, Peter. And can you do me a favor? Lilah and I are both out of eggnog."

He nodded and disappeared with his

envelope. He returned two minutes later with two little cups. "You're all trying to get me drunk," I joked.

"Well, that big smile tells me we're halfway there," Hannah said.

Peter sat down with us in the window seat. "Here we are," he said. "See no evil, hear no evil, speak no evil."

I turned to him; my head felt heavy. "Which one are you?"

"Let's see. You saw evil, so you've got to be one of the other two. And I've been speaking my share of evil, so I can't be that one."

"Peter is a terrible gossip, is what he means," said Hannah fondly. "But he amuses us."

"I actually didn't see evil. I just heard it," I told them.

"Right. So we'll say Lilah doesn't speak it, I don't hear it, and Hannah doesn't see it."

"That passed the time," Hannah joked.

"What sort of evil are you speaking about?" I asked Peter.

He leaned toward me, clearly ready to dish. Parker probably loved people like Peter the music teacher as a means of getting information. "Listen, I didn't know Brad that well, but I do know Cleo a little better. She's a nice girl, and I happen to know that

Brad cheated on her."

"But lately things were better," I said. "He was turning over a new leaf. He even spoke about it, on the day he died. He told me he was a philosopher Santa, or Zen maybe, and —"

Peter pressed his lips together. "I don't buy that, but I'm not going into it here. Oh, shoot, there's Cleo. I never said a word," he said, springing up from his seat and moving to the door, pasting a sympathetic expression on his face.

Cleo Whitefield was indeed there. She looked pale and wan and small next to the tall, dark-haired man on her left.

"That's her brother," Hannah said. "I think she's staying with him, which is a good thing."

Cleo was thanking Emma and Dave. "It's so sweet of you, really — all of you — thank you so much. We can't stay. Ed and I are going out for a quiet dinner, and then he's making me go to bed. I'm lucky to have all these people to take care of me." Her eyes swept the room and lighted on Hannah and me. She brightened with recognition and waved. Hannah and I waved back. She said something to her brother and moved toward us, still wearing her coat. "Hi — Hannah, right? It's been a long time."

"Yes," said Hannah, shaking her hand. "I'm so sorry for your loss."

"And I met you the other day — what a coincidence! It's Lily, right?"

"Lilah. Yeah, isn't this weird? Jenny — the first grade teacher — is my best friend, so I'm here with her. She's the one currently making out under the mistletoe. And as far as I can tell, Dave Brent is taking blackmail photos." I realized too late that liquor had loosened my lips, and that perhaps Cleo didn't want to see a young couple in love while she was grieving for her own husband.

Cleo turned briefly and looked at Jenny, who was kissing Ross with some abandon, although they'd had the decency to move to the shadows of a corner. She turned back to us; her little freckled face had become sad. "I was planning to spend Christmas doing that. Kissing on a Hawaiian island." We sat in an uncomfortable silence, listening to the music one of the Brents had put on their iPod. Right now Leon Redbone was singing "Christmas Island." Cleo smiled wryly at Redbone's lyrics, pointing at the ceiling, as though the song emanated from there. Then she shrugged. "Anyway, it was nice to see you again. What are you both doing for Christmas?"

Hannah sipped her eggnog. "I'll be hosting the family, as usual. Three daughters, two sons-in-law, four grandchildren."

"Sounds lively," Cleo said. She turned to me.

"Oh, just hanging with the family. Nothing special," I said.

She nodded, scanning the room, then froze. "I know that tall man in Emma's den. He's a cop. He talked to me the night that Brad — after it happened. Asked me a bunch of questions. What's he doing here?"

I touched Hannah's hand and said, "Oh, he's not here as a cop. I think he's dating someone here. No worries — he won't interrogate you." I made it sound like a joke, and Cleo looked relieved.

"Isn't it weird, though? I keep seeing the same people. You," she said, looking into my eyes with sudden perception, "and now him. I guess life is just full of coincidences."

"It is. Especially at Christmastime, when everyone is going to parties."

She nodded, looking weary again. Her brother came to join us. "You ready, Clee?"

"Yeah." She touched her brother's sleeve and said, "This is Ed. He's been my rock in all of this." She patted his arm, then held a hand up in farewell. "Have a good Christmas."

"You, too."

Her brother's face had not creased into a friendly smile, as Cleo's had. Still, he seemed protective of Cleo; he slid an arm around her shoulder, and they walked away. At the door she hugged Dave and Emma, and the latter whispered something in her ear. Dave slipped an envelope to Cleo's brother, who shook Dave's hand. Then the siblings departed into the bitter air.

"That was interesting," Hannah said.

"Hmm?"

"Not only that your boyfriend is a policeman, but that you didn't want Cleo to know he was your boyfriend."

I looked into her kind and curious eyes. "If you could stick to the speak-no-evil plan, I'd appreciate it. There's enough gossip at this party."

Hannah nodded. "No problem."

Jenny appeared in front of us, her cheeks flushed, her eyes shining. "Lilah, can you go with me to the bathroom?"

I sent a wry glance to Hannah, who giggled, and I got up from my comfy window seat. "Sure, Jenny. I'd love to hear about your tempestuous love life."

She dragged me all the way upstairs, where it was oddly silent and where our feet made no sound on the blue-carpeted hallway. I found myself peering into an elegant bedroom, then walking into it. This, too, was carpeted in a delicious plush, and I floated toward a window to see a sheen of ice shining on the long driveway. Cleo and her brother were getting into a black car, stepping carefully to avoid slipping. "Weird, to see Cleo twice in such a short time," I said.

"Who?" asked Jenny, who had followed me.

"Cleo. And where's the Christmas clown? I wanted to talk to her."

"Apparently she's in Delaware visiting her grandchildren."

"Doesn't sound very sinister."

"Hmm?"

"Never mind. Did you ask me to this party so that I could watch you make love to a man?"

Jenny put her hands on my shoulders and hugged me against her, saying something like, "Eeeeee," into my ear. Then she let me go. "I asked you here so that you could get a sense of whether he liked me or not. And then he just — grabbed me and kissed me, and neither of us stopped, and it just kept going!"

"Geez. I could have saved a trip out in the cold. I told you; I knew he liked you when I delivered the macaroni and cheese. The guy

239

looks at you like you're steak and he's a Rottweiler."

"Are you drunk, Lilah?" she asked, giggling.

"No. Are *you*? Which of us was just making out in front of a large group of people? And which of us was sedately chatting in a window seat of a rich person's home?"

Jenny shrugged. "I don't even care. I'm just so happy!"

"Then why aren't you with him?"

"He said we should probably make the rounds and pretend we hadn't just become the gossip of the school for the next two years."

"Did he look happy, too?"

"Yes." Now her face was smug.

"Well then, I think you should go down there and grab your new boyfriend and go home. Then you can make out to your heart's content."

She danced a little dance on the soft carpet. "Lilah, I'm so glad you're here. Even if we haven't really been talking."

"Yeah. It's sort of a weird night, but I intend to get a catering client out of it."

Jenny gave me a kiss. "Hang on — I really do have to use the bathroom." She ran into the master bathroom, and I tried out the springs on the large bed.

Jenny emerged minutes later. "Lilah, you can't go to sleep there! Come on, we're going back downstairs."

She pulled me up from my prone position and hooked her arm through mine. "You haven't spent much time with your cute date."

"No — we tend to avoid each other. That's what keeps the attraction alive. I'm sure if I ever spent more than an evening with him I'd hate his guts."

We reached the stairs and began our descent. She squeezed my arm. "You are the greatest friend," she said.

"I know. Go find Romeo."

She didn't have to look far. Ross was walking around with a yearning expression. Jenny practically threw herself at him; I shook my head, slightly ashamed.

Parker appeared in front of me. "Have a minute to exchange notes?" he asked.

"Sure, boss."

He took my hand, as Jenny had just done, and led me down a long hallway, this one on the first floor.

"Do they want us going in this part of the house? And also, how big is this house?"

"You throw a party, you have to assume that people will wander," he said. "Ah, here we go. What do we call this? A mudroom? A

241

study? A library?"

"The chapel where Hamlet finds Claudius at prayer?"

"What?"

"I don't know. This house has a lot of rooms."

"Are you drunk, Lilah?"

"No. Are *you*?"

Parker sat down on a leather couch in a small but cozy room. The brick fireplace was lit, and some dishes of candy sat on the oak coffee table — so Emma did indeed think people might end up in here. "No. I didn't make the mistake of trying that 80-proof eggnog."

"Uh-oh. You might end up firing me as a junior detective."

"I don't know. You're the prettiest junior detective I've ever worked with." Parker shot me a smile and twinkled his blue eyes at me.

"So, you need my report?" I faced him, my hands on my hips.

"Yeah. Come sit here." He pulled me down on the couch next to him. The leather was even more comfortable than the bed upstairs had been. I resisted the temptation to lean on Parker and start snoring.

"Who did you talk to?"

"With whom did I talk, you mean."

"Okay."

I lifted my hand and listed names on my fingers. "Tara, Andrea, Hannah, Peter — oh, and Cleo and her brother. Then Jenny. Sorry, I guess I didn't get far. But I do have some theories."

Parker's eyes were still twinkling. "I'd love to hear them."

I leaned back on the delicious couch. "Relax, Parker. This might take a while."

CHAPTER TWELVE

Parker slid an arm around my shoulders and said, "I'm all ears."

"Okay. First of all, Peter the music teacher knows something, but we got interrupted by Cleo. He's convinced Brad was cheating on his wife, and it sounded like he has evidence. We need to talk to him again."

"Got it."

"And here's the thing. Cleo and Brad were going to visit the Hawaiian Islands over Christmas. Maybe it was an attempt to save their marriage, or maybe it meant that their marriage was solid. But the funny thing is — will you stop *kissing* me, Parker?"

"I'm not," he said, but his lips were pressed against my cheek and moving around.

"This is — we're supposed to be, like — staking things out. Why are you always confusing me?"

He pulled away and waited until I looked

at him. "Maybe we should be straight with each other."

"Okay. About what?"

"Are you still hung up on Angelo Cardelini?"

"What? No! He broke my heart. I could never trust him again, and I'm not attracted to him anymore. I happen to be hung up on you — but you broke my heart, too."

"Wow. That stuff is like truth serum."

"Now you be straight with me."

"Okay."

"How come you said you were proud of me to everyone here, but you've never said it to me? And when I was on television, and Fina and Cam were saying how good it was, you just left the room? I never know what's going on in your head."

Parker leaned back and looked at his hands. "Fair enough. I'll tell you why, Lilah. Because I was jealous."

"Of me?"

"No. Of your brother, and his wife, and everyone who had — the right — to tell you how great you were. But I'm just the guy who treated you badly and . . . now I hear that I broke your heart, too. So no one wants my opinion, even though I have one."

"*I* want your opinion."

"Okay. I thought you were great on that

TV show. Amazing. Photogenic, charismatic, funny, sweet. I wasn't thrilled to see Cardelini leering at you, but — you were great. The truth is, Lilah — I think you're wonderful. I think you're going to accomplish great things, and that you could do anything you set your mind to. And I — would you stop *kissing* me, Lilah?"

"I'm not." But I was — rubbing my lips on his slightly whiskery cheeks and inhaling the scent of his aftershave.

"You are. But I take it back; don't stop."

I slid my arms around him, and he clasped his hands behind my back and yanked me against his chest, and for the first time in months we had a proper kiss — warm, lively, seductive, enthusiastic. "Parker," I said eventually, my mouth moving to his ear.

"Mmm?"

"I think I might be a little drunk."

"How many glasses of that eggnog did you have?"

"Three."

"Oh God."

"I'm not much of a drinker."

"Clearly." He was laughing at me, but then his face grew serious. "You're not going to forget this, are you?"

"No." I squeezed him. "I'm going to

246

replay it like a happy little movie. But wait — there's something I should be mad at you about. I can't remember what it is."

"I hope you never do."

"Huh. I can't remember, and you're distracting me with your handsomeness. And your blue eyes. And that scent. . . ." I rooted around near his collar, trying to find the source of his lovely cologne.

"Lilah, don't. I mean, do, but not here. Are you *licking* my neck?"

"It *tastes* good, too."

"I think we need to get you home."

"Mmm. But wait, I didn't finish with my theories."

"Okay." Parker's expression was a cross between amazement and hilarity, like someone watching monkeys at play.

"So, where was I? Oh yes, the island. You see — on the day he died, Brad Whitefield spoke to me of an island. He said he had found his own little island of escape. That's why he was advising me to follow my dreams."

"Okay. So he was talking about his vacation."

"Well, that's what I'm not sure about. Because you see, I read *The Tempest* in high school, and again in college. I was an English major, did you know?"

"I guessed after that *Hamlet* reference a while ago."

"So the whole play takes place on an island, you see? The main character, Prospero, has been stranded there for twelve years."

"Okay."

"So maybe he was talking about his vacation, but maybe he wasn't. Maybe he was being philosophical. He implied he was into philosophy. He quoted Shakespeare. And if he's speaking of the island metaphorically, then he's not escaping into something *new* — he's escaping into something he already has, right? Like, something he values and has now decided to pursue? He said he was leaving the Mainland forever — but that too could be a metaphor. Prospero became a great sorcerer on his island. He achieved power like he'd never known before, even though in Italy he was a duke. Yet he ended up leaving it all behind. The question is: was Brad staying on his island, or leaving one island for another? Is the island his talent? Is it his life?"

"Those are pretty deep questions for one who's had so much eggnog."

"Jot this down, Parker. There's the music teacher and whatever he knows. Then there are the multiple references to islands. To what was Whitefield referring, and was it important? Enrico Donato's son mentioned that Whitefield had a special talent, and that the Donatos were great patrons of the arts. They wanted to patronize Brad as an artist, and to help him rise to the ranks of the great actors. But the other side of that coin is that Donato Junior is possessive of his wife and clearly aware that Brad had charisma with women. So despite his warm assertions that he and Whitefield were the best of friends, I think you should investigate that area, too."

"That's good to know." Parker was writing now, on a little pad he pulled from his pocket.

"And then there are the rings."

"What?"

"Brad Whitefield had a little hematite ring on his pinkie finger. Sort of distinctive. When Wendy and I had lunch with all the actors, I saw that Isabel had one, too. Same ring, same finger. Seems like an important coincidence."

"Yes."

"And then there are the weird strings of connection."

"What?"

"Everyone we've met has known either Brad or Cleo or both. Is that odd?"

"Not really. We're only seeking out people

who had links to them."

"Huh. Oh, and then there's Tabitha."

"Yes?"

"She's in love with one of the actors. I don't know if it's Brad, or maybe Dylan, or heck, one of the female leads. I don't know her sexual preferences. But I did see a photo of her with an absolutely smitten look on her face, and she was gazing at the four actors. And yet Tabitha claimed to just be a friend to Brad, and she didn't seem to have feelings for anyone at the table when we were all together. Which means that Tabitha is hiding something. She also lied to me; she said she 'heard' that Brad was in *The Tempest,* but she was actually working on the production. Do you have your phone handy?"

Parker handed it to me, and I logged on to the Internet to find Brad's Facebook page. "There's the cast," I said. "Look at that woman — make the picture bigger and look at her face."

Parker studied Tabitha in her headset, standing in the wings. "Interesting," he said.

"Right? And did you know that Dylan Marsh tried out for the role of Prospero, but it went to Brad? And did you know that Marsh will now have the part? Which is noteworthy, because in the play, Antonio plots to kill Prospero for his throne. Could this be a case of art reflecting life? Or vice versa?"

Parker thought about this, puffing out his cheeks and then letting the air out again. "I spoke with Dave at great length tonight. He's an administrator as well as a teacher, and it was he who hired Whitefield. But he did it on the suggestion of a friend — I still need to get that connection clarified. Someone who is reputed to be one of Whitefield's best pals, but who is not in fact an actor. His name is Mark, or Mike, or something. Did that come up in your conversations?"

"No, but — it did somewhere. I can't recall right now. I should take notes, too."

"Lilah, this is impressive work."

"I can impress you in a lot of other ways." I leaned against him, wanting to seem flirtatious, but instead closed my eyes.

"I'm looking forward to it, but right now I think we need to leave. Sleep does wonders for an eggnog overdose."

"Hmm."

"Lilah?"

"Yip."

"I really am proud of you."

I opened my eyes and met his beautiful blue ones. "I'm proud of you, too. I think you're dedicated and smart."

He smiled. "Then I should be able to close this case before Christmas, don't you think? I've got three days."

CHAPTER THIRTEEN

I woke on Tuesday morning to a lacy white pattern that snow had traced upon my bedroom window. I climbed out of bed, expecting to trip over Mick, but he was gone. Surprised, I headed downstairs and into the kitchen, where I found my loyal canine sitting at the feet of Wendy while she drank coffee and read the newspaper. "It's cute that you still get the paper delivered," she said. "I read everything online, but this is fun. It feels like going back in time."

"Hilarious. Did you make plenty of coffee?"

"Yes. And your dog has already been out. He played in the snow a little bit, and he chased a chipmunk."

"That's Scrounger. We've known him for more than a year. I think he and Mick are friends, but they love to taunt each other."

"Cute. Your backyard is like a Disney movie, with all the happy little creatures.

There were little birds hopping around your feeder, too. How was the party?"

"It was nice. My friend ended up making out in the corner like a high school student, but Parker and I got some information that might be helpful."

"Yeah? Did you get anything else out of Parker?" Her face studied the page in front of her, but she was smirking slightly.

"He was surprisingly human last night. We — got along."

"Okay. Let's go back to the good information part. Is he any closer to catching this guy?"

I shrugged. "It's all so confusing. So many names, so many stories. I don't know how you cops do it."

"Well, it's only the cops like Parker who have to deal with this type of thing, but it's a clear pattern: go over it and over it until you notice the anomalies."

"I guess. I told Parker I should be jotting down notes. I think I'll do that today."

She stretched and yawned widely. "Good idea. Let me know if I can help."

I studied Wendy, who was wearing yet another comfortable-looking knit suit with some sort of earth shoe. She was not a fashionable dresser, but her clothes suited her. "I feel bad, like I'm keeping you from your Christmas preparations."

"You are earning me some really nice Christmas overtime. And Lilah? You're the nicest case I've ever worked on. I don't know if you realize this, but police don't tend to meet beautiful specimens of humanity as a rule."

"I guess not."

"Plus, you keep feeding me, and I'm falling in love with your dog, and your cute house. Someday you have to let me show it to Bets."

"Sure. Right after you catch the bad guy."

"Deal." She stood up and stretched. "I'm going to look around."

I swigged down some coffee, scratched Mick on his large, warm head, and then went back upstairs to take a shower. When I emerged, clean, scented, and dressed in jeans, thick socks, and a brown knit turtleneck sweater, I climbed back down and found my laptop, on which I began typing my own notes. I titled the first page:

The Brad Whitefield Murder

Then I made a list.

1. Brad Whitefield was agitated on the day he died, because someone was texting

him and making some sort of demand. He said he would have to run "a quick errand," but then a car pulled up in front of him. He was surprised, and said, "I was just coming to you."

Question: had the person purposely lured Whitefield out of the building with a text, then shot him? If so, had that person been lying in wait nearby? If so, wouldn't that person almost certainly have seen me? Is that why the person took the phone from Whitefield? Because it would reveal his or her identity to the police?

2. People who lied:

Tabitha — said she heard Brad was in a show, when in fact she knew it, and was working on that very show.

Donato's son — said that he and Whitefield were great friends, that Whitefield had a poker debt, but that he, Donato, was happy to forgive it; yet when his wife was mentioned, he grew angry. Clearly Donato is lying about his level of jealousy. Potential affair between Brad and Mrs. Donato?

The three actors — they are actors. Any one of them could have been lying about their grief over the dead man, and all of them seemed weirdly suspicious, as well as narcissistic. Dylan had the best motive, but either of the women could have been involved with Whitefield or jealous of someone who was — or could potentially have been scorned by Whitefield. Hell hath no fury, etc.

Enrico Donato — may well have been lying about his involvement in Whitefield's death, or about the shooting at the studio, or about Serafina's mugging. His supposed protection in the form of Frank could be a blind to conceal his crimes.

3. Suspicious behavior:

Enrico Donato. Seemed distressed to learn about Whitefield's murder. This seems to suggest that either he was acting/lying because in fact he knew about the murder, or that he was concerned someone he knew might have done it, which could implicate his son.

Tabitha, Dylan, Isabel, and Allison. All weird. All dramatic types. I felt neither comfortable with them nor trusting of what they said. Try to meet with them again?

Cleo. Seemed nervous when she saw Parker at the party. Was this merely because she was tired of being interrogated?

Peter the music teacher. Seemed particularly resentful of Brad Whitefield, and sure that he was a cheater. Is Parker following up on this?

Mark or Mike, the guy who recommended Brad to Dave Brent at JFK School. Who might this person be?

I stared at the notes I had just made, and something sluggish started moving around in my brain. I didn't have a hangover, but I did feel rather tired. Mark or Mike. Someone had told me something about someone named — "Esther!" I yelled.

"What?" Wendy moved swiftly into the room.

"Oh — no. I just remembered a little detail that might fill in some blanks. I have to make a phone call."

"Cool." She left again, with Mick at her heels. Clearly Mick thought that things were going to happen wherever Wendy went.

I dialed the Haven number, and Jim answered after two rings. "Haven of Pine Haven. This is Jim."

"Jim. It's Lilah."

"Hey, kiddo. How are you holding up?"

Jim said this in his usual friendly, avuncular way, and for just a moment I was tempted to let loose with a torrent of fears and hopes. Then I cleared my throat. "I'm okay. Are you doing all right with the Christmas jobs?"

"Just a little brunch this morning, and then we're finished for a week or so. We're doing fine."

"Okay, good. Is Esther around?"

"Right beside me."

"Does she have a second?"

"For you, she always has time."

"You're sweet," I said. In the background I could hear Jim's Christmas music: "What Child Is This?" played on a hammered dulcimer.

Jim handed Esther the phone, and she spoke breathily into my ear, as though she'd run across the room. "What's happening? Are you okay?"

"Yes, yes. I'm fine, thanks. I have a bodyguard right now. She's making me feel safe."

"Really? That's great."

"Yes. I'm calling with a question, actually. That night when I came to work with Detective Parker, you mentioned that you thought Mark might know Brad Whitefield.

Did you ever find out?"

"Oh God, yes — didn't I tell you? It turns out that this Brad was one of Mark's friends from that group he's in — those gamers. You know how Mark likes all that virtual stuff? I don't know what they call it. He laughs at me and says no one calls it "gaming," but I hear people say that. Anyway. Long story short, they were friends. Mark has been very upset about it."

"I need to talk to him. Is he going to be around there at any point?"

"He's coming this afternoon; he's going to stay until Christmas and then disappear back to his lair downtown. His brother's coming later tonight, too, but Luke's driving from Indiana, so he won't get in until late."

"Would I be interrupting if I stopped by — maybe around three? I won't disrupt your dinner or anything."

"You're always welcome. You know Mark loves flirting with you. Although I think he might be dating someone now."

I laughed. "That's all right. I might be dating someone, too."

"You're not sure?"

"I'm fairly sure. But — there's some stuff to be worked out."

"You can tell me all about it at three. But

first you can talk to Mark; I'll make some snacks for you."

"No — you will put your feet up and enjoy your Christmas *vacation.* I understand it starts later today."

"Yes! Lovely."

"See you later," I told her.

I sat at my kitchen table, watching the delicate snowflakes and pondering the puzzle of Brad Whitefield. My main question was: how did he find the time to work as a professional actor, yet get side jobs like playing Santa at a grade school? To have what seemed, based on gossip, like a multitude of affairs? To plan trips? To be a virtual "gamer," whatever that entailed? To go regularly out to pubs with a big group of friends? To play poker so often that people suggested he had a gambling addiction? How much time was there in a day? Did Brad Whitefield have more than one life?

Suddenly I remembered Whitefield standing before me in his absurd red suit, quoting Shakespeare and saying that "our little life is rounded with a sleep." Life was short, it was true, and Brad had entered that sleep that Shakespeare had spoken of in more than one play. I had only met Brad for a short time, but I was ready to give him the benefit of the doubt and believe he had been a good man until someone proved otherwise.

"Wendy?" I waited until she came back into the kitchen.

"What's up?"

"I found out that an acquaintance of mine was also friends with Whitefield. Apparently, in addition to everything else, Brad played some sort of online game — the kind you play with other people?"

"Huh."

"I'd like to go talk to Mark — he's the friend. He's the son of my coworkers at Haven. Okay to make that trip this afternoon?"

"Sure. I'll just clear it with Parker, but he was fine about the lunch we attended."

Wendy took out her phone and started to dial, her eyes alert and gazing out my back window. I left the room and heard my own phone buzzing. I grabbed it from a living room table and said, "Hello?"

"Lilah *mia*! You were fabulous." It was Angelo's voice, low and sexy and annoying. In all of the craziness, I had almost forgotten his show, his flirtation, the shooting in the garage. . . .

"Uh — thanks, Angelo. Listen, I have a lot going on right now. . . ."

"My producers want me to tell you this,

as well. They would like you to return."

I paused, staring at the snow that coated the long driveway outside my house. "What?"

"They are thinking one or two shows, to start, but they are wondering if you might work as a Friday feature."

"What? As in *every* Friday?"

Angelo chuckled. At one time that chuckle had sent shivers down my spine. Now I was shaking, but for a different reason. It was exhilarating, terrifying, wonderful, terrible. Angelo was speaking again in his irresistible voice. "The numbers were good, they say. People are asking about you, about me. People are searching for you on Google."

"Google? I guess this is a compliment, right?"

"Don't be afraid, Lilah. You were so good the first time. You would get better and better."

"I have to think about this."

"Of course. But I need to know by the New Year."

"Okay. I'll get back to you, Angelo. And — thanks. I appreciate the opportunities you've been sending my way."

"Lilah." He sighed. Angelo was a great sigher, and his exhalations could express any number of emotions. This sigh hinted at regret. "You know that I care. I will always care. And if I can help you in any way, I will do so."

"Thanks, again. I'll talk to you soon."

I said good-bye and hung up with a sense of unreality. Wendy emerged from the kitchen and did her scanning thing out the front window. "Parker is okay with us going to Haven, as long as you listen to my instructions."

"Of course. Parker doesn't seem to realize we're on the same page about this. I do not particularly want to be shot."

Wendy sat on the edge of the couch. "I'm thinking you can breathe a little easier about that."

"What? Why?" I sat across from her, still clutching my phone. The hairs on my arms were still at attention as a result of Angelo's news.

"I've been thinking. This attack on you and your brother seemed kind of random. But of course we linked it to the crime you witnessed. Yet nothing else has happened — no other attempts to harm you, no warnings over the phone, no visitors to this area. My instincts tell me there won't be another attempt. No, don't worry — I won't stop being vigilant. That's my job. I'm just telling you I think you're safe. Snipers are scary, but if this was a random sniping, it should be a great relief to you."

"Or it could in fact have been related to the crime, but then when we made a point of telling several different groups that I witnessed nothing, maybe someone figured he could back off. I might have looked whoever this is right in the face — do you realize that? Whoever was driving that car. And if they saw me stare at them with no recognition, then they know I'm not a threat."

"Okay — so there are two theories that should make you feel a little better."

"I'll feel best of all when they catch the driver *and* the sniper, which Parker has promised he will do by Christmas."

Wendy sniffed. "Now that's confidence."

"Or wishful thinking." I looked back out the window. "This looks like really good packing snow. How safe do you think we would be if we made a snowman in my backyard?"

Wendy shrugged. "It's enclosed, so I would say very safe."

"We can pretend that he's Parson Brown. 'He'll say "Are you married," we'll say "No, man," ' " I sang.

Wendy didn't let me down — she sang the rest of the line, and then said, "You're on. Let me get my waterproof gloves."

We bundled up and went into the yard, where the snow still fell in magical drifts, and Mick pranced around, biting at snowflakes. For the first time since I'd met Brad Whitefield, I laughed out loud.

Haven was lit in silver and blue, and a large green wreath with a silver bow dominated the front door. Wendy and I, slightly exhausted from the strenuous building of a seven-foot snowman (Wendy used a ladder to put on the giant head), welcomed the sight of Haven's fragrant foyer and polished counter. We found even more satisfaction when Esther ushered us through the door that led to their personal quarters behind the business — a lovely house that was now fragrant with pine and Esther's baking.

"Sit down, sit down," Esther said. "I'll bring you something to eat."

"Don't be silly," I said. "We're just here to talk to Mark, and you should relax and drink eggnog, or wassail, or something festive."

"I will — with you! Let me know when you finish with Mark, and we'll have a nice chat." Esther disappeared into her kitchen, and Mark came loping in. He was tall and thin, like Jim, but he had a head of copious chestnut hair that Jim lacked. His face was narrow and handsome in an intellectual way.

"Hey, Mark."

"Hey, Lilah." His eyes flicked to Wendy, curious. I introduced her, and Mark shook her hand. "So — you're like a bodyguard?"

"Pretty much," Wendy said. "So far, the easiest job I've ever done."

"Cool," Mark said, sitting in a chair across from us. "You need to talk to me about Brad, Mom says."

Esther skimmed back in holding a gold tray, on which she had slices of one of her special treats — caramelized onion squares topped with goat and blue cheeses, along with a chafing dish full of Swedish meatballs. "Don't say a word, Lilah — these are just some extras we made for an event yesterday, and we ended up not needing them. Mark, keep your paws off until the ladies have eaten." She set out some little plates that matched the tray.

"Unfair, Mother. Can't you see I'm thin as a rail and in need of food?"

"You eat all day. Okay, I was never here." She whisked back out as Wendy and I goggled at the food.

"That smells amazing," Wendy said.

"You go first."

She did, helping herself to several of the

little pizza squares and five meatballs.

I took an equally generous amount, since I suddenly couldn't remember when I'd eaten last. Mark waited, as instructed. "Listen, Lilah — Mom tells me that you were there — when Brad got shot."

"Yes."

Mark's face was grave. "I'm sorry to hear that. I just wanted to know — did he suffer?"

"I don't think so. He was immediately unconscious. I don't think he ever knew what happened. He seemed to be focused on something that — the person — had taken away from him. He never sounded afraid."

"Huh." He leaned back in his chair and pushed at a meatball with a toothpick.

"You were pretty good friends?"

He nodded. "Which is weird, because I never was the type to hang out with the actors. You know, in high school and stuff. The thespian crowd always seemed weird to me, and I hung with the computer geeks. But Brad and I happened to meet once at a comic convention — about five years ago — and we just hit it off. Then we found out that we liked a lot of the same shows, and the same games. I discovered this game called *Kingdoms* —"

"Kingdoms!" I said. "He had something on his phone the day that I met him — I saw the word *Kingdom*. That must have been it. It had pretty pictures."

"Yeah, that's it. Anyway, I invited Brad into my realm, and then we started spending time together."

Wendy and I exchanged a glance. "What does that mean — invited him into your realm?"

Mark's face grew more animated. "*Kingdoms* is a game that requires multiple players — it's a virtual community. In it you create your own kingdom — hence the name. It's vaguely medieval, but it's meant to be an experience out of time. It's more about power and relationships."

"Okay," I said.

"Brad loved it. He started out as a visitor to my kingdom, but of course the goal is to build a kingdom of your own and then develop alliances with other kingdoms. Brad was a genius, not just at constructing kingdoms, but at creating characters."

"I thought the characters were real people."

"They are, a lot of them, but you can also create fictional characters who live in your kingdom. It becomes quite complex, because sometimes you're not sure whether you're interacting with a real person or a fictional construct."

Wendy looked blank. "So why would you want to do it?"

Mark leaned forward. "It's the ultimate challenge. It tests your ability to create, but also relies on your skills in strategy, negotiation, compromise. The important thing to note is that these relationships are real — as real as your day-to-day interactions. You can become immersed in the game."

I shook my head. "How did Brad find the time? He was in a Shakespearean play. He had a wife. He had other obligations."

Mark grinned. "Brad was one of those people who didn't need a lot of sleep. We did a lot of our kingdom building at two, three in the morning. Sometimes all night long."

"When do *you* sleep?"

"I have weird hours. A lot of times I work the three to eleven shift, so at midnight I'm just getting home and ready to relax."

"So weird to me," I said. "So you basically did your 'kingdom building' when everyone else was asleep."

"Yeah. I can tell you think I'm just some nerd who wastes time on the computer, but you'd have to understand *Kingdoms*. The people who are really good at it — like Brad was — are artists. They create worlds, and the detail of those worlds is incredible."

Wendy stabbed another meatball. "Do you name these kingdoms?"

"Yeah. Mine is called Hlidskjalf. I borrowed it from Norse mythology — it's the seat of Odin, from which he can view all realms. I figured that was a great way to go in *Kingdoms*."

I was marveling at Mark's imagination, and I told him so. He shook his head. "I'm pretty good, but the game has kind of lost its luster since Brad stopped playing. He was the best. Wait — I can show you some of his work."

He jumped up, left the room, and returned a minute later with a laptop. "Let me just get into the game screen here. Okay — this is the *Kingdoms* main page."

"Wow." It was beautiful — the word *Kingdoms* seemingly woven into a tapestry of great intricacy — filled with knights and battles and lovely women with long, flowing hair, and unicorns and tigers and ships at sea and running horses and castles and shining swords and mysterious, robed beings . . . all in rich color and detail.

"Yeah — that's just the intro page." He clicked a few things, and then turned the screen toward us. "This is my kingdom —

Hlidskjalf."

Before us was a compelling scene, dominated by the color blue. A castle loomed high in the clouds, and around it was azure sky and tossing cerulean waves. As we watched, a man walked out of the castle, wearing kingly robes, but also a chest plate of armor. "That's Godall," he said. "He's my avatar, and the king of Hlidskjalf."

"So if people are playing this game, they can click on your kingdom and interact with you."

"Yes."

"How many players know that Godall is really you, Mark?"

He shrugged. "A handful. The rest just know him as Godall."

"What was Brad's name?"

"He was Thrivven. And his kingdom was called GrandIsle."

"Ah."

"You had to see my page to appreciate Brad's. Hang on — I was always so amazed by his creations I took screenshots of a bunch of them. But I'll show you his home page first."

"Oh man," said Wendy. It was indeed breathtaking — Brad's vision of GrandIsle was colorful, beautiful, and so real that it seemed like a glimpse of heaven. His castle sat on an island lined with the verdure of trees and tall grasses; beyond this could be glimpsed the blue of an unknown sea. The castle itself was many stories tall, with turrets and balconies on which smaller details could be viewed — from knights in the battlements to flowers in the windows to the small cat walking along a parapet. As we watched, a man stepped out onto the largest balcony and looked around at his kingdom.

"That's Thrivven," Mark said.

"How is he moving around if Brad is — ?"

"That Thrivven icon is always walking around."

"But when Brad was playing this game — if you went inside, you could talk with him, interact with him?"

"Yes. That's the essence of the game."

Wendy pointed. "Why would he put himself on an island if this is about battles? He's an easy target."

Mark shook his head. "It's not so much about physical battles as it is about interactions. There's a lot of dialogue in *Kingdoms*."

I had noticed something else — a woman who had emerged on an adjoining balcony and was gazing across at the man. "Who's that?"

Mark smiled. "That's Amoura. She's Thrivven's lover."

"Not his queen?"

"No — that's his queen." He pointed at a distant balcony, where a woman stood facing the sea. Wendy and I must have looked disapproving, because Mark said, "It's not like having real affairs. In *Kingdoms,* you want to form alliances; it doesn't matter whether or not they're sexual. Every alliance is a chance to win. Anyway, let me show you some of the screenshots I made of his best stuff."

He clicked around for a while, then turned the screen to us. Now we were looking at a close-up of a room in Thrivven's castle. It was rich with furs and oil paintings, as well as a wealth of wooden furniture, ornately carved. One of the paintings was clearly a portrait of Shakespeare. In another, a stag lapped at a gurgling brook. Sunlight streamed in the eastern wall through stained glass windows. "Wow," Wendy and I said in unison.

"Here's another one. This is Thrivven and Amoura having one of their illicit meetings."

This, too, was a close-up, which allowed one to see the nobly handsome visage of Thrivven and the pale skin and long, tumbling hair of Amoura. They were joining hands and gazing into each other's eyes. In the background, another man, in a black garment with a red silk necklace, looked on with an envious expression. "Oh God," I said.

"What?" Mark tore his eyes away from the screen and looked at me.

"Amoura is a real person, right? Not just a fictional creation?"

"No, she's real. I've interacted with her. In fact, she and I just attended Thrivven's funeral together last night. We had a ceremony for him, on a cliff that overlooks the sea." Mark shook his head, and I felt his genuine grief.

"But his avatar remains?" Wendy said. "That seems tacky. The game makers should shut down his page."

Mark shrugged. "We like seeing it. It gives him an eternal life."

I pointed at Amoura. "So she came back? She's still involved in *Kingdoms*?"

"Yeah. Amoura's very talented. She's hooked, just like the rest of us."

Esther came back in with eggnog. "That's not spiked, is it?" I joked.

"No, no. Just plain old eggnog. How's it going in here?"

"Mark's been telling us all about *Kingdoms*. What a fascinating virtual experience.

Really — it's like a new art form. Your son is very talented."

"He always was," said Esther fondly, sitting on the arm of her son's chair and riffling his hair.

She and Mark started reminiscing about something from his childhood, and I murmured to Wendy, "I need to call Parker. I know who Amoura is, and she was Brad's lover in real life."

"How can you be sure?"

"I'm sure."

It was perhaps just a coincidence that Amoura looked rather similar to Isabel Beauchamp; but it couldn't be coincidental that both Thrivven and Amoura had worn iron-gray rings on the smallest fingers of their right hands.

CHAPTER FOURTEEN

We chatted with Esther and Mark for half an hour or so, then I told them we had to leave. "But thank you so much, Mark, for telling me about Brad and showing me his talent. What an amazing man."

"He was. And a good friend."

"But I'm not clear on something. How was it that you are the one who told Dave Brent to hire Brad as the JFK Santa? How do you know Dave Brent?"

"Through my mom," Mark said.

I looked at Esther, who smiled at me. "Dave and I went to school together," she said. "Besides, Lilah, this is Pine Haven. Everyone has a connection to everyone else — haven't you noticed that?"

I had. "Thanks again," I said, grabbing the coat that Wendy had retrieved for me from Esther's little coat tree. "Hey, Mark. In that screenshot of Thrivven and Amoura — there's another knight, or king, or something, in the background. Who was he? Why would Brad have put him into the picture?"

"That was Count Fury. Brad didn't put him in there; it was a screen grab of the actual game in progress. Count Fury usually liked to try to invade the private meetings of Amoura and Thrivven."

"But you did, too. You were able to see it, to take a screenshot."

"That's only because Thrivven had invited me, and a few other people. He and Amoura had been about to make an announcement. Right after that, though, he had to confront Fury and have a private conference with him. I don't know what that was about. Private conferences are conducted in a separate screen."

"Do you know who Fury is?"

"No. He didn't play very well — he's not a super popular character, and he doesn't have many alliances."

"So did they end up making an announcement?"

"Yeah. I had thought it would be that King Thrivven was leaving his wife and marrying Amoura, but that wasn't it. They were just announcing that the two of them were taking a journey together to an island near GrandIsle. It was called Idyllia."

Wendy and I exchanged a wry glance. "Do

you know if the queen of GrandIsle was real? That is — assuming she represented Cleo Whitefield — did Cleo ever play the game?"

"The queen was just a fictional construct. She never moved from that little parapet. She was just a reminder of the king's main family alliance. In the game, he married the queen because she brought him important trade agreements with the Kingdom of Tharliss."

"Mark, I think the police are going to want to see this game. Esther — do you mind if I ask Parker to come over?"

Esther gave me a sparkly eyed glance. "Not at all. I'd love to get another look at him."

I handed my coat back to Wendy. "Do you call him, or do I?"

"You do it. I already bugged him once today."

I took out my cell and wandered into Esther's hallway, then dialed Parker from a shadowy, Christmas tree–scented corner.

"Parker."

"Jay."

"Hey, partner." His voice was warm and affectionate, so much so that my stomach started doing weird things. "Do you have anything good for me today?"

279

I was briefly tempted to make a comment filled with innuendo, but it wasn't the time or the place. "Yeah — Brad Whitefield and Isabel Beauchamp were having an affair. And it was she who was going to be accompanying him to Hawaii, not his wife."

There was a pause, and then Parker said, "Okay — how do we know this?"

"Trust me — you're going to want to see this for yourself."

As always, Parker seemed to defy time and speed limits. He arrived at around five o'clock, and we ushered him straight to Mark and the computer. Mark ran through his spiel again, explaining *Kingdoms.* Esther managed to hold a plate of food under Parker while he listened, and Parker proceeded to devour Esther's delicacies with his mouth while he took in the screen before him.

After a while he started firing questions at Mark, some of which, I was proud to note, were the same questions I'd asked. Wendy noticed, too, and gave me a thumbs-up. I really liked Wendy.

Finally Parker sat back, stretched, and looked at me. "You're brilliant," he said.

"What?"

"You noticed the rings long ago. We never would have noted them here if you hadn't seen them on the actual people. That's crucial, Lilah."

Wendy gave me another furtive thumbs-up.

Parker was solemn. "Despite all of this evidence, though, we can't prove any of it."

"There was something else," I said, remembering. I turned to Wendy. "Do you remember that when we all had lunch at the pub, Cleo said that she and Brad had been planning to go to Hawaii? Right then Isabel spilled her water, and everyone was distracted, and we didn't talk about it again."

"That's true," Wendy said. "You think Isabel did it on purpose, as a distraction?"

"Or because she couldn't bear to hear another woman talking about her vacation."

"Aw, man," Mark said. "I didn't know all of this. I must be the dumbest person in the world."

I swung back to him. "You're telling me you didn't know Brad was having an affair?"

Mark shrugged. "Well — no. Cleo was my friend, too, and Brad really loved her. Sometimes the three of us would go out for pizza. She called me when she heard about Brad. I was trying to calm her down for an hour."

"Okay. What about Amoura?" I said.

281

He shook his head. "You don't understand the game. Lovers in the game aren't necessarily lovers. They're alliances. I mean, it's true, you could fall in love with an alliance, the same way a person could fall in love with an e-mail pen pal or something. I never really thought of Amoura as a real lover. I just figured it was a friend of Brad's who wanted in on the game somehow. Brad had so many friends. I'm not kidding — like hundreds of them. He had so much charisma."

Mark faced the three of us, his expression earnest, and saw our skepticism. Then he bowed. "Oh man. I need to spend more time with real human beings."

"I thought you had a girlfriend," I said.

"I do. But I met her in *Kingdoms,* and we — do a lot of our interacting there," he said.

"You have . . . met her in real life, haven't you?" I asked.

Mark and Esther laughed. "Yeah. Mom's met her, too."

"Her name is Rebecca. She's lovely," Esther said.

Parker was looking impatient, which was his specialty. "I actually spoke to Isabel Beauchamp today. She denied any involvement with Brad Whitefield, aside from being in a play with him."

"She's lying," I said.

"Looks that way," Parker said to the room in general. Then he turned to me. "You figured this out. Want to be there when I question her again? I could use your knowledge of all this."

This was new. Parker inviting me inside some police work? I was both shocked and flattered. "Yeah, I do."

I had one more question for Mark, though. "Wait — when you talked to Cleo — did she seem to know about Isabel?"

"What? No — *I* didn't even know about Isabel. I only knew her as Amoura."

"So you don't think she knew that Brad was having an affair?"

"No. But I suppose other people could have known. I mean, you figured it out."

This made Parker look thoughtful. He took one more of Esther's hors d'oeuvres, shoved it into his mouth, and chewed with an appreciative expression. "Thank you. I didn't have time to eat much today," he said. Poor Parker. He never seemed to eat while he was working on a case.

We bid farewell to Esther and Mark (Jim was still mysteriously missing, and I suspected Christmas shopping) and made our way to the door.

In the driveway, Parker turned to Wendy.

"You were in on this good police work, too, and you've been doing a great job as Lilah's protection. You're absolutely welcome to sit in on this interview, or you can have some well-earned home time."

I couldn't read anything in Wendy's expression, but I sensed calculation, and on my behalf. "You know what? I'd love some home time. I appreciate it. Just call when you need me to return to Lilah's. Meanwhile I can have dinner with family."

"Sure thing," Parker said. "Lilah? We have some work to do."

CHAPTER FIFTEEN

Isabel lived in Trenton Tower, one of the tallest buildings in Pine Haven. It was mostly full of condominiums, although there were businesses on the first couple of floors. Parker and I headed straight through a plush lobby with piped-in Christmas music (the current song was an instrumental version of "Pat-a-Pan"). In one alcove near the elevator was a particularly ugly Santa Claus figurine; Parker turned to smirk at me, and I laughed.

"I should arrest them for that," he said.

I followed him, realizing with a burst of euphoria that he was being playful on my behalf.

We climbed on the elevator; Parker was glancing at some notes on his phone, but then he put it in his pocket, smiled at me, and touched my hair. "Hey," he said.

Before I could respond, the door opened and I was following a newly focused and

285

brisk Parker down a blue-carpeted hallway to a door that bore the gold numbers 612. He knocked.

"Who is it?" said Isabel's voice after a moment.

"It's Detective Parker of the Pine Haven Police."

The door swung open, and Isabel stood there, lovely and petite in a red sweater and black velvet pants, and dwarfed by her cloud of hair. "Detective, I believe you just left here?" She was very adept with her facial expressions; currently she projected both indignation and confusion.

"And I believe you lied to me," Parker said curtly. "May I come in? Or would you like to talk at the station?"

Her eyes flew to me, the unknown in this equation. "What is she doing here?"

"Lilah provided some information, and I need her to be present for verification purposes."

Isabel's eyes had been darting around while he talked; now her face changed again and she seemed to be aiming for a playful, flirtatious attitude. "Oh, come in, then." She stood aside, and we walked into an elegant main room filled with expensive-looking furniture. I wondered what sort of money she made. I recalled Parker saying, *The origin of people's money is always a mystery.*

"Please sit down," she said, although her tone said, *Please go away.*

Parker and I sat on her couch together; she faced us in a plush blue armchair.

"I wonder, Miss Beauchamp, if you would like to change your story regarding your relationship with Brad Whitefield."

"I don't know what you mean." Her eyes were large in her small face.

"Explain the rings that you and Brad Whitefield wore on your pinkie fingers. The ring you still wear, I see."

Her eyes widened, and she looked down at the ring on her hand, then back up at Parker. Her expression was suddenly helpless. "My ring has personal value. It's not for public discussion."

Parker stared her down, but not without gentleness. "If the ring means you were sleeping with Brad Whitefield, then that is not a secret you will be able to keep any longer. I am investigating a murder, Miss Beauchamp, and affairs often provide motive."

Now her eyes seemed to be the only thing on her face. They were sky blue, bright and compelling. "I was not — having an affair. What we had was deeper than that. It was not about sex. We were soul mates."

"Did you sleep with him?"

She shrugged. "No. We had kissed, many times, in the real world, but —"

"But you had done more in GrandIsle," Parker said.

Her mouth dropped open, and then she shut it and shook her head. "You know about *Kingdoms*. Aren't you a good detective."

Parker sent me a glance, acknowledging my work. Then he turned to her. "Did Mrs. Whitefield know of the affair?"

She shook her head. "I told you — it wasn't an affair. Brad loved his wife. He wanted to stay with her. But he needed me, because I spoke to something higher in him."

I scowled. That was a mighty flimsy excuse to see someone behind your wife's back. Parker's face expressed the same skepticism.

Isabel sighed. "You have to understand. Brad liked his wife when he married her, very much. But he wasn't in love with her. He was persuaded to marry her by her family, who thought that Brad would benefit from the — alliance."

I sat up straight. "Just like in *Kingdoms* — Thrivven married his queen for trade routes to her kingdom. What exactly did marrying Cleo do for Brad?"

"It wasn't quite so crass. He thought he could make a life with her. But he had a certain — weakness — and her family said that they would help him with it. If he became a member of the family."

"Gambling," I said.

"Yes. Cleo and her wealthy family knew of Brad's addiction. She loved him; all women love him, I think. But they promised Brad a sense of security that I think he truly valued. And yet, he found he could rarely talk to Cleo. Brad was a man of great intellect, a philosopher. He had two advanced degrees. Cleo had only graduated high school. Often he wanted to talk to her about acting, or about Shakespeare, or about the various theories of life and death, and she — was limited as a conversational partner. This is why I say that Brad and I were not really lovers as much as we were — companions. We loved to talk together; we could do it for hours and hours, and not just about the play that we were in. We could talk about any-thing. It was effortless with us. Brad intro-duced me to *Kingdoms* so that we would have more chances to talk without his wife growing jealous or suspicious. We needed each other." She held up her finger, where the hematite ring gleamed under the ceiling light. "Brad said that this was a symbol of

Thrivven's bond with Amoura. But what it really meant was that we were joined for life."

"Was the Hawaiian vacation for you?" Parker asked.

She bowed her head. "Yes. We were going to talk about our lives — should we stay as we were, should Brad divorce his wife, or was there some other way to accommodate our need for each other."

"So why did Cleo think it was her vacation?"

"She found the tickets at home. Brad was careless. So he had to say that they were for him and her. He still had not decided — would he take Cleo, or run off on a vacation with me and explain to Cleo later? The latter was not very likely; he was intimidated by Cleo's family, and he did not want to hurt her more than was necessary."

I lifted a finger. "But he told me that he was escaping. He said he had found his own little island of escape."

Isabel nodded. "Then perhaps he was planning to go alone. Brad was trying to work through some things. Not just about me, but about life. I think that Prospero was a life-changing role for him. It made him think of higher things. It made him examine his own life. But more and more he felt —

constrained. Trapped. And I don't mean by women. He loved women. Perhaps more by his flaws and limitations."

This didn't sound right to me. "Everyone we talk to speaks about Brad's specialness — how talented he was, and how creative. How he seemed to exceed other people's talents."

"Yes," said Isabel sadly. "But people like Brad are the people who feel they are not good enough, do not reach high enough. They want only to achieve more." She stood up and walked to a little Christmas tree that sat in front of her window. It was only about three feet tall, but it was decorated with pretty, delicate ornaments, some of which looked imported. She saw me looking at the tree and pulled off one of the ornaments. It was a little fairy, a three-inch doll dressed in gold, with long blonde hair. On its dress were painted the words *Delicate Ariel.*

"Brad bought this for me, and added the words. He loved that we could interact on-stage each night, especially in those roles. You see, Prospero and Ariel were not lovers — he was a man, and Ariel was of the elements. But theirs was a marriage of the minds. Like Brad's and mine."

Parker and I exchanged a glance. Isabel was very convincing, but the story didn't seem real. Didn't most people want sex from an affair? Or did they, perhaps, want something more?

"So if Brad had gone to Hawaii alone — would that have upset his wife and her family?"

Isabel shrugged. "Probably not. He's asked Cleo before for these little retreats. Sometimes he wanted to go away to be alone — and he really was alone. I think his reputation as a philanderer was unearned. People often assumed he was off with women, but Brad wasn't a two-timer. No, not even with me. At least, not in the traditional sense."

Parker said, "If Brad wasn't your lover, do you have one?"

She blushed. "I am — seeing someone, yes."

"And was he jealous of what you have with Brad?"

"I think that he understood. I think I made it clear to him. He didn't always like it, but — now he will not have to like it anymore." Her eyes were so sad that I felt ready to cry.

Parker took out a pad. "I'll need his name, Isabel."

Her eyes darted to mine, where she saw sympathy. Then she shrugged. "His name is

Dylan Marsh."

I gasped, and Parker jotted it down. "Marsh got Brad's role, and he got his girlfriend back."

"Dylan had nothing to do with it," Isabel said wearily. "Believe me. He loved Brad, as a friend."

I had a sudden thought. "Is Dylan Count Fury?"

She looked at me with her uncanny blue eyes. "What? No. I don't think so. We don't actually know who Count Fury is."

"What did he always want to talk about with Thrivven?" Parker asked.

"I don't know. Brad didn't want to talk about that. Here's something you need to know about Brad: he kept confidences. People seem to be maligning him left and right, calling him a gambler, a cheater. But he was a good man."

Parker tapped his pen on his pad, thinking. Isabel looked more frail than she had when we had entered the room.

"Isabel?" I said. "I suppose no one has said this to you, but I'm very sorry for your loss."

She sat up straight, her eyes impossibly wide, and then she burst into tears. I moved to the couch and offered a tentative hug, and she threw herself into my arms and

293

cried elaborately on my shoulder. Parker looked startled and uncomfortable, and made a point of jotting lots of notes until the scene was over.

Finally Isabel was dabbing her eyes and telling us to please forgive her. She sent me a grateful glance. "I appreciate what you said. More than you know. . . ."

Parker stood up. "And we appreciate the information. Please don't talk to Mr. Marsh until I've had a chance to do so. And one more thing — I need the name of Cleo's family. I'll be wanting to interview them all."

Isabel, looking distracted, was trying to put her hair back in place. "Oh, it's a big family, and they're all over the city. Her maiden name was Donato. Cleo Donato."

For a moment we stood and stared at her, suspended in time. Then Parker was swearing under his breath, and he was on the phone before the door had closed behind us.

CHAPTER SIXTEEN

Parker sat in his car, shouting into his phone and demanding that all the Donatos be brought into the station for questioning. "I want them all," he shouted. "Enrico, his son Tony, whatever other kids he has, and what's Enrico's brother's name? Vincent? That's what she told us Cleo's father is called. All of them, and whatever other Donatos you can find in the woodwork." Then he clicked off and fumed for a while. "Not once, not once, did that old man mention that Cleo was his niece," Parker said.

"His son did mention something. He said that Brad was family. But I thought he was just speaking in an Italian, *abbondanza* kind of way."

"What?"

"You know — like that old commercial? It's like a welcoming generosity, or abundance or something. Anyway, I didn't think he meant it literally."

"A sin of omission," Parker said darkly. "He could have been much clearer. And now we have another one in the mix: Cleo's father, Vince."

He started the car and pulled away from the curb. His jaw was set, his eyes narrowed. Parker did not like to be crossed. "I'll take you home, Lilah. I already called Wendy and asked her to meet us at your place."

"Parker?"

"Yeah."

"It was impressive, watching you question Isabel. You're so good at your job."

His mind was elsewhere, but he said, "Thanks," with a quick smile.

"It's sexy, Parker. How focused you are."

Now I had his attention. He darted a glance my way. "Yeah?"

"Yeah."

"I thought you said I had a rod in my spine."

"Well, you do, sometimes, but it's mainly very alluring. All the cop stuff."

Now he was grinning. "That's good to know. I will tuck it away for future reference."

"Meanwhile, it is very satisfying to know that you're going to read all the Donatos the riot act. I don't trust those people."

"And you will no longer interact with

those people. Not on the phone, not in person. If I find out that you did, without consulting me, I'll be upset, Lilah. The rod will be back in place."

"Got it." We were approaching my street. I said, "Thanks for letting me tag along, Parker. I felt like a real cop there for a minute."

"Like I said, you could do anything."

I leaned over and kissed him on the cheek. He was about to say something, but as we turned into my driveway, Wendy came running up and pounded on the door. Apparently she hadn't gone home for dinner after all. "We've got trouble," she said.

She led us up the driveway, where my landlords Terry and Britt stood on the walkway that led to my porch, looking grim. Mick sat at their feet, but he ran to greet me when he saw me. "We let him out because he was so upset in there," Terry said.

Parker was on his phone, but now he clicked off and said, "What happened?"

Terry scratched his shaggy blond head. Even now, under stress, he looked sort of relaxed and casual, like a handsome surfer who had been teleported to Illinois from the Malibu coast. "We happened to see

297

Lilah leave earlier, so when a guy appeared in her front yard, we were kind of watching to see who it was. Then this man pulled out a gun —"

"Recognize him?" Parker asked.

"No, not at all. He was tall and dark — that's all I noticed. Dark hair."

"Go on."

"Britt practically tackled me to keep me inside; I wanted to go confront him." Britt snorted behind him, still indignant. Her dark bob of hair, silky and elegant, swung forward, briefly concealing the fear and anger on her face.

"What did he do?"

Terry pointed at my beautiful picture window, which was now a ruin of broken shards. "He shot a hole in that window, dropped the gun, and took off."

"He could have hurt Mick!" I yelled. Mick leaned against me, pleased to have been mentioned. I scratched his big head.

Parker studied the ground as he processed details. "You call it in?"

"Yeah. And I tried to chase him. But by the time Britt let me get out of the house, he had already disappeared into the back-yard. I did chase him then, but he had gone through Lilah's back gate into the alley. There was no sign of him out there."

"Someone waiting for him, maybe," Britt offered.

"Where's the gun?" Parker asked.

"We left it where he dropped it. Didn't want to, like, disturb a crime scene."

Parker nodded. "I'll be back," he said. He moved gingerly around the area, taking some pictures on his phone and bending over the weapon, which still lay like an obscene thing in the snow.

Britt moved to me and slung an arm around my shoulder. "We called a window guy Terry knows. He'll have this fixed as soon as the police are done with it. But you might want to stay in our place tonight. It's going to be freezing in yours."

I sighed. When would I be able to live in my own house again? In the last two months I'd had to stay with my parents, my brother, and now probably with Terry and Britt. It was good to have friends and family, but it was also good to have a home. "Thanks," I said. "There are three of us, though. Mick, me, and my bodyguard, Wendy."

"Bodyguard?"

"It's a long story, which I shall tell to you and Terry tonight."

"We'll have a nice dinner." She looked at the broken window with some trepidation. "Is someone trying to kill you, Lilah?"

I had an epiphany in that moment, standing in the quiet snow on my front yard. "No, I don't think so. Give me a minute."

And I went to tell Parker my theory.

That night I introduced Wendy to the amazing experience that is Terry and Britt's house. Terry is an Internet entrepreneur who officially calls himself a "broker" who helps rich people spend their money. His house is a whimsical collection of everything a rich guy with a lot of style might buy himself because he has no children and a lot of disposable cash.

We sat eating a sumptuous feast (ordered from Elderberry, a wonderful restaurant just outside Pine Haven) at Terry's conversation piece of a dining room table. It was an American antique walnut table with a split pedestal base and lovely carved medallions on the legs. Terry said he had gotten it for a steal, which probably meant thousands of dollars. Whenever I sat at it I felt as though I were dining in a castle.

"So Parker is inclined to agree with your theory about the shooting?" Terry asked, handing Wendy a plate full of roast beef. She grinned at me; she joked that she was going to gain ten pounds being my body-guard because everyone kept feeding us.

Mick, too, was benefitting from Terry's largesse. He sat in the corner with a gargantuan dog bone that Terry had produced from somewhere; if hosting guests were a profession, Terry could have made millions.

I poked my fork into a lovely new potato. "About this shooting, yes. The way you describe it, Terry, he was purposely doing everything out in the open. He shot into the front of the house, not bothering to hide himself. He was clearly not aiming at anyone, since no one was inside. He left the weapon behind on purpose, and then he ran off. He wanted someone to find the gun. Parker thinks so, too. The question is why."

"Not to mention who the hell is he?" Britt said indignantly. She turned to me, her hair swishing on her shoulders. "But we have three gunmen here, right? The one who shot this poor Santa, the one that shot at you and Cam, and now this one."

"Which might all be the same gun. Or not. Who knows? This gets more confusing as it goes along." I put the potato in my mouth and said, "Mmm."

Wendy finished her last bite and smiled down at her plate. Then her brows creased. "So let's see . . . who have we encountered with dark hair? You said this man was young, Terry?"

"Well, youngish. I didn't get a great look at his face. He wasn't old. He was trim, and he moved fast."

Wendy held up her hand and counted on her fingers. "So who has dark hair? Tony Donato, the son. Dylan Marsh has brown hair, if that meets the dark criterion — and he is suspicious for a few other reasons. Your friend Mark, Lilah — who was also Whitefield's friend. And there was the other young man at the party — the one from the school. His name was Reese?"

"Ross," I said. "But he didn't have anything — I mean, I assume he knew Whitefield, but he's not involved in this. He's just a friend of my friend Jenny." Even as I said it, though, I realized I couldn't vouch for Ross. Anyone could have known Brad or held a grudge against him — hadn't Mark said that Brad had hundreds of friends? What if one of them had become an enemy? Could Ross have come out the front of the school and driven around the back? It wasn't likely.

Wendy was still listing. "And then there was the guy with Cleo Donato. She said he was her brother, right?"

"Right. Another Donato. What was his name?" I asked. "Did she say?"

Wendy closed her eyes. "It was Ed. Wasn't it Ed?"

"Yes! Ed. That doesn't sound very Italian."

"Probably Eduardo," said Britt.

I sighed. "Is that it? Did we mention all the dark-haired men?"

"Don't forget Frank," Wendy said, and we frowned at each other. Frank continued to be an unknown element, despite what Enrico Donato said.

Terry must have seen something in my face, because he pounded the table with his hand like a judge with a gavel. "Okay — enough worrying over this. That's the job of your cop friend."

"Yeah, what's the story on him?" Britt asked, flipping some silky dark hair behind her left ear. "He was here at Halloween, and this time you pulled up in the car with him!" Her eyes were shining. "Is he your boyfriend, Lilah?"

All three of them looked at me expectantly, and I shrugged. "More to come on that. We're in a limbo stage right now."

Terry nodded. "Anyway, as I was saying — Lilah, why don't you take Wendy over to your favorite room? I have a surprise in there."

He was referring to his big front hall,

303

which held a spectacular old Wurlitzer jukebox. Of all Terry and Britt's amazing possessions, this was the one I coveted the most. I had whiled away many an hour visiting my friendly landlords and enjoying the wonderful music of their jukebox.

I led Wendy from the dining room to the front door; this allowed us to pass through a large main hall that made me think of castles — or of Mark's *Kingdoms* game — and past a living room with a splendid, fragrant Christmas tree. Then I brought Wendy into the foyer, where she practically dove on the jukebox. "Oh my *gosh*! This thing is awesome. Does it work?"

Terry was right behind us, smiling and proud. "Not only does it work, but I just had a guy I know add some special selections."

"A guy you know? You know every guy," I said, half resentful of Terry's amazing connections.

"Yeah. Anyway. Name your favorite Christmas song."

Wendy was enthralled. "Oh, that's easy. 'White Christmas.' "

Terry nodded. "Great choice. Have a seat." He pointed to two armchairs that faced the jukebox. Its lights, glowing in primary colors, comforted me and made me

304

feel festive. "Tell me if you've ever heard this version before."

He pushed a couple of buttons, and we heard an opening, then a woman's voice singing the introduction that Bing Crosby's version never included. It was a big, familiar, lovely voice. "Is that — Linda Ronstadt?" I asked.

"Yeah. But wait — it's a duet." We listened some more, and a new voice took the solo.

"I know that voice," said Wendy. "That's Rosemary Clooney!"

"Got it!" Terry yelled. "It's a great version. Enjoy — I'm going to get some hot chocolate going."

Wendy turned to me; I could swear there were tears in her eyes. "Your friends are always feeding us. I'm getting so spoiled I might never return home."

I laughed. "Poor Betsy. That reminds me — I'm supposed to make Christmas cookies with my mom tomorrow. I guess you have to be there, right? Unless Parker does something amazing in the meantime? So I wonder if Betsy would come and join us."

Wendy looked almost mournful. "More food," she said.

"Yeah — and it's fattening."

Then she brightened. "Bets will love it. I'll text her." She took out her phone and

305

began typing, and I looked out Terry's hall window, from which I could see his shoveled driveway and a glimpse of my own little house, sitting forlornly at the end of the drive, its front window boarded. I hoped the men would come back to repair it before Christmas. Much as I liked Terry and Britt, and thrilled as I was that I would now get a chance to see their alluring second floor, I longed to be in my space on Christmas, baking food in my oven and watching Mick sleep in his basket by the fireplace.

As if he sensed my thoughts, Mick came padding in to show me the large bone Terry had given him. He set it down briefly, and I said, "Wow." Then he picked it up and started to gnaw, contented as could be.

The song had ended, Wendy's text had been sent, and Terry was back at the jukebox. "Get a load of this. I found all these rare covers of other great songs. Listen."

This time he played us Judy Garland singing "Have Yourself a Merry Little Christmas." No one sang it the way Judy did — sweet and sad — and the melancholy lingered in me long after Terry stopped the music and Britt led us up their grand staircase to a carpeted hallway and to the adjacent rooms that Wendy and I would borrow for the night. It truly looked like the floor of a castle — there was even a full-size suit of armor in one corner.

In my room, which had hardwood floors and a giant maroon rug with thick gold tassels, the large bed dominated the space and faced a stone fireplace that housed not flames but a basket of pine branches. The heater was modern and functional, and the room was warm as toast. "Let me know if you need anything, sweetie. Terry and I are at the end of the hall," Britt said, patting my hair.

As I pulled back the feather bed and climbed between soft sheets, I could still hear Judy singing in my ear, telling me we'd have to muddle through somehow, because next year it would all be better. Next year, I realized, was only a couple of weeks away. Poor Brad Whitefield hadn't made it out of this one.

I looked at the bedroom window, illuminated by Terry's subtle Christmas lights, and saw a light snowfall swirling in a winter wind. How many days in a row had it snowed? It was beautiful, but relentless. Judy Garland, Brad Whitefield, and an anonymous gunman twirled in my thoughts like the helpless snowflakes. Despite it all, I was asleep moments later.

CHAPTER SEVENTEEN

By the time Wendy and I left Terry's house the next morning, still voicing our extravagant thanks, we saw that my window had already been repaired. That, it was clear, was another debt to Terry and his generosity; I was sure that he had secretly paid someone hefty overtime to get it done quickly. Wendy and I went to examine the new window, which was just as lovely as the old one, but seemed thicker.

"He probably got bulletproof glass," Wendy joked. She was holding Mick on a leash, and he sniffed the newly cleaned area with interest. When he looked up, there was snow on his nose. "He cracks me up," Wendy said, grinning. Then she handed me Mick's leash and opened the door with my key. Mick and I entered the warm foyer, but Wendy insisted on checking the place out first. She returned after five minutes. "It's fine," she said.

Relieved, I went to my kitchen and saw my answering machine light blinking. My mother was one of the few people who still called my landline. "Looks like I need to call Mom. We're baking cookies today."

Wendy groaned. "So much food," she said.

"Did you ever talk to Betsy? It would be fun — a girls' day out. And then my mom will get to know you both before our Christmas dinner."

"That's right! Let me call her and check in." Wendy took out her cell and moved into the living room to talk.

Meanwhile I returned my mother's call. "Are we on for today?" she asked brightly.

"Yes, we are. But you know I have this bodyguard, right? Wendy. She's been great. Can I invite her and her roommate Bets?"

"Of course! The more the merrier," my mother chirped. She loved company, and she and my father had recently revamped their kitchen, which she liked to show off to visitors. "Try to be here by noon," she said. "I have all kinds of ingredients."

I promised that I would, and hung up the phone, only to have it ring again. It was Parker.

"How are you?" he asked. He sounded affectionate, but distracted. I imagined him at his desk, sorting through his notes.

309

"I'm fine. Terry treated us like royalty, and he's replaced my window."

"Great. And what are you doing today?"

"We're making cookies with my mom."

"Good, good."

"Is something wrong?"

A pause. "I don't know. And I'm probably stupid to bring it up, but it's been nagging at me."

"What?"

"You said, at the Christmas party, that you were angry with me, but you couldn't remember why. I know I'm opening Pandora's box, but . . . I need to know what it is. Especially because — things went so well with us the other night. I don't suppose you remember it now?"

With a muffled sigh I walked to my back door and looked out at my white yard. "I do."

"Okay."

"The thing is — the other day, your mom called me and told me she'd had a cancer scare. She said she hadn't told me because she didn't want me to worry unless I had to."

"Right," Parker said.

"But she called you, when we were at Cam and Fina's, and she told you how worried she was. And I asked if it was your mother

310

on the phone, and you said no."

"She asked me not to tell you."

"Exactly, Parker. The way Pet Grandy asked me not to tell *you* that I made the chili that ended up being poisoned. She didn't want her secret to be revealed, and I was trying to respect her wishes."

"That's not the same." His voice was defensive.

"Why?"

"You lied to the *police,* Lilah! It's against the law. The law that I respect."

I understood this about Parker. He loved his profession because he was an idealist, and he believed in rules and in justice, however flawed they might be. "Yes, I did. But only because I knew I was innocent, and so it didn't matter to the case whether I was the chef or not."

Another pause. I knew that Parker was making his rumination face — the one where his eyes darted around like his darting thoughts. "I understand what you're saying. But I still see a distinction between the two."

"Well, here's my dilemma, Jay. You cut me out of your life, didn't speak to me for two *months* because I failed to tell you the truth about something I cooked. Then you looked me in the eye and hid the truth from me

311

about your mother, who happens to be my friend. But I understand: Ellie asked you to keep silent. If you hadn't treated me so badly for similar behavior this wouldn't be an issue at all."

"Lilah, I don't know what you want me to say." He sounded miserable.

"I don't know, either. But it dawned on me that if two people disagree on something as important as the truth —"

There was commotion on Parker's side, and a voice speaking to him. Parker said, "Lilah — something's happening here. I'm sorry — this is not where I wanted to end this conversation, but —"

"I get it. Go catch the bad guys. I'll talk to you later."

"Thanks," he said, and the line went dead.

Wendy appeared behind me. "Everything okay?"

"Hmm? Oh, I don't know, really. Nothing a boatload of cookies won't solve."

"I agree. And Betsy said she'd be happy to join us."

We arrived at my parents' lovely house, and Wendy did a quick surveillance before letting me emerge from the car. My father, who had been shoveling the driveway, looked on with interest. I introduced him to

312

Wendy and then to Betsy, who had pulled up behind us. She was a small woman with brown hair and glasses; she wore a rust-colored ski jacket and expensive-looking jeans and boots.

"So nice to meet you all," she said in what could only be called a sweet voice. And just like that, Betsy fit right in. When we arrived in the kitchen and my mother took our coats and bustled out of the room with them, I saw that Betsy wore a red sweater that bore the embroidered words *Jingle, Jingle, Jingle* in happy Christmas lettering, and every letter bore a tiny bell.

My mother returned, took one look at Betsy's sweater, and clapped her hands. "I love Christmas sweaters!" she said. This was obvious, since her own holiday attire was a pair of black leggings and a long red Christmas sweater that said, *Not a Creature Was Stirring,* and had a detailed rendering of cute animals sleeping in front of a Christmas tree.

The two women admired each other's sweaters and talked animatedly while Wendy and I stood sniffing the air. Clearly something was already in the oven. "What are we making next, Mom?"

She had just told Betsy to go to her iPod and find some fun baking music (whatever that might be), and now she turned back. "Okay. I have our favorite recipe cards lined up over there" — she pointed at one counter — "and I have four bowls set out here. Then all the ingredients are on the side. The big blue containers are flour and sugar, and I have several cartons of eggs here. And here's the food coloring and the various types of sprinkles. Just pick something and have fun!"

A thought occurred to me. "Wasn't Serafina going to join us for this?"

My mother nodded. "She was, but now she and Cam have to run a bunch of errands before their trip to Rome. We'll see them tomorrow, I think."

Her eyes were sparkling; my mother loved Christmas, especially when her house was full of people. I gave her a quick impulsive hug, and then we did as she suggested. Twenty minutes later we were flour speckled and singing along with Dean Martin's cover of "It's Beginning to Look a Lot Like Christmas."

My mother's Russian tea cakes were already cooling on the rack, and we had all sampled more than one. They were buttery perfection, sugared green and red. I was contemplating getting another one when my phone rang. I wiped my hands on my apron and went into the hall, away from the music, before I answered.

It was Tabitha. "Hi, Lilah. I just wanted to let you know that the show is opening again today, and I have complimentary tickets for you if you want to go, as sort of a holiday treat. You probably have plans, but —"

"Hang on. Let me see if I have any takers," I said. I asked the women in the kitchen, who, at their current level of hilarity and female bonding, were all for a road trip and a free show. My father, who had emerged from the snow red-faced and cold, said no, thanks, but he gratefully accepted the hot chocolate that Betsy pressed into his hands. The bakers had made it especially for him and then added artful swirls of whipped cream and chocolate sauce on the top. He gave me a quick kiss, took his sweet beverage into his office, and shut the door. He wore the rather solemn face that he always brought to the paying of bills.

I lifted my phone. "Tabitha, sorry to keep you waiting. I will take four tickets, if that's not too many."

"That's fine. I'll leave them at the box office under your name."

"Thanks so much. We'll look for you after the show!"

It seemed strange that the theater company had decided to begin the play again before Christmas, but then again they wouldn't want to lose too much money, and the holidays must be big box office days.

Back in the vanilla-scented kitchen the women were red-faced from the oven and concentrating on their tasks. Betsy was squeezing spritz cookies in the shape of wreaths from the press and onto a pan; Wendy was pressing tiny red-hot candy buttons into the bellies of gingerbread men; my mother was making a green frosting to put on some sugar cookies that cooled under the window. John Denver was singing "Aspenglow" in the background, and the music gave the moment a charmed, almost blessed feeling, accompanied by the occasional jingling of Betsy's sweater bells.

I joined them in the warm room and began to make a thin glaze for the Italian walnut cookies I was making in Serafina's honor (and in honor of my once-beloved Italian teacher, Miss Abbandonato).

"This is so nice," my mother said. "It's been a long time since Lilah brought a bunch of girlfriends home. I don't think she's done it since college."

"When did I ever do that?" I asked, sprinkling more powdered sugar into my glaze.

"You brought half of your dorm here one Halloween. Don't you remember?"

"Oh, right. That was fun."

"It's such a lovely house," Bets said. "And this kitchen! I love that backsplash behind the oven. The whole thing is so happy and warm. And I love that lemony color on the walls."

My mother brightened. "We just finished renovating. We're both Realtors, Dan and I, and we get such good ideas from looking at the houses we show. This was a kitchen we agreed on. And the backsplash is imported from Austria."

Bets moved closer to the wall, and my mother went over to detail the improvements. Wendy raised her eyebrows. "Someone's going to want a new kitchen."

"Do you own a house?"

"We rent one. With the option to buy someday, if we want. Bets has all these great decorating ideas. She's like an encyclopedia."

"It's great to have someone like that around. I've been thinking, with all the things we're trying to process about this whole Whitefield thing — all the suspects, and —" I had been looking out my mother's window and into her nicely shoveled driveway. Now I paused, my mouth still open, as something dawned on me.

"What is it?" said Wendy, stiffening.

I turned to her. "Where was Frank?"

"What?"

I pointed out the window. "And where is he now? Didn't Mr. Donato say that Frank would be with us until we caught whoever killed Whitefield?"

Wendy nodded.

"When's the last time you saw him?"

She shrugged. "I can't remember."

"And where was he yesterday when my house was shot? He wasn't guarding me while I was with Parker, so shouldn't he have been waiting at my place? If so, shouldn't he have seen the man who shot the window?"

Wendy was finished with her gingerbread men. She took the cookie sheet to the oven, her expression thoughtful.

"Hang on — it's time for mine to come out, and you can slide yours in," I told her. I donned some oven mitts and removed the Italian cookies, fragrant with walnut and almond paste, and nudged my mother aside so I could set them on the counter. She was still showing Bets the new tile and trim and raving about the workmen they had found.

I set my cookies on a rack to cool, and moved toward the window, where Wendy joined me. "As we said when we put him on the list, Frank has dark hair," Wendy said. "Do we now consider him more of a suspect?"

"We need his picture. We can text it to Terry and see if he recognizes him."

Wendy nodded. "Let me see if Parker has anything."

As was her habit, she took her phone into the next room and made her call in relative quiet. She came back grinning. "I should have known; Parker didn't have to look in the database. He photographed the guy himself on the first day Donato assigned him to you. He sent me the picture."

"Great. Let me give you Terry's number and you can send it to him."

Moments later Wendy had sent the photo, and we awaited Terry's response.

"Did you tell Parker that Frank's been MIA?"

"Yeah. He said he noticed that yesterday. He tried to call Donato about it, but the man has suddenly disappeared, or at least is incommunicado. No one at the salon has seen him in two days."

"Why does this seem ominous?"

"Not necessarily. Lots of people leave town at Christmas. We are just two days away."

"Right."

My phone rang; Terry didn't like texting. He preferred to call and boom at me with his perpetually happy voice. "Hello?"

"Lilah! I looked at this photo Wendy sent me, but this isn't the guy."

"Have you seen him at all, lurking around my place or yours?"

"I don't think so. He has a pretty distinctive head of hair."

"Okay. Let me know if you do see him, okay? Or anyone out of the ordinary."

"You got it. Be careful."

I thanked him and said good-bye; Wendy sent me a questioning look, and I shook my head.

My mother and Betsy were back at the kitchen island.

"I have four giant Tupperware containers, so that everyone here walks home with a sampling of every type of cookie we made. You'll be all set for the holidays," my mother said.

"I've never been to a cookie party," Bets said. "This was great fun!"

My mother was so happy it looked as though she'd been dipping into the eggnog I'd drunk the other night. "And now we all get to go out on the town!"

■ ■ ■ ■

Many Chicago-area theaters are tucked into old storefronts or hidden in unlikely looking buildings, but this production of *The Tempest* was playing at the Theatre Downtown in Wallace Heights. I'd been there once before to see a production of *Hedda Gabler* with a college English class.

The lobby was alive with that holiday feeling that comes close to Christmas; people with bright coats and stripy scarves milled around, enjoying their pre-holiday activities. I found myself briefly distracted, focusing on individual faces and wondering about the lives they lived. My brain was playing the "busy sidewalks" melodic line from "Silver Bells." My mother appeared at my side and gave me a hug. "Let's go, dreamy." We picked up our tickets and found that Tabitha had scored us seats in the second row.

"This is wonderful," my mother said as we moved down the carpeted aisle. "I haven't seen a live show in years!"

My father didn't like theater as a rule, which was a bone of contention between them, especially when my mother wanted to watch the Tony Awards.

"Bets and I have season tickets to the Goodman," Wendy said.

My mother shot her an envious glance. We had reached our row, which had people already seated in it. "We'll have to climb over some folks," Bets murmured.

A face turned toward us, and I recognized Cleo, who waved. "Hello!" she said. Her brother was with her, too. Had Parker not questioned him? I wondered. Cleo seemed happy to see us, but the tall and silent Ed seemed scowlingly uninterested. I noticed that, for the first time, Cleo looked pretty, and probably more like her regular self. Her red hair was styled into waves, and she had taken some trouble with her makeup. I understood, looking at her, why Bart had referred to her as Brad Whitefield's hot wife. Or had he said sexy? Or something else? I didn't know what words were popular with high school freshmen, but I remembered that Bart had made a point of mentioning Cleo's attractiveness. I hadn't agreed with him until now. Cleo was pretty, and her hair gleamed like copper under the theater lights.

We moved past Cleo and her brother and tucked into our seats. Cleo leaned over and said, "Tabitha invited us."

"Will it be hard to watch the play — without him?"

Cleo nodded, her eyes moist. "Yes. But Dylan is my friend, and I'm curious to see his interpretation of the role."

I took out my phone and set it to camera mode, then held it up. "Are we allowed to take pictures? Oops, I just took one." I stared at my phone and its apparent malfunction.

Cleo shook her head. "I don't think so. No flash photography. Maybe if you turned off that bright flash."

"Okay, thanks." No flash, in a darkened space like this, would produce barely any image at all. I wasn't really interested in taking pictures of the theater, though.

My mother was between Cleo and me, so I introduced her to Cleo and her brother. Being my mother, she immediately offered her condolences and then started a bright conversation that seemed to be keeping the interest of both Donatos.

Using the moment of distraction, I texted Terry and sent him the picture of Ed-possibly-Eduardo Donato, the silent brother. Was this the guy from the driveway? I wrote.

Next I texted Parker. Did you question Ed Donato, Cleo's brother?

A voice over a loudspeaker was asking us to silence our phones. I left mine on vibrate, in case someone texted me back, and stowed it in my pocket.

The lights went out, the curtains opened, and we were sinking with sailors on a tempestuous sea, who cried, "All lost!" as though their hearts would break.

I, too, was lost, for the next three hours, in the magic that is Shakespeare. I rarely came out of the story, except to notice how beautiful Isabel Beauchamp looked in her sparkling nude bodysuit, meant to convey Ariel's ability to blend in, but sequined to remind us of Ariel's magical powers. Her hair tumbled down her back as she ran back and forth on the stage, explaining to Prospero the way she (he, as Ariel) enchanted the sailors. Claudia Birch looked tall and noble as Miranda, and there was a clear chemistry between her and the young man who played her lover, Ferdinand. Dylan Marsh was impressive as Prospero: handsome, clever, humorous with some of his interpretations. The audience seemed to like him, and I noted Cleo smiling now and again. I found myself wishing I'd had a chance to see Brad Whitefield in the same role; while Marsh was good, he was not great, and Whitefield had been said to have put forth a stunning performance of this magical character.

I had not known Brad Whitefield, yet I found myself missing him. How much more of a void had he left for those who actually knew and loved him?

These thoughts lingered in my head when the cast assembled on the stage for a final bow. Dylan Marsh exchanged an affectionate glance with Isabel as he took her hand and bent forward, at the end of the play, to much applause. I thought I saw a moment of pain flash through Isabel's eyes as she faced the audience for the first time without her hand in Whitefield's — her cast mate and soul mate. Was it my secret knowledge of their relationship that made Marsh's expression seem so triumphant, so gloating as he took his bows? His face, still a combination of handsome and evil, looked boldly out into the audience, at one point making eye contact with me and showing both recognition and surprise. I sent him a little wave, and his gaze moved on.

I looked to the left and saw that Tabitha, normally in the wings, had moved slightly onto the stage to clap for the actors. She wore the obligatory stage tech black and a red theater lanyard that said, *Staff,* along with her headset. Something in her face looked familiar. . . . I stiffened and grabbed Wendy's arm. "I need to talk to Tabitha," I said. "You should probably come, too."

She nodded. I made an excuse to my mother, and we slid out of the row and moved out and into the lobby, seeking a backstage entrance. A young person with a telltale red lanyard and a headset stood in our way. "Only staff in there," she said.

For the first time since I'd known her, Wendy flashed her badge. "And police," she said. "We need to speak with Tabitha."

The young person stepped aside, her mouth agape, and we walked down a long, dark hallway that led us to a wooden-floored backstage area filled with scenery and props. A few people milled around, but most were standing at the edge of the stage, watching the cast take their bows.

We spotted Tabitha and moved up behind her. "Tabitha," I said, tapping her shoulder.

She turned, surprised, and then grinned at us. "Hi, guys! How did you get back here?"

"Is there someplace we can talk?" I said.

"I really can't right now. They're about to flow off the stage, and I need —"

"I know you're Count Fury," I said. "I know about *Kingdoms*."

"What?" she and Wendy asked in unison. But on Tabitha's face I saw a red-faced shame that supported my suspicions. In that moment on the stage, she had looked exactly like the count at the edge of Thrivven's kingdom: always looking from the outskirts, in a black outfit and a red sash (her lanyard), wearing an expression of bitter disappointment at her perpetual exclusion.

Now Tabitha pursed her lips. "Fine. But we have to wait," she said, pointing at the actors still taking their bows.

Wendy and I stayed close to her until the curtains had closed. She finally acknowledged us with a loud sigh. Then she lifted a curtain and ushered us through. "We can go back here." She led us behind the stage itself, into another little hallway that housed tiny actor makeup rooms. I glimpsed Dylan Marsh in his room, peering into his mirror as he dabbed away his makeup with a cotton ball. Apparently he wasn't planning to go out and meet any fans; he seemed to be in a hurry, and his hand looked as though it was shaking. I wondered if he had been drinking. . . .

But then we were past his room. One of the doors had Tabitha's name on it, written in pen on a piece of loose-leaf paper and affixed to the door with scotch tape. Production values of community theater, I thought. The room held only a table and chair and was cluttered with papers and props. "How do you even know about *Kingdoms*?" Tabitha asked.

I studied her face. She wore a hangdog expression, and her shoulders drooped slightly in a sort of "you got me" pose, yet her lips were curled into almost a smirk, as though she considered the whole thing a funny prank. It disgusted me, but I couldn't put my finger on the reason why. A part of me was angry that she had lied about her connection to the show in the first place. And she certainly hadn't mentioned the Count Fury thing, although there would have been no reason for her to tell that to anyone — except maybe the police? And Parker didn't know, I was sure.

"Do you admit that you're Count Fury?"

"Yes, okay. I created the count. I heard Brad and Isabel talking about the game so often, I decided I'd join myself. In a weird way, I got to spend more time with him there than I ever did here." She looked around the cramped little room with its cement floor. "Alone time, I mean."

"You were in love with him," Wendy said.

"Duh. Who wasn't?" Tabitha said, shrugging. "But it was just an innocent thing. I mean, it's not like I ever went after him."

And yet she had managed to be in his life, again and again. Had she ever had to

328

manipulate things so that she was in shows with Brad Whitefield? Had he even been a friend of hers, or was she more of a stalker? With a rush of anxiety I realized we had only Tabitha's word for any of it — their closeness, their fond relationship, their "alone time" in *Kingdoms* as a positive thing. What if that had been her perception only?

"But you resented Isabel, didn't you? Because Brad wanted to spend time with her," I said.

"Yeah! Time he should have spent with his wife." Tabitha's face took on a blurry look.

Wendy and I exchanged a glance. "It wasn't his wife you were upset for, was it?" I asked.

She sank into the chair and scowled up at us. "Cleo's my friend. Yeah, I loved her husband, but I wouldn't have cheated with him. I'm the one who called there and told them about the tickets!"

Wendy stepped closer to her, looming. "What tickets? The Hawaii tickets? What did you know about them?"

She seemed to diminish under Wendy's stare. "Brad asked me to pick them up for him at a travel agency. I went and this guy who worked there was also a guy who knew

329

Brad from his Santa Claus gig. Some red-haired guy who taught at the school."

"Peter from the Christmas party," I said to Wendy under my breath.

"Anyway, that guy was saying snipy things about how Brad ordered the tickets with some woman, and that woman wasn't his wife."

"So you took it upon yourself to tell — whom?"

"I told them both. Ed and Cleo. Ed answered the phone when I called."

I thought about it now. Almost everywhere Cleo went, her brother accompanied her. Was this family solidarity, or was it custody? Did Ed want to prevent Cleo from talking about something? At the pub she had seemed almost worried, and that was the one time we had seen her without Ed. . . .

"How did Ed respond to the news?" Wendy asked now.

My phone vibrated in my pocket. I took it out and read the note from Terry: That's the guy! just as Tabitha answered, "Well, naturally he was upset. Actually he was furious."

CHAPTER EIGHTEEN

Wendy was on the phone and requesting backup as we ran back down the long, dark hall. I kept looking behind us, convinced that someone would be giving chase.

Out on the theater floor, Ed Donato was making his way out, his hands clamped firmly on his sister Cleo's arm. I spotted her red hair and pointed. "There, Wendy!"

We ran to the back through a side aisle, avoiding the crush of people in the main aisleway, and then waited near the entrance for Ed and Cleo to reach the back. When they arrived, Ed Donato glanced at us and then looked at his watch. "Hello, again," said Cleo with mild surprise.

"I wonder if I can ask you a couple of quick questions, Mr. Donato?" Wendy said, flashing her ID. My mother and Bets joined us, but then held back as they realized that something official was happening.

Cleo looked up at her brother, her eyes

wide. Ed's face remained unfriendly. He had none of the charm of his uncle Enrico or his cousin Tony. "We have to get going," he said. Cleo struggled slightly in his grasp.

"What's going on?" she said.

"Mr. Donato, we can talk here, or you can accompany me to the police station," said Wendy. She put her ID away and rested her right hand on her hip, near her gun.

His eyes were on her hand. Then, suddenly, he summoned up a charming smile, and I saw Enrico Donato's eyes looking at us. "What do you need to know, Officer?"

"I would like to know why you shot a hole in Miss Drake's window on Dickens Street yesterday."

"What?" Cleo asked, almost laughing. "You have the wrong man. Ed doesn't even own a gun."

Ed continued smiling. "I don't know what you're talking about. But I also know I'm not going to address your accusations. If you want to question me, then I want my lawyer present."

Wendy nodded. "That's your right, sir. But then we will need to go downtown. You can call him on the way."

He sniffed. "I'm not going anywhere with you."

I was filled with admiration for Wendy,

who met his gaze with steely resolve. "You will indeed go with me, Mr. Donato, one way or another."

The moment was both terrifying and compelling; we had drawn the notice of some people who were still departing the theater, and they lingered around us, eavesdropping. My mother and Betsy were among them, their eyes wide and uncertain. Looking from Wendy to Ed Donato, I decided that my money was on Wendy, despite an intimidating gleam in the tall man's eyes.

Wendy's hand was still resting on her hip when two uniformed cops moved toward us from the entrance. "Backup's here," I murmured.

"Mr. Donato? I think these officers will be happy to offer you a ride in their cruiser," Wendy said.

His smile disappeared. He glared briefly at both of us and then said, "Fine. Come on, Cleo."

"Just you, sir. Your sister is not required for this interview."

He seemed reluctant to let go of her, and I saw fear dart across Cleo's face before she looked down at her shoes. "Go on, Ed. I'll call Don Giovanus and tell him to meet you there."

Ed Donato darted a particularly evil glance at me before he snorted and walked toward the cops. Wendy said, "Be right back," and followed them toward the exit, speaking to her colleagues in low tones.

I turned to Cleo, who still wore a look of surprise. "Are you okay?"

"Yeah, I guess. I mean, what's all this about?"

"Someone shot my window out yesterday. They think it was your brother."

"But why? Ed doesn't even know you."

"No." I thought about this for a moment. "And I have no idea why. You would know better — he's your brother. I just know that a witness put him at the scene of the shooting."

"This is ridiculous! Why is all this stuff happening to my family? And at Christmas! It used to be my favorite time of year." She shook her head, then lifted her chin, her eyes on the back exit. "Oh no — Ed has the keys to the car. Do you think I can still catch him?"

I turned. The lobby still thronged with people, but the uniforms were no longer visible among them. "I think they're gone."

Wendy emerged from the lobby then, jogging down the aisle to join us. "Sorry about that," she said.

Cleo gave her an unfriendly glance. "I don't think you had to haul my brother away like that."

"I disagree." Wendy shrugged. "He discharged a firearm in the middle of a residential area. We have reason to believe this may be connected to the death of your husband, Mrs. Whitefield, and it's not something that we can wait on."

"Why would it be connected to Brad?" Cleo asked. Then she looked at me. "And why would that have anything to do with you?"

I shrugged, following Wendy's lead. "I don't know."

Cleo looked suddenly small and deflated. "Oh God," she said.

"Do you need a ride home?" I asked. "We can give you one, although our car's a little crowded."

"Yes, thanks. Ed had the keys, and he didn't think to leave them with me. That or he didn't want to; he's insane about that Caddy."

"Where do you live?" Wendy asked.

"I'm just outside Pine Haven, off Crandall Road. Ed has been staying with me for the last few days because he didn't want me to be alone."

"That's a nice area," Wendy said as we

made our way to the lobby with its grand chandelier and then out into the snow. My mother and Betsy were following us at a distance, speaking to each other in low voices.

It was cold outside, but not as bad as it had been on Monday. Some of the snow was melting on the sides of the parking lot. We had driven out in Wendy's Ford, and she unlocked it now so that we could all board. Cleo got in front with Wendy while I climbed into the backseat between my mother and Bets.

Cleo was texting rapidly on her phone. "Ed already contacted his lawyer," she said to us. "I guess they'll meet at the station." She looked at Wendy. "I wish I knew what the heck was going on."

Wendy's face was serene as she backed out of her parking space. "That's what your brother is going to clear up for us. Oh, Lilah — look who it is."

I followed her gaze to see Frank, a cigarette hanging out of his mouth, getting behind the wheel of a black car, seemingly with the intention of following us. "I think I'll make his job hard," Wendy said, speeding up. And then, "Oh, shoot." We turned into an exit lane only to find ourselves behind about thirty departing theater lovers.

"Looks like we're here for a while," said my mother. "Would anyone like some chocolate? I hung and filled Christmas stockings this morning, and I tossed some of the extra treats into my purse." She passed them around now — brightly wrapped Lindor balls and tin-foiled Santas — which we took eagerly from her red-gloved hand.

All of the women thanked her, and the crinkling of candy wrappers was a sort of music in the back of my thoughts, the most dominant of which was that my mother was sweet to keep hanging the family stockings, more than twenty years old and rather worn, with the names *Cameron, Lilah, Mommy,* and *Daddy* embroidered on them in gold thread. I felt a burst of nostalgia and a desire for Christmas, for holidays, for normalcy, and a lack of fear.

Now my mother, brimming with sympathy, leaned forward toward Cleo. "Do you have someone to spend the holidays with, dear?"

Cleo had flipped up her hood in the chilly car, and she nodded now, looking like a grim Emperor Palpatine. "Yes, I have plenty of invitations from friends and family. I'm still weighing my options. I won't be alone,

337

though — thanks for asking."

"Of course. I can't even imagine what you're going through," my mother said, patting Cleo's arm. "I don't know what I would do without my Daniel."

"Ah!" said Wendy as the traffic started moving again. We made it to the exit, then turned left and headed for Crandall Road. Cleo turned toward us so that more of her face was visible.

"The worst thing is that I just keep picturing him — dressed as Santa Claus and lying in the snow." She wiped at her eyes.

I leaned forward, too. "They made you identify him?"

"No — but I came to the hospital when I heard. They — filled me in on the circumstances."

"Ah." I leaned back again. What if it had been Cleo that Brad was texting in the parking lot? Tabitha had said that she told Cleo and Ed the truth about Brad's Hawaii tickets. Wouldn't that have made her angry? And yet she sat in the front of the car, alone and palely loitering like the lady in Keats's poem — what had been the name of it?

"Lilah," my mother said, poking my arm.

"What?"

"Wendy asked if you will be staying in your own place tonight."

"Oh — yes. Yes."

Cleo turned. "Why wouldn't you be staying in your own house?"

If only she knew. "Uh — it's a long story. Basically Wendy has been my bodyguard for the last few days."

Cleo's brows rose. "This is intriguing. Why in the world do you need a bodyguard?"

"She's not allowed to talk about it," Wendy said. "It's still under investigation."

Cleo smirked. "So you and I are both subject to police scrutiny this Christmas."

"Yeah, I guess so." I smiled at her and ate another one of my mother's chocolates. Cleo didn't seem to be a likely candidate for crime. Even if she had known Brad was having an affair — and she hadn't seemed to know at the Christmas party — she couldn't have been the person who shot at Cameron and me. How would she have known that I would be at the studio? It was just too unlikely. Just as all of the other suspects seemed unlikely. As time passed, the whole thing seemed more illusion than reality. *We are such stuff as dreams are made on.* It was almost as though I heard Brad Whitefield saying it again, now that my thoughts had turned to things imagined. On a whim, I pulled out my phone and texted a question to Mark.

"This is my street; turn left," Cleo said.

I tucked my phone in my pocket, and Wendy pulled onto Mainland. "What a lovely street," Bets said, gazing out her window. "It must be so nice to have the forest across the road. What terrific views you must have!"

Cleo's voice was as tiny as a child's. "Sometimes you can see deer. Especially in the early morning."

"How wonderful," said my mother. "You can take great comfort in the beauties around you. That's something my mother always used to say."

Cleo smiled at her. "You are all so sweet! You've all cheered me up." She pointed at my mother and Bets. "You two with your Christmas sweaters, and this one with the bows in her hair, and even you, the cop who detained my brother — you seem like a nice person." She made a wry face at Wendy, and we laughed.

My mother was in nurturing mode. "Well, we're just a phone call away, sweetie." She patted Cleo's arm.

"Is this it?" Wendy asked.

"Yes. This white one," Cleo said.

Wendy pulled into the driveway of an attractive one-story ranch house lit with stylish landscaping lights in green and blue. Cleo sat still. "I'm suddenly paranoid. Will you guys come in for a minute? Just until I get all the lights on? Maybe have a cup of tea?"

"Of course we will," said my mother, opening her door. The rest of us followed suit, getting gingerly out of the car and stepping delicately on the icy driveway. I slid a bit and grabbed onto the car; my braid flew up onto my shoulder, and my head flipped backward until I saw not the car, but the streetlight glowing over the Mainland sign on Cleo's corner.

Two things happened in my mind at once: I heard Brad Whitefield's voice saying, "I'm finished on Mainland forever." *Mainland.* And then I heard Cleo saying, "and this one with the bows in her hair." She had been looking at me, but I had no bow in my hair, nor did I tend to wear them. But I had been wearing one on the day that Whitefield died — a bow that Jenny made for me.

The others were walking away from the car. I wanted to speak to Wendy; something was not right. But it was cold and icy, and the women were moving determinedly toward the house.

Cleo was the first to fall; she took one wrong step on the slick ground, and her feet slid right out from under her. She lay there, looking up at the sky. "Geez, that was embarrassing," she said, and then they were all laughing. Cleo's purse had gone flying toward me, and I bent to retrieve items for her, tempted to laugh myself.

She got up and moved toward me, saying, "Let me grab my spare key out of the garage. The other one is on Ed's stupid key chain."

I tossed the items back into her purse, but hesitated when I saw one of them. She made eye contact with me, and I hastily put everything away and stood up. "Here you go," I said. "I think I got everything." I stepped forward to hand it to her and hit the same slick spot Cleo had. One moment I was looking at Cleo and the house behind her, and the next I was staring at the dark sky and the sprinkling of autumn stars.

I sat up, rubbing my elbows, and watched as Cleo, still laughing, opened a side door of her garage and flipped on the light. For a moment the whole room was illuminated, casting a bright light on the metallic blue car inside. My mouth went dry.

"Wendy," I croaked.

She was at my side, helping me up. "I saw," she said under her breath.

In a similar low tone I said, "There were

two phones in her purse."

Wendy knew what this meant. She and I exchanged a deadly serious glance while Bets and my mother still leaned on each other, unable to stop giggling in what they felt was a holiday atmosphere.

"Let me go in alone," Wendy said.

She moved forward carefully, ready for the unexpected, and the rest of us followed. Cleo had not emerged from the garage. Wendy moved on, her posture tense, her hands on her hips. "Cleo?" she asked.

She peered around the corner of the garage door and yelled, "Cleo!" Then she disappeared inside.

I ran to join her, almost falling once more, and leaned in to see that Cleo Whitefield was lying on the floor of the garage, her body jerking spasmodically, her eyes wide with terror.

CHAPTER NINETEEN

Wendy knelt next to Cleo, who seemed to be having difficulty breathing. My mind flashed back to a night two months earlier, when I had seen a woman poisoned before my eyes. Had Cleo been poisoned? All she had eaten were my mother's chocolate candies. I tried to make these bleary connections while Wendy attempted to loosen Cleo's coat and my mother and Bets crowded in behind, saying, "What's happening? What's going on?"

My phone buzzed in my pocket; confused, I took it out and saw Mark's response. Yeah, I hope U don't mind. I told Cleo all about UR TV spot and how excited my mom was.

I looked up again, an instant too late to see Cleo, her thrashings ended, sliding the gun out of Wendy's holster, turning it on Wendy, and pulling the trigger. "No!" Wendy yelled, and then she was dragging herself behind the blue car, leaving a bloodstain in her wake.

Cleo was standing now, holding the gun on three frightened women. "You saw the phone, right? You figured it out there in the driveway. But of course you might have known it was me, anyway. I know I saw you that day, with your long blonde braid and your narrowed eyes. I knew you were suspicious."

"The sun was in my eyes. But I certainly know now, Cleo. You shot a cop. You shot your husband. You're going to jail forever."

"What?" my mother cried. "You killed your own husband? Oh, Cleo." Her disappointment was more evident than her shock, and Cleo heard it. Remarkably she wanted to defend herself. My mother had that effect on people.

"He cheated on me. With Isabel! She's everything that I'm not — smart, sophisticated, talented, beautiful. There was no way I was going to win him back from her."

"He wasn't going to her," I said. My voice sounded weary, something separate from myself.

"How do you know?" Cleo looked vulnerable again, but the gun was steady in her hands. She had killed Brad with one shot. This recollection made me tremble.

"Because Isabel said so. She said he

wanted to be alone. To make some decisions about his life."

Two tears ran down Cleo's face, but her gun hand didn't move.

Betsy and my mother were making distressed sounds behind me, and Betsy was calling, "Wendy? Wen? Are you okay?"

There was no response from Wendy, but behind Cleo I could see her legs moving, slowly, changing position. Perhaps Betsy could, too, because she went silent.

I pointed at my pocket. "Did you see that I just had my phone out? I texted Detective Jay Parker of the Pine Haven Police. He's on his way."

"I don't believe you," Cleo said with a curl of her lip. "That's a bunch of BS. Why would you have his number handy on your phone?"

"Because he's my boyfriend," I said.

"Oh, Lilah!" said my mother with what seemed like delight. A gun pointed at us both, and she was probably already making mental wedding plans.

Cleo looked slightly uncertain. "In any case, we're not going to be here even if that's true. We're leaving right now, you and me." She gestured toward my mother and Betsy. "You two go over there, by the cop."

She pointed with the hand that didn't

hold the gun. They moved slowly, carefully, and then Betsy flew toward Wendy and knelt down behind the car, out of my sight line. My mother went, too, and stood there, her lips in a thin, disapproving line. "I don't know what you think you'll achieve," she said, a hint of distress in her voice. "Where can you possibly go that the police won't find you?"

"I have an idea," said Cleo with an unpleasant smile. I wondered now why I had never noticed that her eyes had a strange, unfocused quality.

She turned to me. "Go out the door and back to your friend's car. She left the keys in there, I saw. Do it!"

I turned and went back into the cold. I didn't have much desire to argue with an unbalanced woman holding a gun. My mother said, "Don't worry, Lilah. He'll be here soon."

I sighed. If only I had actually texted Parker. I doubted I could get away with grabbing my phone now. But surely Wendy, if she were still conscious, would have contacted someone? We walked out into the driveway, and I had a brief hope that Cleo would hit the same ice patch that had us all in stitches a few innocent moments earlier.

Instead she walked on the crunchy grass

and sent me across the same route. We remained upright, and Cleo ordered me behind the wheel of Wendy's car. "Get in and drive. I don't want to shoot you — I'd rather have you as a hostage — but if you want to be dead, that's your choice."

I did not want to be dead. I got behind the steering wheel and started the car. "Head to the city," she said. "Take the Lake Shore Drive exit. My uncle has a boat, and we're going to spend some time on it. My cousin Marco should be taking care of everything."

A boat? None of the boats were left on the water; it was December, for goodness' sake. The boats were in winter storage. Perhaps, though, Cleo's apparent ignorance could work to my advantage. "Great. Sounds like a nice place to spend the holiday," I said through chattering teeth as I backed out and started driving down Mainland. The woods across the way seemed sinister now rather than beautiful. I glanced into the rearview, hoping to see red and blue lights, but I saw only darkness. Surely Wendy had called it in by now? Was Wendy even okay?

"Faster," Cleo said. "Good. Now we'll just stick to the back roads until you get to the expressway."

"Sure." For a while there was silence. Perhaps if she relaxed, she'd set down the gun, and then — what? Would I have the courage to crash the car or slam hard on the brakes in an attempt to set off the air bags? And what if that didn't work? Then I'd just have an angry murderer with a loaded gun.

The car moved in silence through the cold night. Cleo pointed at an expressway ramp, and I got on, heading for the city. Random images bounced in my mind, jumbled by fear. Parker's blue eyes. My mother, hanging stockings. Wendy, dripping blood on the garage floor. Betsy and her jingling bells. Serafina and her red purse. Mick's wise, nodding head. My father, drinking hot chocolate. My brother, a brand-new husband, in love with his wife. Brother. Brothers.

"Hey. Why did your brother shoot a hole in my window?" My voice shook slightly, but my mind said, *Keep her talking.*

Cleo snorted. "He found the gun. I guess he figured things out. He thought if he could leave the weapon somewhere, have witnesses connect it to some anonymous gunman, then no one would suspect me. I told him it was stupid."

"Why me?"

"I told him you were there, when Brad died. I recognized you, but you didn't seem to recognize me at the restaurant. But I wasn't sure — you seemed to be everywhere I was. Like the police planted you there or something. He thought it might intimidate you into keeping quiet."

My phone rang. Shoot. Cleo raised her eyebrows and then reached across to my jacket pocket. She took the phone and glanced at the caller. "So you weren't lying. Some cop is really calling you. Dammit." Then she looked closer. "I recognize this picture. This is the guy from the Christmas party. What was he doing there?"

"We were there together. On a date."

"Why? Do you teach at the school where Brad was Santa?"

"No. Friend of a friend."

She clicked on my phone. "This is Cleo. You cops need to stay away from me or you'll be putting your girlfriend in danger."

I heard Parker's voice, loud, angry, but I couldn't make out words.

Cleo giggled. Despite everything, it wasn't until then that I realized there was something wrong inside her. "Just stay away, and everything will be fine." She clicked off the phone and then looked at me. "Your boyfriend just threatened me. He threatened to shoot me."

"He did not."

"I swear. He didn't sound very professional at all. I think his feelings are getting in the way." She rolled down her window and threw my phone onto the expressway. "They can trace that. I left mine back at the house. Now hopefully they'll have no way of finding us."

Except for Wendy's license plate. But I kept that thought to myself.

We drove some more; it was about seven o'clock now, and there was still plenty of traffic on the road, but I didn't know how to signal someone without alerting Cleo, who still held the gun perilously close to my side.

"The funny thing is," I said, "you seemed so sad. Like someone else really took your husband away. Not like you lured him out of a building so you could shoot him yourself."

"I am sad! I did that in anger; I didn't think it through, obviously. Because now I'm stuck here with you and I'm going to have to make arrangements to leave the country. But that's fine. I'm sick of Chicago winters. I want to go somewhere warm." She pointed at the Lake Shore Drive sign, and I got into the exit lane.

"Who exactly is going to make those arrangements for you?"

"That's none of your business. Just get me to the lake." She had pulled something out of her purse and was texting on it one-handed while somehow keeping her weird eyes on me.

"I thought you left your phone behind," I said. I couldn't seem to keep my mouth closed, despite my fear.

"I did. This is my iPod. They probably don't know about this, right? Or they won't think to check until later."

"Are you going to kill your cousin, too? The one we're meeting?"

She pouted. "No, but I might kill you if you don't stop criticizing me. I loved my husband. That's why I was so angry when I heard that the tickets were for *her*. How could he do that to me?" Her jaw thrust out aggressively, and she leaned closer with her gun. I tried to keep my eyes on the traffic even as they kept darting toward her, gauging my level of danger. It was an absurd situation all around — an ill-fated, chance meeting with a Santa Claus who just happened to have a homicidal wife, then a few surreal days with a bodyguard who now lay bleeding even as a murderer forced me to drive into the darkness toward an unknown destination and a boat that couldn't possibly be there when we arrived.

On our right, the lake glimmered in the dark. A seagull who hadn't been told his bedtime sat on a wood piling and stared at me for a moment before we sped past. He, too, was alone and palely loitering. . . .

"Ah!" I said.

"What?"

"Nothing. I was just trying to remember a poem earlier, when I saw you, and now I remember it — 'La Belle Dame Sans Merci.' John Keats. I read it in college."

"So?"

"So it means I knew it was you, unconsciously, before I figured it out."

"Why? What does that title mean?"

"It means 'The Beautiful Woman Without Mercy.' "

Cleo stared at me, her eyes weirdly pleased. "You think I'm beautiful?"

Her device buzzed in her hand, saving me from having to respond. She clicked it on and read something.

There was silence while Cleo read and typed a brief one-handed response.

"Okay," Cleo said. "We're almost there." She said something under her breath in Italian.

I struggled to remember any Italian words

that Fina had taught me, but it didn't help. I had no idea what Cleo had said. Poor Fina and Cam. Did they know what was happening? Were they worried about me? I knew my mother must be, although she was convinced that Parker would ride up on a white horse and save me. I let my mind play with the image of blue-eyed Parker astride a horse. It calmed me slightly.

"Here," said Cleo. "Take the Belmont exit."

I did as she said. I was numb, and not from the cold. "How about if I let you out and then I drive away?" I said.

"I still need you. I need you until I'm on my boat and headed out of here. I might even have to take you to my next destination. No one's going to shoot when there's a hostage, right?"

"Cleo. You'd be better off going in, saying it was an accident. You don't want anything else that they can charge you with. You're already at murder and abduction."

She instructed me to turn right into a little wooded parking area. I stopped there, the only car in an otherwise empty lot. Prompted by Cleo, I got out of the car and began walking with her toward the Lakefront Trail and Belmont Harbor. It was dark now, and a few harbor lights twinkled on the black water. The city, to our left, looked festive with Christmas decor and bustling people. I felt jealous as I thought of what might await those little rushing figures: warm meals, smiling families, Christmas trees, hot chocolate. My eyes burned, and I wiped at them so Cleo wouldn't see my tears and interpret them as weakness.

We were still walking; this was where the boats normally sat, gently rocking, their hulks covered with tarps. I felt weirdly detached from my body as we walked, and I barely felt my feet as they touched the ground. I wondered vaguely if I was in shock or if it so was cold that I was frozen. I waited, nervous, for Cleo to notice that the boats were missing.

It took her a while, distracted as she was, but she finally stopped and stared dumbly at the black water. "Where the hell are the boats? I told Marco to meet me here; we're going to leave in the dark, and no one will realize we're not on land anymore."

"Not even when they find Wendy's car at Belmont Harbor?"

She waved this thought away. "They won't find it for a long time. Why would they? They're not going to be looking here."

"Doesn't your cousin know that boats are in winter storage?"

"He doesn't usually get to drive the boat. It's my uncle's, like I said. He doesn't trust Marco with it."

I wondered which uncle this was. Her uncle Enrico? Or another Donato brother that Parker knew nothing about? Certainly Donatos seemed to have a way of multiplying. In any case, cousin Marco sounded about as bright as Cleo was. Perhaps he was driving up from some suburb and unfamiliar with the city boating policies. If that were the case, though, then could he be trusted to pilot a boat? None of this made sense; I wanted to be gone.

"How about if I leave you here, Cleo?"

She flicked her red hair over her shoulder with her free hand, then looked at her watch. "You're going where I tell you."

"Find your cousin and go. You're running out of time." Police sirens wailed distantly. I wondered if they could be for me.

Cleo focused in on me. Her eyes shimmered resentfully in the dark. "Don't threaten me!"

"I'm not threatening you; I'm trying to help you."

"No you're not. This is because of *you,*" she said. She raised her gun and pointed it at my chest. "This is all because of you!"

I fought to find words in my own defense,

but my body was frozen with terror. Was this really how I would die, at an empty boat harbor in the dark, with Christmas lights shining all around me? Had Brad Whitefield believed he would die in a Santa suit?

"Don't, Cleo," I managed.

"Why not? Give me one good reason why not?"

My mind, dulled with fear, supplied me with only one answer. "Brad said I deserved a second chance."

Her eyes grew huge. "He said that? When you two were there in the parking lot?"

"Yes. We were talking about life. He said some beautiful things."

She scowled at me; this had clearly not been the right thing to say. I was about to die.

The gun seemed to tremble in her hands. Then her eyes widened, her body stiffened, and she crumpled to the ground. Behind her stood a man with some type of weapon in his hand.

"Hello, Miss Drake," he said.

It was Enrico Donato. Even in the dark I saw that he was still wearing his slippers.

CHAPTER TWENTY

I stared at him, my mouth open and ready to scream. "Did you kill her? Did you kill your niece?"

He sighed and shook his head. "As I assured you long ago, Miss Drake, I am not in the habit of killing people. This is a Taser, and I regret that I had to use it, but Cleopatra had become unstable. She always was a difficult child."

"Cleopatra? My God, this family," I said, staring down at Cleo, who looked like a cement statue of herself.

A suspicion entered my mind, and my head whipped up so that I could study Enrico Donato, who held very still with his Taser in his gloved hand. "How did you know we would be here? You couldn't possibly have known unless she told you."

He shook his head. "Or unless Frank told me, which he did. Frank is loyal to me, and for the last few days that meant he was loyal to you."

"Then why didn't he report the shooting of my house? He must have seen it?"

Donato shrugged. "He recognized my nephew. We weren't sure what he was up to, but we were confident that Eduardo had not committed the crime, since he was with us at the time. I told Frank to watch things more closely. That is how we found out that my niece had betrayed us all and killed a good man."

He shook his head and slid the Taser into his pocket. "I owe you an apology, Miss Drake. I assured you that no one in my family had hurt Brad Whitefield; now I find out that is not true. I can promise you I did not believe at the time —"

"I understand," I said. There was genuine grief in Donato's voice, and despite everything — my fear, my anger, my almost overwhelming relief — I felt sorry for him. "But you do know we have to call the police, right?"

"I have already called them. This is a matter of family honor, and we will do the right thing."

The sirens had grown louder; they had been for me after all.

I shoved my hands into my pockets. "If you're here and Frank came with you, then who was going to drive the boat? The supposed boat, I mean," I asked, pointing at the empty harbor.

Donato sighed again. "I fear it is one of my less than intelligent nephews. Cleo likely lured him with talk of Brad's sizable life insurance policy." He met my eyes with his arresting gray ones. "But I do not believe murderers can collect on those contracts."

"No — I don't believe they can."

We stood there in the cold. I could hear the police cars as they screeched onto the Belmont exit and toward the path. "Thank you for saving my life," I said.

He looked down at Cleo. "I saved both of you. She makes unwise decisions, and too often we have not made her face consequences. Even now, her father and I will provide a team of lawyers for her defense. Yet she will face stern consequences, I fear."

"Yes. She's already facing some. She misses Brad."

"Love is a mysterious thing," said Enrico Donato, looking past me, and I turned to see Jay Parker running down the path toward me, his coat flapping in the cold wind.

"Parker," I said, walking to meet him. Then suddenly I was in his arms and squeezing him too tightly and realizing just how afraid I had been. Other police officers flowed past us, but I never let go of Parker, who in turn was holding me with a fairly solid grip.

"I seem to always show up too late, after you've already been through danger. I wanted to protect you, to save you," he said, squeezing me spasmodically. "When I talked to Cleo on the phone, I could tell she was unbalanced. I've never been so afraid, Lilah."

"You and me both."

He let me go and looked past me to the deck, where people were tending to the stiffened Cleo. "What happened?"

"Her uncle tased her," I said, and suddenly I was laughing. It was unforgiveable and inappropriate, and it drew more than one glance from the team at work behind us, but I couldn't stop. Parker looked concerned; he probably figured this was my last fall from sanity. He pulled me back against him.

I stayed there, giggling into his chest, enjoying the warmth of him, the familiar smell of him, the security of his arms around me. Finally I was able to stop laughing and take some deep breaths. I pulled away and looked at him more carefully. His normally perfect hair was in utter disarray, and his face, for the first time since I had known him, was unshaven. "This has been rough on you," I said.

"It's been a tough week. It got a lot better when I saw that you were all right."

"I was scared, Jay. She had a gun, and I thought she might kill me. She shot Wendy!" I cried.

He stroked my hair. "Wendy is okay. They're going to release her tonight. She was shot in the arm, but it was — a lucky place to take a bullet."

"Oh God." I shook my head at the weirdness of it all. "Enrico Donato saved my life."

Parker glanced past me to Donato, who was speaking in his quiet voice to the authorities around him. Then his eyes were back on me. "Let's get you home," he said.

CHAPTER TWENTY-ONE

On Christmas Eve, my parents' house was a Christmas fantasy, with real pine swags wound around the stair rails and a magical tree filled with the ornaments I remembered from childhood. Cam and Fina sat close together on the couch, and Fina displayed her wedding ring to my beaming parents. Across from them sat Wendy and Bets, my mother's new best friends (and mine). Like all people who go through trauma, we found ourselves compelled to talk about it, to tell the story to one another even though most of us had been a part of it. We had spent much of the evening rehashing our harrowing adventure, all of us occasionally touching Wendy's bandaged arm as a sort of talisman of good fortune.

Mick was in his element. He wore a red holiday scarf and strolled from person to person, getting endless petting and probably too many treats.

Wendy had been distressed since the previous night when Cleo turned on us; she felt it was unprofessional of her to allow her weapon to be taken in that way, although all of us had assured her that we, too, had been fooled into thinking Cleo had been in real danger. Parker understood the situation, and after a couple of interviews with Cleo, he told Wendy that she had in fact succeeded in keeping me safe, since Cleo had admitted being put off by Wendy's presence and had been unwilling to approach me, despite her fears that I might remember something about her involvement in the crime.

I was hovering near a gold plate covered in generous pieces of my mother's homemade fudge, eating too much of it, as I did each year. I occasionally switched to a different plate and retrieved a piece of cheese for Mick, who had relocated to a spot under my table. His red scarf brushed softly against my arm.

"Lilah, come back to us," my mother said. She had been beaming widely all evening, a smile that was mostly due to relief and partly due to spiked eggnog. I had learned my lesson about that particular drink and was sticking to hot tea.

"I'm here," I said. "Eating fudge, just like

every Christmas. But we need to change the subject. We should be talking about holiday things. Baby Jesus and the snow outside, and the stockings hung by the chimney with care."

My mother laughed. "This is the best Christmas ever. I'm so happy that you are all here and safe. All my children, by birth and by marriage and by adoption."

That last part was for Bets and Wendy, who smiled and lifted their glasses.

When the doorbell rang, everyone stiffened for a moment; my father left the room, and we heard his voice mingling in friendly tones with the voice of Jay Parker. The two men appeared in the doorway. Parker's eyes sought mine, but whatever he might have said was drowned out by Serafina screaming. "My purse! My beautiful bag!"

She leaped from the couch and dove on Parker, who was in fact holding Serafina's lovely Italian leather handbag. "Where did you find it?" she cried.

Parker shrugged. "I just had to check a few Dumpsters near your apartment."

I stared at him, openmouthed, while Serafina continued to hug him until her husband stood and pulled her away. I said, "You went Dumpster diving on Christmas Eve just to look for Serafina's purse?"

Serafina was on the couch now, examining the inside of her bag. "It is all here — everything — just the money is gone. Money is the least important thing, yes?" Now she transferred her joy to Cam in the form of hugs and kisses, and he accepted them with a smug expression.

He did manage to say, "Thanks, Jay. That was really cool of you. I should have thought to look there."

It was the first time Cam had ever called Parker by his first name, and Parker's face brightened with surprise. Then my family closed around him, patting his back and asking him questions and (in the case of my mother) plying him with food. I went into the kitchen and retrieved Mick's leash and my coat. Parker was still wearing his, but he wouldn't be for long if he planned to stay.

I went back into the living room and waved to him. "I was just about to walk Mick. Do you want to go with me?"

Six people around Parker now suddenly found reasons to walk away from him, talking among themselves. "I would like to, yes," Parker said.

We went out into the early evening cold. It wasn't snowing, but the occasional random flake hit our faces as the weather sorted out what it wanted to do. I handed the leash to Parker so I could zip up my coat. He looked very natural walking Mick, so I let him keep doing it.

"Lilah," Parker said.

"I didn't mean to interrogate you over the phone yesterday."

"I don't want this to be a problem. I want to be with you. I made a mistake the first time, and I missed you."

"I missed you, too. And I don't want to create problems. But it seems to me the truth is a pretty big thing to have a disagreement about. I can't be with someone who thinks I'm dishonest."

"I don't."

"But what if you do, deep down? And then there comes a time that you need to trust me, really trust me, and you find that you can't?"

Mick stopped to sniff a patch of snow, and Parker faced me. "Lilah, I regret the way I handled a lot of things. And I am sorry that I lied to you about my mother. All I can do is try to start from this point."

I took his gloved hand, the one that wasn't holding a leash, and held it. "When I was driving down the Lakeshore last night, wondering if Cleo was crazy enough to shoot me, I tried to think comforting thoughts — of my family and Mick — but

367

mostly of you. I've only known you for a couple of months, but I can't seem to stop thinking about you."

Parker looked earnest. "What if we just made a pact right now to only look forward? And we'll both promise not to lie to each other ever again?"

I studied his face, strong and finely chiseled in the evening light. "So we're at that point when we're talking about second chances, like you said in my house, when this all started?"

"We are at that point, yes."

"I would like a second chance with you, Jay Parker. And I will never lie to you again."

"I won't lie to you, either, Lilah."

"Okay. Can I kiss you now?"

"I wish you would."

I stood on tiptoe and pressed my lips against his. Parker slid one arm around me. Mick's nose had moved to Parker's shoes. Finally Parker broke away and laughed. "He's licking my feet."

"He's affectionate, like me," I said. "Hey, do you have time to come back in and celebrate Christmas with us?"

"For an hour or so. Can you spare some time after that to come over to Mom's with me? Nothing would make her happier than to see me come home with a girlfriend."

"Am I your girlfriend, Parker?" I said, batting my lashes at him.

He let go of Mick's leash and slid both his arms around my back. "Do you know what? I hear your name in my head all day. When I first met you, I thought it was a pretty name, but now it's almost like music to me. *Lilah.*" He kissed me. Mick sat down directly on our feet, clearly not pleased to lose our attention. "And yes, you are my girlfriend. Tell that to your Italian chef."

I sent him a regretful look. "He's offered me a regular spot. Is that going to be a problem?"

His mouth was near mine; I could feel the warmth of his skin. "I know he's good for your career. Just keep it in the studio, okay? I don't want to have to compete with that guy."

"You never would, Jay. He had his chance, and he lost."

"And I won."

"You did. I keep thinking of what Brad Whitefield said, about his island of escape. Maybe he did want to be alone, but I think he would have chosen to be with Isabel eventually. I think he was in love with her; I understand, because that expression on his face — I see it on my own in the mirror, when I'm thinking about you."

■ ■ ■ ■

Two hours later we drove to Ellie Parker's house. Ellie, my good friend, had tried to initiate a relationship between her son and me back in October, and the attempt had failed. Now Parker and I had reconciled, but Ellie didn't know that yet.

Parker got out of the car, looking like a mysterious sailor in his dark coat, then came around to my side to help me out. "You look pretty," he said.

I smiled, and we made our way up the driveway, past a couple of other cars. Parker's brothers were there with their families.

Parker had texted his mother that he was coming, and she met us at the door. "Hi, sweetheart. I'm so glad you could make it, and — is that *Lilah*?" Ellie practically dragged me across the threshold and gave me a big hug. "You worked things out?" she said in my ear.

"We did," I murmured.

She turned to hug Jay and wish him Merry Christmas. "Thanks for getting me the present I wanted," she said to him.

He grinned. "It's the present I wanted, too."

I said nothing, but I realized it was what I

had asked for, when I spoke with a cos-
tumed Brad Whitefield on that fateful day
when we stood together in a delicate snowfall. I wanted a second chance, I'd told him,
and he had smiled at me and told me to
believe in my dream.

Now Jay Parker and his mother and I
walked together to the main room, where
Jay's two brothers, their wives, and three
little children sat around the tree. They
looked up at us, their faces bright and ex-
pectant.

Parker stepped forward, holding my hand,
and said, "Everyone? This is Lilah."

RECIPES

SERAFINA'S PIZZELLES

(Italian Christmas Waffle Cookies)

For this recipe, you need a pizzelle baker, similar to a waffle iron, which imprints a beautiful, snowflake-like design on each cookie. The dough takes only minutes to prepare, and the cookies themselves can be hot on your table in less than half an hour.

My sister-in-law, Serafina Bellini Drake, assures me that these cookies, when made with love and just the right amount of butter, taste like Christmas itself, whatever that means.

Ingredients
1 1/2 cups flour
1 teaspoon baking soda
1 1/2 sticks (3/4 cup) butter

3 large eggs

3/4 cup sugar

2 teaspoons vanilla (or almond extract, if you prefer)

Powdered sugar for sprinkling

First preheat your pizzelle baker.

Mix flour and baking soda and set aside.

Melt butter and mix with eggs, sugar, and vanilla in blender until smooth.

Add the flour mixture until you have a sticky dough.

Check to see that your baker is ready; spray the inside lightly with a baking spray to avoid sticking.

Place a rounded teaspoonful of dough on each of the pizzelle pattern grids.

Lower the lid and hold for 30–40 seconds (you may have to experiment with timing).

Lift and gently pry up the cookies with a fork tine or thin knife, then set cookies on a baking rack to cool.

When cookies are finished, sift powdered sugar over them to create a lacy, holiday effect.

Your finished pizzelles will be thin, delicate, snowflake-like cookies that are sweet and addictive.

LILAH'S FRENCH TOAST CASSEROLE WITH GINGERBREAD FLAVOR

(Adapted for Christmastime)

Ingredients:
1 loaf of soft French bread (or soft rolls)
8 large eggs
2 cups half-and-half
1 cup milk
2 tablespoons sugar
1 tablespoon vanilla
1/4 teaspoon cinnamon
1/4 teaspoon nutmeg
Salt to taste

Streusel Topping:

(This can vary, but here's one option.)

2 sticks (1 cup) butter
1/4 cup molasses
1 cup brown sugar
1 cup corn syrup
1 cup chopped pecans (or walnuts)
1/2 teaspoon ground ginger
1/2 teaspoon cinnamon
1/2 teaspoon nutmeg
1/4 teaspoon cloves

Slice bread into twenty slices (or separate ten rolls) and lay out in buttered baking dish.

Blend all of the ingredients and pour them over the slices of bread, making sure that the wet mixture gets under and in between the slices, and that all of the bread is saturated.

Cover the mixture with tinfoil and refrigerate overnight. In the morning, make the streusel mixture and spread on top of the saturated, chilled bread; bake for 40 minutes at 350 degrees.

Serve with pats of butter and maple syrup. (Gingerbread also tastes delicious topped with whipped cream.)

Be ready for a scrumptious surprise to share with friends or family! Toby's five children love this recipe, but adults love it, too!

LILAH'S HENRY-BEAR CHOCOLATE CHIP COOKIES

Made Exclusively for Henry of Weston

This particular recipe is sure to please any cookie-grubbing small people in your environment. Since children have surprisingly large hands when it comes to taking cookies, you might consider doubling the recipe so that you have plenty on hand.

Ingredients
3/4 cup granulated sugar
3/4 cup light brown sugar
1/2 teaspoon cinnamon sugar
1 teaspoon vanilla
2 eggs
2 1/4 cups flour
1 teaspoon baking soda
1 teaspoon salt
1 teaspoon baking powder
1 bag semisweet chocolate chips
Chopped walnuts to taste (For those with a nut allergy, these can be omitted or replaced with a candy substitute. Check candy bag to make sure it is nut-free.)

Preheat oven to 375 degrees.

Combine sugars, vanilla, and eggs (use a blender for a smooth dough). In a separate bowl, mix flour, baking soda, salt, and baking powder. Gradually fold into the blended mixture. Finally, stir in chocolate chips and nuts, if you choose.

(If a tiny child is present, he will try to eat the dough at this early stage — watch for little fingers.)

Capture dough between two teaspoons

and flick balls onto greased baking sheets. (Alternatively you can buy cookie patterns in various child-friendly shapes. Henry is fond of the knight patterns.)

Bake for 12–15 minutes or to desired crunchiness.

This recipe is also excellent aromatherapy, as it fills your house with the smell of chocolate and sweet cake.

Take cookies off the pan (they might continue baking slightly) and put on wire racks to cool. Seal cooled cookies into airtight containers.

Freeze half the batch so that you can have them fresh and ready when company comes.

Henry's rating: Five Batmans (the highest number possible)

ABOUT THE AUTHOR

Julia Buckley is the author of the Undercover Dish Mysteries and the Writer's Apprentice Mysteries. She is a member of the Mystery Writers of America, Sisters in Crime, and the Romance Writers of America, along with the Chicago Writers Association. Julia has taught high school English for twenty-eight years, and currently lives in Chicago, Illinois.

The employees of Thorndike Press hope you have enjoyed this Large Print book. All our Thorndike, Wheeler, and Kennebec Large Print titles are designed for easy reading, and all our books are made to last. Other Thorndike Press Large Print books are available at your library, through selected bookstores, or directly from us.

For information about titles, please call:
(800) 223-1244

or visit our website at:
gale.com/thorndike

To share your comments, please write:
Publisher
Thorndike Press
10 Water St., Suite 310
Waterville, ME 04901